Ask the Fellows who Cut the Hay

also by George Ewart Evans

THE CROOKED SCYTHE
An anthology of oral history
edited by David Gentleman

ASK THE FELLOWS WHO CUT THE HAY

by

GEORGE EWART EVANS

with decorations by

THOMAS BEWICK

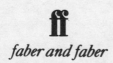

faber and faber

First published in 1956
by Faber and Faber Limited
3 Queen Square London WC1N 3AU
Second edition 1962
First paperback edition 1965

Printed in England by Clays Ltd, St Ives plc

© George Ewart Evans 1956, 1962

A CIP record for this book is available from the British Library

ISBN 0 571 06353 5

9 11 13 15 14 12 10

TO
MY WIFE

COUNTRYMAN: We old men are old chronicles, and when our tongues go they are not clocks to tell only the time present, but large books unclasped; and our speeches, like leaves turned over and over, discover wonders that are long since past.

(From a XVII Century Tract)

'*Sustine modicum: ruricolae melius hoc norunt.*
"Wait a bit: let us ask the country folk"—as the senior clerk said to his junior in the exchequer in 1177, when he asked him a tricky question.'

(*History:* Feb. 1953: *Representation in Mediaeval England*)

From a different line of work, my colleagues,
I bring you an idea. You smirk.
It's in the line of duty. Wipe off that smile, and
as our grandfathers used to say:
Ask the fellows who cut the hay.

(From *The Decade of Sheng Min* translated by Ezra Pound)

Preface to the Second Edition

The original manuscript of this book was completed six years ago. Since that time many of the people who so generously co-operated in preserving the lineaments of the old Blaxhall community have died—Robert Savage, Joseph Row, George Messenger, Aldeman Ling (Senior), and Henry Keble. And this second edition can well stand as a tribute to their memory. A year after the book was written we left Blaxhall to live in another part of Suffolk; and it has been possible to estimate it against the background of five years spent in another not greatly dissimilar rural area. My findings in the Stowmarket district of Suffolk have confirmed and amplified the original attempt to record the pre-machine village life in Suffolk. They have also enabled me to understand it more fully; and in the light of this new understanding, fresh material has been added to the present edition.

But living in this area has also persuaded me that the old hand-tool methods of farming, and many of the old domestic crafts, lasted longer in the Stowmarket area than they did in Blaxhall. The evidence is chiefly in the number and variety of old farm tools still to be found in this district; and the occasional survival even today of such methods as the brick-oven weekly baking of bread. The main reason for this survival I believe to be the rather later change-over to the full mechanization of farming. It was easier to introduce the machine on the light land of the Sandlings than on the heavier soils of mid-Suffolk; and the lay-out and size of the fields were better suited to the new scale of farming that so rapidly developed as soon as the machine got into its stride.

If I were writing the book today, it would be planned in a

very different way. This, I suppose, is a natural development. But I have withstood the temptation to recast the book drastically. Such a re-writing might have improved it as an historical record; but it would no longer have been the record of living in a village just at the point where the last evidences of an old way of life were disappearing.

Needham Market, Suffolk. April, 1961

Contents

Contents

Acknowledgments

The author wishes to thank all those who have helped him in the making of this book, especially those who have answered his many questions and so willingly supplied him with information.

He is grateful to Sir James Scott Watson and Mr Ezra Pound for permission to quote from their works; and acknowledgment is made to the following for permission to reproduce maps and photographs: the Air Ministry for the aerial photograph, and H.M. Stationery Office for the map of Blaxhall for both of which *Crown Copyright is Reserved;* the Department of Education of the International Wool Secretariat for the wool burial certificate, Aldeburgh Corporation for the extract from John Kirby's map, the *East Anglian Daily Times,* Lieutenant Colonel W. Manning, Reverend T. Waller, Mr J. W. Ling, and all those who have kindly lent photographs.

Acknowledgment is also made to the Editors of *The Countryman* and *The Village* where parts of this work have already appeared. The author is grateful for help from the following: Mr Brian Vesey-Fitzgerald, Miss D. A. A. Rope, the Blaxhall Local History Committee, the Staff of the Ipswich Borough and East Suffolk County Record Office, the Staffs of the Ipswich Borough and East Suffolk County Libraries, the Staff of the Ipswich Museums.

For reasons of economy photographs were dropped from the second edition of 1962 and from this paperback version.

9

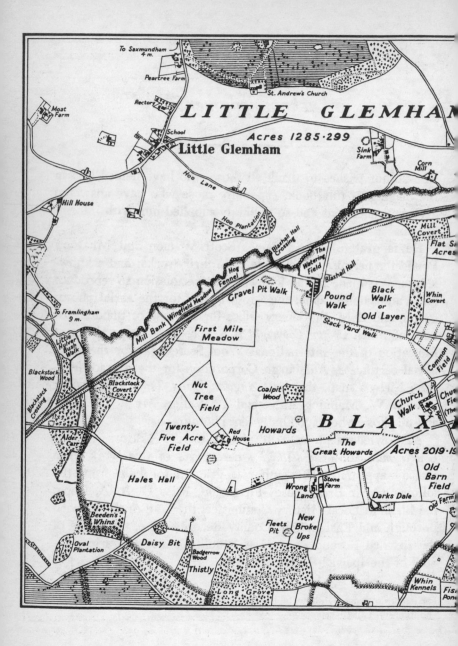

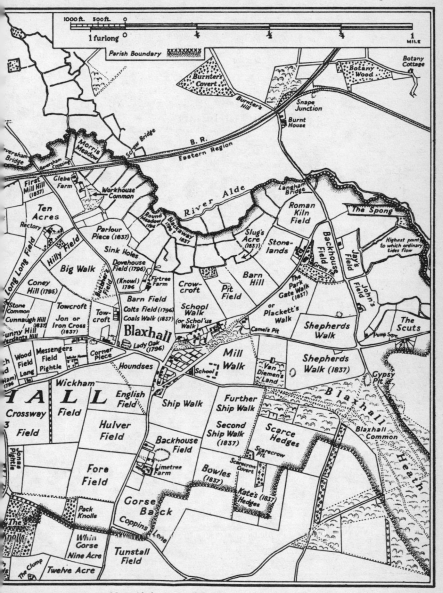

1000 ft. 500 ft. 0

1 furlong   0   ¼   ½   ¾   1 MILE

Parish Boundary XXXXXXXX

Botany Cottage

Burnter's Covert

Botany Wood

Burnter's Hill

Snape Junction

Burnt House

B. R. Eastern Region

Feversham Bridge

Morris Meadow

Screw Bridge

River Alde

Langham Bridge

The Spong

First Mill Hill (1837)

Glebe Farm

Workhouse Common

Roman Kiln Field

Highest point to which ordinary tides flow

Ten Acres

Rectory

Parlour Piece (1837)

Round Meadow 1796

Buckaway 1837

Slug's Acre (1837)

Stonelands

Backhouse Field

Jay's Field

Long Long Field

Hilly Field

Sink Holes

Dovehouse Field (1796)

(Knowl) 1796

Firtree Farm

Crowcroft

Pit Field

Barn Hill

Grove Rd.

John's Field

Big Walk

Coney Hill (1795)

Stone Common

Towcroft

(Knowl) 1796

Barn Field

Colts Field (1796)

Coals Walk (1837)

School Walk (or Schol'us Walk)

The Park Gate Walk (1837)

or Plackett's Walk

Shepherds Walk

The Scuts

Cunnaugh Hill (1837)

Jon or Iron Cross (1837)

Towcroft

Blaxhall

Lady Oak (1796)

Camel's Pit

Pump Spng.

Sunny Hill

Aberdene Hill

Wood Field

Lang

Messengers Field Pightle

Corner Piece

White Barn

Houndses

Mill Walk

Shepherds Walk (1837)

Gypsy Pit

(1796)

(1896)

Wickham Field

English Field

Ship Walk

Further Ship Walk

Van Diemen's Land

School

Blaxhall Heath

HALL

Crossway Field

Hulver Field

Backhouse Field

Second Ship Walk (1837)

Scarce Hedges

Blaxhall Common

Jones Pightle

Limetree Farm

Bowles (1837)

Scarecrow Pit

Scarecrow Covert

Fore Field

Pack Knolls

Gorse Back

Coppins Lane

Kate's Hedges (1837)

The Knolls

Whin Gorse Nine Acre

Tunstall Field

Twelve Acre

The Clump

Introduction

An attempt has been made in this book to record what is left of the old rural community as seen in the East Suffolk village of Blaxhall and the district around it. For this purpose, the experiences and memories of a group of old people have been set down. Each section of the book has been associated with one or two old people because they have given a great deal of information relevant to it; and again because each typifies the aspect of the old community dealt with in that particular section. Not all, however, of the material contained in the book has been collected orally: much of it has been taken from books and manuscripts; but in nearly every section the oral material has given the initial impetus to search, check and amplify wherever it has been possible to do so. The old people, it is hoped, dominate the whole work.

The book has taken this particular shape from the writer's conviction that the oral tradition is at this time of the greatest historical importance. During the past fifty or so years the life of the countryside has been revolutionized and the rate of change within this period has been greater than it has ever been in recorded history; and if we were to extend the period by another hundred years it could be said that more changes have taken place during this time than in the previous fifteen centuries. At present, old people in this countryside are survivors from another era. They belong essentially to a culture that has extended in unbroken line since at least the early Middle Ages. They are in some respects the last repositories of this culture; and for this reason should have some of the respect given to any source of valuable historical information. Their knowledge of dialect, folk tales and songs, old customs and usages, and craft vocabularies, and their ability to identify and describe the use of farm implements that are now going into limbo after being used for centuries, are sufficient reasons why they should have the local historian's greatest attention. That this attention is urgent is too obvious to need stressing; and if, as often happens, the local historian—with limited time and means at his disposal— has to choose between helping to dig out a site and collecting oral information in his town or village, it is to be hoped that he will choose the less popular and in many ways the more exacting task. For an unexcavated site after waiting in the soil for perhaps a couple of thousand years will not suffer from the neglect of a few more; while the sort of knowledge that is waiting to be taken down from the old people is always on the brink of extinction. Tomorrow may be too late; and once this knowledge is under the soil no amount of digging will ever again recover it.

But the history of the last fifty or sixty years deserves attention for another reason. For just as we tend to assume that anything written by a man who is still living can hardly reach the level of literature, in the same way we think—perhaps unconsciously—that anything that has happened within the present century is hardly worth the name of history. It is as if we have told ourselves: 'Why! my grandfather remembers that, therefore it cannot possibly be history.' The result is that the historical foreground is in many respects a blank, and we have more knowledge about people distant in place and time than we have about our own immediate forbears. That we have now a special reason for scrutinising our particular foreground has already been stated.

Much of the book is concerned with farming: it has been given this bias advisedly. For farming is the basic rural industry— certainly the chief occupation in the area here studied—and it is probable that when the history of the countryside in the twentieth century comes to be written, the revolution in agriculture, particularly the application to it of the internal combustion engine, will be considered the chief agent in the final break-up of the old community. Farming, moreover, has until recent years contained vestiges both in implements and vocabulary, and more rarely in actual farming practices, of the old rural way of life that has its roots in a past far beyond the longest memory of man.

It may be objected that the method of treating the past followed in the present book tends to paint too rosy a picture of the old way of life and to idealize a village where the *sequelae* of retarded development and past neglect are only too evident. Stated baldly like this the objection is hard to meet, for no farm worker of the present day would wish to go back to the old conditions; and no thinking person would advocate a return of the old domination by squire or near-squire that most villages have suffered in the past. But the fact has to be met that the old community was organic, at however low a level; and since its fragmentation village life, and therefore the life of the nation, has suffered because nothing comparable has taken its place; and while it would be foolish to wish for its return, the gap it has left nevertheless emphasizes the need for a conscious attempt to build up a new community to replace it. The Rural Community Councils, the Women's Institutes and the Cambridgeshire Village Colleges are some of the institutions that have done a great deal towards repairing the gap; and the Parish Councils have shown that they have the capacity to give some sort of binding to the disparate elements in a modern village. But it is a herculean job, and it is very doubtful whether any sort of new community can consciously be built up with any hope of permanence until the new farming, which is still evolving at a great speed, has reached an equilibrium; and until land tenure is made more uniform and farm land is planned in units that are best suited to present-day farm mechanization. For just as the shape and manner of organization of the mediaeval village was conditioned

Introduction

by the way the people worked the land, so the village community of the future will have to bear organic relation to the way the land has been used since the coming of the tractor and rural electrification; and while the land is still bought and sold on an estate market in units that have no relation either to present working conditions or to local needs there is no hope of an integrated village community, however great the conscious efforts to help it evolve. In human terms the problem may perhaps be summarized by a remark of a farm worker in this village: 'The trouble with farming today is, it's such a lonely job. When I started as a back'us boy about thirty years ago at least you had plenty of company.'

It is only fair to warn the reader at this stage that there is a slight didactic purpose lurking in this book, related in a way to the village of the future that has just been discussed. For although it is a commonplace to say that we cannot build the future until we know the past, it is a truth worth stating here once more. A move into the past gets the best start from the sure ground of known and *felt* facts about one's own immediate environment, and the main task, and probably the most difficult one, is to help the 'backward traveller' not so much to *know* the past as to *feel* it. For history is not merely the mechanical acquisition of knowledge about the past: it is more than anything else the imaginative reconstruction of it. 'Fiction,' it has been said, 'is history's fourth dimension.' And if by fiction is meant the re-making of the past in term's of one's own emotional and imaginative experience, this statement is sound sense as well as a piece of harmless provocation. For unless the 'traveller' is given an opportunity and helped to make his own *fiction* of the past, it will always be dead to him—a series of stodgy facts and a masquerade of characters that will never properly live and therefore will soon be forgotten.

To end with a personal note: after all has been said I have to confess that the book, as originally conceived, had no purpose at all. Shortly after coming to live in this village seven years ago I became aware of the material that was waiting to be collected

Introduction

and went out in a desultory way to do so. Later the colour and
wealth of the material overcame my natural laziness and hesitation about starting a new project, and eventually worried a pen
into my hand. Even then it is likely that this book would never
have been written had I not the help of my wife both in collecting
the material and ordering it into something like readable form.

Blaxhall: A Note

Blaxhall is a village of about four hundred people, six miles away from the Suffolk Coast; and the east wind often blows the smell of the sea over the heathland. The cottages are tucked away in isolated groups between the fields. They are small brick-and-tile, boxlike buildings, functional rather than picturesque. Their usual pattern is two rooms down and two up-stairs; but there are a few *bedroom cottages* (bungalows) built originally by squatters on the common.

Most of the old people mentioned in this book are natives of Blaxhall, but not one of them has lived continuously in the same cottage all his life: a change of master or retirement meant usually a change of house. Many of the cottages are still *tied* today, so there is often a certain amount of moving about, but nearly always within the village. The cottages are so much alike that the moves do not seem to break the continuity of the various households: each family has its own nest of particular possessions —a pair of china dogs, a few old photographs, a couple of old chairs and a few pieces of old-fashioned china and a nineteenth-century clock; and these fit without any difficulty into the new home.

There is a sense of community existing among the old people,

Blaxhall: A Note

and they are secretly proud of belonging to Blaxhall. New-comers, hardy enough to attempt to settle in the village, are at first regarded from a distance and their behaviour is minutely observed just long enough to confirm the old judgment: 'Only the rum 'uns come to Blaxhall.' But during the last four years there have been innovations: eight council houses, piped water and electricity are modifying the pattern of life and bringing more strangers into the village. Blaxhall is being swept late into the flood of twentieth-century change.

PART ONE

ROBERT SAVAGE

1 Back'us Boy and Shepherd

Robert Lionel Savage, the last of a long line of shepherds, died in his seventy-seventh year. But he 'gave up the sheep' some time before, badly crippled by the rheumatism that attacks so many of his calling. After years of rigorous lambing seasons when he was exposed to all kinds of weather and when the needs of the sheep were preferred to his own, he was anchored to his chair; and his mind easily swung back to the time when he started his career.

He left school at the age of twelve after satisfying the local schools inspector that he had reached a sufficient standard of learning to seek a job. He then went as *back'us* (back-house or kitchen) boy to a big farm in the village. The back'us boy was at that time the lowest rank in the rural hierarchy. He was under the command of the farmer's wife. She called and the back'us boy answered; and the calls he answered were many and various. A list of Robert Savage's duties gives an idea of the back'us boy's working day.

He rose at six-thirty in the morning and his first job was to give the milking pails to the cowman. These were kept indoors for the sake of cleanliness and the cowman would have to come to the kitchen door to fetch them. He next made the copper-fire so that there would be plenty of water for the maids to carry upstairs for the family to wash. After the copper came the *black-stocks*—the open, barred fire-grates in which would be lighted either for warmth or for cooking. Then as he turned from the blackstocks he would see numerous pairs of boots and shoes which the maids had set out in the back-kitchen waiting to be cleaned. These were the footwear of the farmer's family and of the guests who happened to be staying in the house; and had to be taken upstairs by the maids before 'they' rose. His next job was to grind coffee for the cook; and he was also under her eye as he did his next job which was cleaning all the knives. The knives were made of steel and they were cleaned daily with bath-brick and a board specially kept for the purpose. He would just have time to feed the fowls before breakfast time at nine o'clock.

The fare for breakfast was usually herrings and salt pork. 'They were wunnerful people for herrings.' The herrings were smoked or bloatered and enough were bought to last a week: they were strung up on a line across the back-kitchen. Robert Savage was not happy with the breakfast when he first went to the farm because, as he said, 'Warm herrings and cold fat pork didn't fare to go right togither.' The girls used to go for the pork as they also went for the oatmeal porridge: the back'us boy, however, preferred the hominy—coarsely ground maize, boiled with water—that was an alternative to the porridge.

After breakfast came prayers. The girls filed into the drawing-room first and knelt down at the front. The back'us boy with the groom and any other male members of the household knelt behind them. Robert Savage confessed to tickling the girls in front of him to make them laugh: he was bored during prayers and would loiter over his breakfast purposely to get out of attending them. But after one of the family had read and a hymn had been sung, the servants would be released to their various tasks. The back'us boy's duties now took him outside: first to get the vegetables for dinner—potatoes, cabbages, roots, *sparrow-grass* (asparagus), anything that was in season. Then he chopped the kindling wood and filled the old brass-bound coal-scuttles and carried them into the house; next he peeled the potatoes for the cook.

Dinner was eaten about one-thirty, after the family had eaten theirs. The fare in the kitchen was the food that was left over from the dining-room. In the afternoon the back'us boy fed the fowls again; fetched the cows from the marshes; collected the eggs and did all kinds of jobs about the kitchen—any job that would turn up. Then came tea; and as soon as tea was cleared away and one or two little odd jobs completed, the last task was to take the letters up to the post office, about three-quarters of a mile away. This had to be done before six-thirty. If there were no evening jobs he could stay up in the village; this gave him a chance to visit his home and play with his friends. Whatever he did he had to be back at the farm before nine o'clock. But on some evenings he had to go back to dig in the garden; or if there were visitors he had to stand by to help with their horses when they went home. This was a better job than digging in the garden as the visitors invariably gave him a tip. There were other occasional and seasonal jobs such as churning the butter. This was done once a week during the winter; twice a week during the summer.

Wages were £1 a quarter, but there were some perquisites. He received a penny a score for the eggs he picked up about the farm. If one of the farm-workers discovered a hen's nest in a hedge or in the stack-yard, he would mark it by putting up a stick near it so that the back'us boy could find the nest and get his penny, or at least part of it. There would be occasions when the back'us boy was able to repay this kindness: for instance, when he was told to go down the cellar and draw beer for the gardener or the groom or any one of the workers who were entitled to a daily fixed amount, he would not be over-scrupulous about passing the fixed mark in the beer can.

The back'us boy also received a penny for plucking each fowl that was sold from the farm. The plucking of fowls that were consumed in the household was considered as part of his duty and there was no extra payment for these. For *drawing*—removing the entrails—and plucking a fowl to be sold he received twopence. All the little sums accruing to the back'us boy would be entered in the egg-book. The farmer's wife kept this in the knife-drawer in the kitchen, and often Robert Savage used to examine the book surreptitiously to see how much money he was accumulating.

But his estimate of the backhouse boy's lot is worth recording: it was a good job for a boy in spite of its arduousness: 'They looked after you and larned you well; they gave you a proper cultivation, and you were not brought up rough like the boys who went straight on to the land. Not many boys could stick at being a back'us boy, though I got on well enough. But they were wunnerful strict with you: I had to be in bed every night just after nine o'clock; and if they were to come in and see me a-settin' in the kitchen, talking with the girls, after this time they'd look at me some serious and I'd hev to go to bed. I used to sleep in the old part of the house, in the little room on top of the dairy, up the little steps. And Miss Jessie—she was kinda in charge— used to come through every night to go to her bedroom which was further along. The door opened and she could bolt it on the other side so the servants could git no further. She used to be on to me allus about sleepin' on my lift side. She would wake me up as she went through and git me on to my other side. I used to be half asleep and she'd cetch my elbow and I used to wonder what was happening. "You'll niver make a man," she say, "unless you sleep on your right side." It was the heart, they reckon. They say there's too much pressure o' blood on it if you sleep on your lift side. But I fare to sleep on my lift side allus—I can't sleep on my right; and she was allus on to me. She'd tell me if I worn't brisk enough in the morning: "There! Thet's through sleeping on your lift side; you may depend!"

'Sometimes I used to stop up to see to Old George's—the master's—horse if he was out late. Ephraim Row, the groom, would say to me sometimes that he didn't fare to be well and he'd ask me to see to the horse when the master came back. Old George used to go out in a *sulky*—a light kind o' trap; you was all boxed up in it and you couldn't fall out. So I would set up in the kitchen a-talking to the gels: sometimes it would be nigh midnight before the master came back; but they niver said nawthen to me when I was settin' up for him. I remember Old George didn't come back one night till close on midnight. I saw to his horse; fed him and wiped him down; and then I went to the back'us door to go in. But I found it was locked. Young George had gone out to feed his dawg afore going to bed and he'd locked the back'us door thinking that Ephraim Row had seen to his father's horse and had gone home—he used to sleep at his own house did Ephraim—so I was locked out. I was thirteen or fourteen at the time and I didn't want to go round to the front door: there was nothing for it but to go home. So I went off up the road and I knocked up my father with the linen-prop and I told him: "I hevn't got a bed to sleep in." And he came down tidy quick and opened the door, and I turned in that night with brother Will. I didn't go down to the Grove till nine o'clock next morning. There was something to do down there, I can tell you: no hot water to wash or nawthen! There was a kind o' official meetin' after I got down there to find out what it was all about. But it couldn't be helped and it all passed over.'

After he had been a backhouse boy for about two years Robert Savage went to help with the horses. He also assisted the shepherd at various times, especially during the lambing season. Shepherding was, in fact, his true interest; and when he was sixteen he 'drew off'—he ceased to live in the farmhouse—and went to tend the sheep; and he spent the rest of his working life with them. Sheep-tending was in his blood; therefore when the shepherd fell sick and the farmer offered to put him in sole charge of the flock with a man's wage he could not resist.

He went straight from being a shepherd's *page*, as he termed himself, to take the full responsibility of the flock. This must have caused him a certain amount of hesitation at the time: 'I was so young,' he said, 'that I dursn't stay out in the dark by myself. I was not man enough to stay with the flock throughout the night; so for a little while my father used to come out with me at night and sleep in the little ol' cabin along o' me. But I soon got used to it by myself and I took no notice of the queer little noises you hear in the night. I kept with the shepherding at the Grove until they gave up the sheep altogether; then I moved to a farm in the next parish.'

The shepherd was one of the most skilled and respected members of the old village community. He worked by himself; made his own decisions; and as far as the sheep were concerned laid down his own policy. And a farmer would have to be sure of his man before entrusting to him a flock of sheep whose welfare depended solely on the skill and trustworthiness of the shepherd and his occasional assistant. As our old shepherd says: 'Us shepherd chaps had to be serious chaps. The farmers would let us git on by ourselves. You were independent and you had to think forrard. You can't say with sheep: "I'll do this now and maybe I'll do that tomorrow." You got to wait and do everything in its turn. You got to think forrard. And you can't break into something different when you a-shepherding. I couldn't give my hid (head) to anything else until after I'd given up the sheep. Though you got plenty of time to think when you are with the sheep, 'cos shepherding is a lonely life. You got no one to talk to. For the whole fore part of the day, when you took them up to the walks you wouldn't see a soul.'

Robert Savage's wages when he started with the sheep were eleven shillings a week. This was a little above the ordinary farm-worker's wage and was fixed by a yearly agreement. When he got married a few years later he got twelve shillings a week. In addition to the weekly wage he also got lambing money. Lambing is the shepherd's harvest, and Robert Savage got sixpence for every lamb he reared. During the First World War this rose to ninepence: later it went up to a shilling.

The shepherd would have to wait until the lambing sales before he got his lambing-money; but some years he was compelled to ask for it before in order that he could buy shoes for his growing family. As well as the actual wages there were two or three perquisites. First the shepherd got a half a coomb of malt (two bushels) during lambing times in the same way as the other farm workers got a similar amount during harvest. Also, every time he killed a sheep he was entitled to the *hid and pluck*.

Back'us Boy and Shepherd

The head was cleaned and the *pluck*—the liver, etc.—was boiled with it in the same pot to 'make a wunnerful stew for poor people'.

The Savage family have lived in this parish for many years; and on Robert's mother's side the men have been shepherds for generations: as far back as memory extends. Shepherding was in fact, one of the rural skills that was carefully nurtured in families, with little secrets and knacks being handed down from generation to generation. Not long ago our shepherd was asked by a farmer, who grazes a very large flock of sheep in a parish at the other end of the county, if he could give him a cure for foot-rot. He produced an old tattered piece of paper with a cryptic formula written on it—a formula which the farmer managed successfully to decipher and to apply. An ancestor of Robert Savage had a similar reputation as an authority on sheep ailments. Lionel Richardson was born at the beginning of the last century, and his name appears as a cottage holder in this parish in the Tithe Commutation Returns of 1838. A contemporary account reads:

'Liney (Lionel) Riches or Richardson was a shepherd known far and wide as an authority on all matters relating to sheep and their ailments. His opinion and advice were much valued by neighbouring shepherds, who in important and critical cases, would "walk across" and consult the sage.

'He and his family lived in a lonely cottage on the heath near the Blaxhall and Tunstall boundary, in the garden of which, notwithstanding the poverty of the soil, he grew good crops of greengages. Much of his time was spent with his flock on the heath; with certain parts of which his presence came to be so intimately connected that they still bear his name. A small pond at which in dry weather he used to water his sheep is even now spoken of as "Liney's Drink". A tumulus or artificial mound of some kind, on high ground much frequented by the shepherd, was and probably is still known as "Liney's Mount". Here he would stand and overlook his large flock of Down and Norfolk scattered abroad among the whin bushes.

Robert Savage

'Liney Riches was about middle height. He had good, regular and rather refined features. His gait, like that of many whose work is entirely restricted to the tending of sheep, was quite free from the swaying, rolling movements so often acquired by those who have long been accustomed to follow the plough. With his shepherd's *slop* or smock flowing gracefully behind him; with crook on shoulder and dog at heel he would sail grandly in front of his sheep at a steady, even pace, his body leaning slightly forward and head thrown back—a picturesque figure in the landscape; but also a personage of some importance in the district: the consulting surgeon and physician of the parish in all cases of injury to sheep.

'He used to discourse learnedly on the various mixtures (drugs) he made use of, and of sundry mysterious "iles" of great virtue and efficiency; "green iles" being held in particular estimation. Oil, be it noted, is in Suffolk spoken of as in the plural. "Rub on a few iles night and morning" is a piece of advice one often hears in cases of sprains. He had a remedy for the foot-rot on which he set great value. He described it as containing, "Nine different mixtures asidus-o-witterol"; which being interpreted means, "Nine different ingredients besides vitriol". The number of these was evidently considered to ensure the potency of the remedy.

'It is impossible in writing to give any idea of his fine rendering of the pure Suffolk dialect; or the true pronunciation of certain vowels and diphthongs. Liney had the courteous and respectful but dignified manner often notable in the elder shepherds and farm labourers of his time. His greeting was usually, "Sarvent, Sir", or "Sarvice tie yer, Sir". As to his language, a conversation between Liney and his old friend John H. would be hardly intelligible to one unfamiliar with the pure Suffolk dialect as it existed before the days of railways, board schools and so on.

'In pointing out the position of some particular member of his flock he would say: "Hin owd on laid agin the hid o' the trow"; or "She stan' agin the holl (ditch) hinder a chowin' o' the quid". His speech was rather slow, deliberate and free from all hesitation or uncertainty. For many years he had charge of a large flock of black-faced sheep owned by old Mr H. referred to above.

'Liney was, as before stated, an acknowledged authority on the management of sheep; and it also appears that he was well aware of the fact, and resented any interference. The story goes that his new master's son, in conversation with the shepherd, said something about his father's opinion as to some matter concerning the treatment of sheep which differed from that adopted by Liney: whereupon the latter is reported to have exclaimed: "Yar father! What d'yar father know about a *ship* (sheep) I ha' forgot more about a ship than yar father iver larned!"

'Liney was a skilful trainer and handler of a sheep-dog and almost always managed to have a good one. His old yellow and white Bob used to go about in summer with his head and ears bound up in a crimson handkerchief as a protection from the flies. Liney Riches was, I believe, one of the first in his district to make use of "Scotch dorgs"—collies—for his work.'

This account was written by George Rope (1846–1929), an artist and naturalist, who was called *Young George* to distinguish him from his father *Old George* who was born in 1814 and died fifteen months before reaching a hundred. But another and more intimate account of the old shepherd survives; and it shows him in a different light altogether. It comes from Robert Savage's family. His mother, who lived until she was over ninety, was brought up in Liney's household; and her stories about him are still remembered in the family.

Liney's life as a shepherd followed the pattern that was typical of a farm-worker's life at that period—long hours, a large family and almost constant poverty, if not actual want. There were, however, two ways of relieving this poverty: poaching and smuggling. Both were unlawful; but at that time, in spite of heavy penalties, they were both so commonly practised as to be thought of hardly as crimes at all. Liney's way of relieving the poverty of his family was by smuggling. The sheep walks extended right down to an inlet in the coast where cargoes of contraband goods were regularly landed on dark nights. Liney was in league with the smugglers, and his job was to help them to put away the cargoes in a safe place before the morning; he also kept them well informed of the movements of the 'preventive men'.

It was quite a common thing at that time for a farmer to hear two or three of his horses, and perhaps a wagon, being taken out of his yard in the dead of night. Usually he was wise enough to turn over on his pillow and go off to sleep. He knew that the horses would be back in their stables before the next morning; and though he knew that the people who were borrowing them would—as the Suffolk saying is—ride a black horse white, he realized that it would not do to complain or to ask too many questions about the condition they were in. He recognized, too, that next day he need not be too curious about the tub of wine, the canister of tea, or the roll of silk or lace he found hidden under straw in the corner of his barn.

Old Liney's chief task on the night when a cargo was being *run* was to keep his eyes open and to turn his flock of sheep from the fold and quickly cover up the tracks of the wagon when it returned full—particularly did he do this near the spot, either barn or cottage—where the contraband was being hidden. It was a clever excise man who could trace exactly the route of the wagon after Liney's sheep had been walking the road.

The story comes down that Liney's wife knew well when a cargo was being run. And on these occasions it was her practice to gather all her children round her and sit by the kitchen fire; and not one of them dared move or utter a word until their father returned safely. Many people from this area had suffered transportation for life, ending their days in the penal settlements of Australia, for smuggling offences; and Liney's wife knew the risk he was running. She was, therefore, in dreadful suspense the whole time her husband was away, waiting anxiously for the sound of his returning footsteps, when the children would be released from their enforced silence. As far as we know, Liney Riches was never caught; and he finished his life, to all appearances, the peaceful, rather idyllic shepherd of George Rope's word-picture.

Although, at the time of writing, there is not a flock of sheep left in our parish, the rearing of sheep and the selling of their wool was at one time at least as important as the growing of corn. Methods of farming have since changed, and sheep are not considered as essential to the present-day farms as they used to be. But some of the older people say that it was a bad day when they left the sheep out of farming in this district. For, they say, sheep fertilised the land, giving back to it the goodness taken away in the form of crops; and giving it back more efficiently than can ever be done by artificial manures. And it is fairly certain that in the past no farming at all would have been possible in the light, sandy soil or heathland of this district had it not been trodden and manured by countless generations of sheep. There are few districts in England where the old proverb—the foot of the sheep turns sand into gold—could be repeated with more truth. Another aspect of this change in farming is the resulting loss of the old shepherding skill which is traditional in this parish. Robert Savage has trained two of his sons as shepherds; but neither at the present time is working with a flock; and it is likely that when sheep become popular again it will not be an easy job to find skilled shepherds to look after them.

The rearing of sheep also formed a part of the closely-knit economy of the countryside. Every activity and calling in the old village community that has been passing away since the coming of the machines was dovetailed into the whole; and when one ceased the effect of this was often much wider than one would suppose. To give an example: one of the direct effects of the absence of sheep along the Suffolk coast was pointed out after the disastrous flooding of February 1953. Formerly, the sheep ate the grass on the sea-walls which have been built and kept in repair for hundreds of years along parts of this coast. They kept the turf on these walls firm by their constant cropping; and by their regular tramping and treading, filled in the rat-holes and rabbit burrows that would naturally appear from time to time along the surfaces. When the sheep were removed, the sea-walls gradually became weaker and less able to withstand an ordinary tide, much less an exceptionally high one. Steel and concrete sea and river walls were built in their stead; but these in the opinion of many local people who know this coast are not standing up as well as the old walls. These turf-covered banks—although not as spectacular to look at—were more effective as they were constantly renewing their own strength by their natural growth; and the sheep helped them to do so.

As has already been stated the sheep have gone from this parish chiefly because of the general change in the method of farming; but the occasion when they went is worth noting. This happened during the 1914–18 war. There was quite a lot of enemy activity along this coast. Submarines and surface vessels sometimes came inshore and shelled the coastal towns and villages. Robert Savage reports that the sheep did not like these happenings at all, and often panicked in their folds, becoming 'hurdlers' and jumping out and scattering over the countryside. It was decided to send them further inland. Many flocks were taken into West Suffolk; but when the war ended the sheep did not return to this parish in any numbers. In Robert Savage's early days there were over two thousand sheep in the seven or eight farms in the parish: after the First World War this number dwindled considerably.

2 Shepherds' Dress and Gear

Another old shepherd of this parish, a contemporary of Liney Richardson, is also remembered. He was William Meadows, and his is another example of a family living in the same village for generations. He himself, his son and his grandson all worked on the same farm at Dunningworth, on the site of the old decayed Domesday village mentioned in the Appendix. Between them they have a record of over 150 years' service on the same farm. William E. Meadows, grandson of the first William Meadows, died two years ago. He had a long service certificate for fifty-three years' service on this farm; and his father, also called William Meadows, was in 1922 awarded a certificate for sixty-two years' continuous service. In the eighteen-eighties, when all three Williams were alive together, they were known as Old Billy, Young Billy, and Young Billy's Son.

We have an accurate picture, taken from family memories, of the way shepherds dressed in Old Billy's days. For work they wore a shepherd's smock or *slop* made from eight yards of drabbet—drab twilled linen. The material was 'honeycombed' across the chest and occasionally on the sleeves as well. Inside the slop were two long hanging, or *poacher's*, pockets so that a shepherd could very easily conceal a couple of rabbits in its generous folds. It can be be gathered from this that the honeycombings, although the most picturesque additions to the slop, were not the most useful. This can be illustrated by one of Robert Savage's stories:

He was up on the Heath one morning with his sheep and he heard someone shooting near an adjoining copse. He saw the man go away, and a little later he himself left a boy in charge of the sheep and made for the village. As he walked he came across a hare lying dead in the grassy pathway. It had a gunshot wound and it was still warm. Without hesitating he picked it up and put it in one of his *slop* pockets. But the hare was so big—he found afterwards that it weighed nearly a stone—that it would not stay in the pocket. So he took off his *slop*; bound it tightly round the hare and slung it over his shoulder, walking home in his shirt sleeves. 'As I came down the lane from the Heath I saw the policeman a-talking to old Billy Whitehead, the schoolmaster. Billy sees me a-coming and he says: "I see you got your smock off, Bob. You must be kind o' warm." So I said: "It is right warm—wery close indeed." And I thought to myself right close it was! But there's a rum 'um for you! I'd been a-going down that lane hundreds of times, and the first time I had something in my pocket I must see the policeman. But you couldn't be too particular in those days. With the house full of children and wages as low as they were, you couldn't pass by nawthen at that time o' day.'

There were no openings in the slop either at the front or the back; no wind could get into it and for that reason it was very warm. It also kept out the rain. When it was very wet, with the wind driving the rain across the heath or the pastures, the shepherd carried a large *gig* umbrella. Sheltering under this he could spend a whole wet day up on the Heath and return home dry at the end of it. He took his food with him; and for drink he would have home-brewed beer carried in a wooden keg strapped around his shoulder. He might have a costrel instead of a keg. This was an earthenware bottle and was also much used at harvest time. It was designed in the same way as the mediaeval 'pilgrim' bottles—so as to hang by a cord from the waist. Costrels were made at the pottery at Iken—the next village towards the coast. A very fine example, made at Iken in 1834, still exists.

The shepherd's boots were made by one of the village shoe-makers—*shummackers* as they were known here. During Robert Savage's early years there were two shoemakers, who also did some cobbling, and one man who did nothing but cobbling. One of the shoemakers, called Benjamin Newson, had a small hut for a workshop; and he let the boys go inside during the evenings to watch him work. Many boys here learned to cobble shoes that way. Children had to treat their shoes or boots with great respect in those days—forty or fifty years ago—because they would only possess one pair. Every Saturday night they would be given an extra cleaning in an attempt to convert them into 'Sunday' boots. The shummacker's bill was paid once a year, at Michaelmas—with the extra money gained by the harvest work. But the shummacker was never grudged his money, for the boots he made were good ones. The boots he sold were called *made* boots to distinguish them from *bought* boots which came from the town shops. Made boots were very strong; they kept out the weather much better than factory boots, and they lasted much longer. They had flaps over the lace-holes and double tongues that made them quite waterproof. These boots could be worn constantly for a year. At the end of this time, they would be *clumped*—a clump or extra sole of leather would be riveted on to them. They would last for about three years, having almost constant wear in all weathers.

For walking out and going to sales the shepherd wore a sleeved *weskit* (waistcoat) with breeches and *buskins*. Old William Meadows wore buskins—canvas leggings reaching to the knees—regularly. Even on ceremonial occasions, for instance when he walked out with his wife, he wore them with a long *slop* and very tall felt hat. Chief of the shepherd's tools was the crook. One of Robert Savage's sons has in his possession a very old *nut-tree* (hazel wood) crook. This was the one used by Liney Richardson; and had probably been in use in the family before him. Wooden crooks have not been much used in the last hundred and fifty years, and Liney Richardson's crook has been preserved for many years just as a family heirloom. The iron crook was generally used during the last century as it is today. Often it was made from the barrel of an old muzzle-loading gun, according to the shepherd's own design. Shop-bought crooks would be of no use to him—'only good for shepherd-girls in a play'! The shepherd would sketch out the size and the shape of the crook he required and get the local blacksmith to fashion it exactly as he wanted it; for the size of sheep varied from county to county, and one shape and size of crook would not do for all.

The crook is used for picking out and holding a sheep in the fold. If a shepherd wants to examine a particular sheep that is limping a little, or has something about it he wants to see to, as it runs past him he shoots out the crook, holding it firmly near the end of its long wooden handle. The crook slides up the near hind-leg of the sheep and the thigh is fixed immovably in its curve. By a neat twist of the wrist the shepherd throws the sheep onto its back; in that position the sheep is examined without any trouble. In some districts, though not as far as we know in ours, shepherds used to carve designs on the wooden handles of their crooks.

The shears or clippers used for taking off the sheep's wool, were made of steel—all in one piece, with a spring handle. The shape of the old hand-shear did not vary for centuries: old memorial slabs, dating from the Middle Ages and commemorating wool-staplers or clothiers, show clippers of an identical shape to those used right up to the introduction of the mechanical shears at the beginning of the present century.

The sheep-bells were among the shepherd's most important *tools*. In Blaxhall there were often five or six flocks of sheep on the Heath, or sheep-walk, at the same time: to distinguish the flocks the leading sheep of each flock wore a bell round its neck. Each bell would have a different note so that a shepherd could easily pick out the direction of his flock even if he could not see them—as sometimes happened when a *dag* or heavy mist came down; or it got dark more quickly than he had expected. Normally, however, he would take the sheep back to their fold in the early afternoon. Robert Savage had a collection of these bells: they are of varying age and design and each has a different note. The leading sheep or *cosset* was one that had 'taken a fancy' to the shepherd since it was very young: perhaps the shepherd had reared it himself after the death of its mother; perhaps it had taken to attaching itself to the shepherd as soon as it could walk. Whatever the reason, the cosset carried the bell and he followed the shepherd wherever he went. The rest of the flock would follow the cosset. This enabled the Suffolk shepherd, as distinct from shepherds of many other parts of Britain, always to walk in *front* of his flock, opening the gates and in fact guiding his flock like the traditional biblical shepherd, while his dog followed on behind whipping up the stragglers, like a deacon zealous in his master's business.

Another tool the shepherd found essential was the turnip-pick. With this he broke up the turnips into pieces so the sheep in the fold could more easily eat them. Especially was it necessary to cut up turnips for the *crones*—the old sheep without any teeth; otherwise they would be likely to starve. A *beet-chopper* for chopping up cattle-beet (mangel-wurzels) served the same purpose. The roots were often placed in a box and the chopper was used to cut them, rammer-fashion, into small pieces. It is worth noting here that the shepherds in the sixteenth century illustration to Spenser's *The Shepheardes Calender* have crooks with an attachment at the bottom of the handle; this might well have been used for root-chopping. There was also the old *horn-lantern*, a candle lantern with its windows made of horn. This gave a dim glow, rather than a bright light which would have frightened the sheep and disturbed them unnecessarily when they had been folded down for the night. There was also the *fold-pritch*, a heavy iron-bar about four feet long, having a square end brought to a point. This was used for driving holes into the ground so that the hurdles for the fold could more easily be erected.

Robert Savage

Thomas Tusser reminds us that the shepherd had a *tar-box* which held the tar-ointment he smeared on the sheep's cuts and wounds. Here are contemporary instructions for a shepherd: although written in the sixteenth century they are far from being out of date:

'The Sheepheard (must) have a little board sette fast to the side of his little fold to lay his sheepe upon when he handleth them and a hole bored in the board with an auger and therein a grained stake of two feet long to be set fast, to hang his Tarre box upon so then it shall not fall. And a Shepheard should not goe without his dogge, his sheep hooke, a pair of sheares and his tar box. . . . and hee must teach his dog to barke when hee would have him, to runne when he would have him, to leave running, or els hee is not a cunning Sheepheard. The dog must learne it when he is a whelp, or els it will not be, for it is hard to make an old dog for Sheepe.'

The dog has always been the shepherd's essential helper. Robert Savage had many different types of sheep-dog during his shepherding days. One of the best was a bob-tailed dog—an old English sheep-dog. He was a 'rare good dog'; very quick and intelligent and as gentle as a maid. But he had one fault; he was lazy in the summer. This, however, was not due to any inherent bad nature; his drowsiness was caused by the thickness of his coat. For in the heat of a summer's day he would have to slink panting into the shade; and there he would lie down at odds with the weather and with himself; and there he would stay irresponsive to his master's call. Yet if there was a pond or a full ditch into which he could plunge he came out refreshed and worked the sheep with vigour.

Many *crosses* with the old English sheep-dog were tried: the cross with a terrier was of no use because the dog would *hang*—bite the wool and often actually nip the skin of the sheep; the cross with the wolf-dog (alsatian) was more successful: 'Some people didn't trust the wolf-dogs, but they were whoolly fine dogs and bred for sheep over in France; and the cross would make a fine sheep-dog. The red collies were stately, good-looking dogs, but they were not as useful as the crosses. The best dog iver I had was the first cross of an old English sheep-dog with a red collie. She wor called Nellie—a bitch she wor. She would do something that no other dog I had iver did; and the rum thing was, no one iver larned her to do it (it must have been in the breed) as soon as iver I'd make for the gate—I didn't want to lift a finger or say nawthen—she'd up and round the sheep in a twinkle. And she'd soon have them following arter me: she kept behind them and had them as close together as folk at a wedding. I remember one morning I was working her and she suddenly walked off and wouldn't come back when I called. I was whoolly roiled. Then I went up to the hut and found she got underneath, made a kind o' hollow and had pupped. I took her and the family home; but I had to keep working her because I had no other dog for sheep. So I used to take her and her pups to the sheep in a donkey cart; and during the day the family would be underneath the cart and she'd lay with them whenever she got a chance.'

3 Sheep Shearing

U nder the old method of farming it was a poor year when
the farmer could not gather his rent from the back of his
flock: it is not surprising, therefore, that the sheep-shearing was
as important to him as the corn-harvest. The shearing was also
just as much a country occasion as the harvesting. It was so in
the time of Shakespeare and his contemporary, Tusser. Thomas
Tusser, who according to his own testimony, 'Then tooke I wife
and led my life in Suffolk soile', has given a comprehensive picture of Elizabethan farming. A fellow writer said of him: 'He
spread his bread with all sorts of butter, yet none of it would ever
stick thereon'; and it is true that he died in a debtors' prison,
thus seeming to confirm the contempt practical husbandmen feel
for mere book-farmers. But Tusser gave much sound advice, and
his verse is far from being unreadable, in spite of its jog-trotting
rhythm. He can still be read with profit, especially in East Anglia
if only to help fix the meaning of old words that now survive in
the dialect.

But before the actual shearing, the farmers in our parish, up
to thirty or forty years ago, would first have their sheep washed
as the fleece or *clip* of the sheep could be marketed in a much
better condition and could thus demand a higher price. But the
sheep are rarely washed today, at least in this country: probably
the modern farmer has found that his unwashed wool at a
greater weight but lower price is worth as much as a smaller

quantity of washed wool sold at a higher price. There is an added reason why sheep are rarely washed nowadays: the grease which is present in unwashed wool is valuable for the making of lanoline, much used as the basis of ointments, shampoos and so on.

The washing of sheep in this parish used to be done about a fortnight before the clipping or shearing. After the lapse of about eight days some of the grease begins to return to the sheep's wool, and it *comes up*, assuming its normal position and texture. It would be impossible to *clip* before this. In the summer the wool comes up, is *frizzed out*, naturally; in winter it *stays down* to keep in the warmth. That is the reason, or at least one of the reasons, why it would not be possible—even were it desirable—to clip in the winter.

A large square tub was taken and placed on the bank of the river beside a pool. One or two men were engaged in filling up the tub with water from the river, while two more stood over the tub to handle the sheep into the wash. Each sheep was first *breasted*, that is its underside was washed; next it was turned on its back. It was then lifted out of the tub on to a platform of straw that had been arranged near the tub. For a few moments the fleece would be so heavy with water that the sheep could not stand. Presently, however, it would get up and shake itself and drift away to its fellows who had already been treated. But even at this period the wash was just as unpopular with the shepherd as with the sheep: they were so likely to catch cold after it and it meant extra work for him in doctoring. In fact, there is no animal so prone to ill-health as a sheep that has not had the shepherd's constant care: ticks, foot-rot and accidents demand that he be always ready with his *tar-box* or its modern equivalent.

Tusser in his *June Husbandrie* devotes his first two stanzas to the subject of sheep-washing:

> *Wash sheep—for the better—where water doth run,*
> *and let him go cleanly and dry in the sun:*
> *Then shear him, and spare not, at two days an end,*
> *the sooner the better his corps will amend.*

Robert Savage

Reward not thy sheep, when ye take off his coat,
with twitches and patches as broad as a groat;
Let no such ungentleness happen to thine,
lest fly with the gentils do make it to pine.

Gentils are maggots which breed in any break in the sheep's skin. Tusser appears to recommend only two days should elapse between the washing and the clipping. Possibly the explanation for this short period is that the sixteenth century sheep did not have as heavy a fleece as the present-day sheep: we know that they were much smaller in build. And with a lighter fleece the wool would *come up* more quickly.

In addition to being washed the sheep were regularly *dipped*. Dipping was done after shearing, before the sheep was taken to the sales. The process of dipping killed the lice and ticks or sheep-scab; also the smell of the dip persisted for some time afterwards and gave the sheep a rest from flies. The sheep here were dipped twice a year: once in June and again at the latter part of September. In our village sheep-dipping or *dressing* is a skilled craft which has been handed down for generations in one family. The man who practised this trade at the beginning of this century had a board outside his house: it read CHARLES SMITH: SHEEP DRESSER. In the village he was known as *Ship-dresser Smith*; and he owned a special dipping wagon, used solely for this trade. He used to point out humorously that sheep-dressing was a very different thing from sheep-shearing which you could describe accurately as the *undressing* of a sheep.

On the sheep-dressing wagon was a large tub which was lifted to the ground and filled with a special *dip* or mixture that had been a secret in the Smith family for generations. From the tub was a ramp leading onto the wagon: the sheep was lifted into the *dip;* allowed to stay in for a few seconds and was then assisted up the ramp. A gate across the opposite end of the wagon prevented them from proceeding straight down another ramp which led to the ground. But when most of the dip had dripped off them, running back into the tub, the gate was opened and they scampered off into the fold.

In this parish the sheep-shearing used to be one of the big occasions of the year. The clipping was done by a body of men known as the Blaxhall Company of Sheep Shearers. At the turn of the century, and earlier, it was no use for a farmer to try to hand-shear his own flock of sheep: it would take too long. Moreover the shearing came at that time of the year when most of the workers would be busy at the *haysel* or hay harvest. Therefore it was the custom for companies of men to be formed: these went round to each farm specially to shear the sheep. The Blaxhall Company goes back further than local memory or written records, and it probably has its origin in the sixteenth or seventeenth century or even earlier.

The men who made up the company fifty years ago were not all-the-year-round employees of any one farmer; they were independent men working on their own account at such jobs as hedging and ditching on piecework; bark-peeling or any other seasonal occupation connected with agriculture. During the six or seven weeks of the sheep-shearing season any one of the company could earn as much as the average farm-worker would during six months of continuous work. His was a skilled job, and the expert sheep-clipper who could take off an entire fleece without once snipping and injuring the sheep was well thought of and of great use in the old farming community.

Before the clipping started, the Blaxhall Company elected a captain to command it; the captain in his turn chose a lieutenant who would write the letters and would be a kind of clerk dealing with the business side of the company. The procedure, it may be noted, is very much like that of the harvest company and the Lord and Lady who organized the harvest.

On the Sunday night before the shearing season started, the company gathered at the village inn, appropriately called *The Ship* (Sheep) Inn. The landlord used to reserve a special room for them, and help them in a general way—by ordering a supply of whetstones which they used to sharpen their shears, and by cashing their cheques for them when they were paid by the farmers. To the Ship Inn would be summoned the shepherds of all the flocks the company proposed to shear during the ensuing week. The captain would arrange with each shepherd the day that would suit him best for shearing; and the shepherd would undertake to have his flock ready on the appointed day. This was called 'allotting the sheep'. Having made their arrangements for the week the company would disperse. Next morning at six o'clock they would assemble at the first farm on their list.

Their first job was to prepare the shearing platform. For this they lifted the two big barn-doors off their hinges and laid them on bricks to form a raised table. The shepherd would have his flock ready penned for them. At this time of year there are frequently heavy dews; and if the flock was left out all night the clippers' work would be delayed until the fleeces had dried out. Therefore if the shepherd was at all able he placed his flock under cover—either in barn or cow-byre—on the night before the shearing, thus making sure that there would be no hold-up in the morning.

There were eight or nine men in the Blaxhall company when it was at full strength; and these could clip the wool off a whole flock during one day. A sheep-shearer using the hand-shears could clip nearly two score of sheep during the day; he would take from eighteen to twenty minutes for each sheep, depending on the state of the fleece. The length of the working day would be from twelve to fourteen hours. Every three sheep clipped— so was the Blaxhall custom—the shearer rested for a *horn* of beer. Every five sheep he had what was known as a *pull-up and sharp*—beer with a drop of gin and time to sharpen his shears with the whetstone. If the wool had not *come up* properly he would have to sharpen more often. The pay, about fifty years ago, was five shillings for every score of sheep sheared: when one considers that an ordinary farm worker here was at that time getting not much more than ten shillings a week, this was good pay. But it was gruelling work, especially for the first few days, before the muscles of the wrist had become hardened to the constant gripping and working of the shears. After the first day, each man's wrist would be swollen up and painful; but gradually this wore off as the week went on.

The company worked the farms within a radius of ten miles of this village. While they were away from home, they *slept rough* —that is, wherever they could. They would lie down on some hay in the barn after they had eaten their suppers; or if it was a fine warm night they would even sleep out on their shearing platform. A story told by Priscilla Savage, wife of Robert Savage, concerns the time when the sheep-shearers were working a few miles from home and were sleeping where they could in this manner. Priscilla Savage when a girl lived near a village called Snape, in a lonely house overlooking the estuary. This house had been mixed up with smuggling and like many of these houses had the reputation, spurious or otherwise, of being haunted. When her father, Aaron Ling—one of the sheep-shearers—was papering one of the rooms he found a piece of glass cemented into the wall as though something had been fixed behind it. He and his wife decided to leave it untouched and cover it up again with paper. Shortly before this time the family had been disturbed by the front door opening, presumably of its own accord; on each occasion at about the same time during the night. Following the opening of the door a noise 'as of chains' would be heard on the stairs and something would ascend to the upper part of the house. Then came the sheep-shearing season and the company were working towards Hazelwood and Aldeburgh way. To save them going home each night to Blaxhall, Prissy's mother let four or five of them sleep in the back-room upstairs, on blankets laid on the floor. This was the room that the *Thing*, whatever it was, seemed to make for. The first night the shearers slept there they heard a noise on the stairs and the *Thing* came into the room. But Humpy Sam Ling, one of the shearers, jumped up. He was short and had a deep voice. 'He was a Christian man was Humpy Sam and he got up bold and said to the *Thing*: "What seekest thou?" And whatever it was went away and niver came back for weeks.' If one had known Humpy Sam perhaps one could imagine the ghost's dismay: he was a very short man with wide shoulders and a dark fringe of beard outlining his broad face.

At the end of each week the shearers returned home to this village; and on Sunday night they met again in the Ship Inn to get out their programme for the following week. They moved their gear from one farm to another in a horse and trap owned by the *ship-dresser*. Some of the shearers also owned donkeys and when they were harnessed to their little carts they would follow the ship-dresser's pony and trap without any trouble.

When the company was working at a farm in, or not very far from the village their families would go out to them to have their main meal of the day—usually after the work had been completed. The wives and children carried out the food in big baskets covered with cloths. The sheep-shearing platform would then be cleared and covered with white table-cloths. The food was then placed all together on the improvised table and shared in common by all the clippers and their families. The fare eaten at these open-air dinners was traditionally pork, dumplings, spring cabbage and new potatoes, followed by suet pudding. The meat and the vegetables would all be boiled in the same pot. The dumplings were called *fillers*, as the father would have most of the meat while the rest of the family filled up with the dumplings and the gravy; but the children often called them *swimmers* as they always floated on top of the pot of meat and vegetables. The men had home-brewed beer to drink, the children *small* or very weak beer. As at harvest-time this was kept in large earthenware bottles and was served in horn-beakers, one of which each man would carry in his bag with his shears and whetstones. As it was horn it was less likely to be broken. Often the farmer would supply drink—beer or cider—for the shearers. It was brought to them in a large earthenware jug called a *gotch:* on one farm in this village the beer was brought into the fields in a copper jug called a *ranter*.

After the sheep-shearing season was over there would be a settling up and the company would disband and each man would go back to his seasonal job—some of them went back to sea to the herring boats, others to ditching; bark-peeling would not claim them until the early spring when the sap in the trees would begin to rise and the bark would come off more easily. This bark was sent away to the big tanning centres. But before the company dispersed there would be a Sheep-shearing Frolic or Supper. This would roughly follow the lines of the Harvest Frolic; but instead of songs like the Barley Mow, old sheep-clipping songs would be sung. Here are two verses from one of them:

Come all my jolly boys, and we'll together go
Abroad with our masters to shear the lamb and ewe;
All in the merry month of June, of all times in the year,
It always comes in season the ewes and lambs to shear;
And here we must work hard, boys, until our back do ache
And our master he will bring us beer whenever we do lack.

Our master he comes round to see our work is doing well,
And he cries, 'Shear them close, men, for there is but little wool.'
'Oh yes, good master,' we reply, 'We'll do well as we can.'
When our captain calls, 'Shear close, boys!' to each and every man.
And at some places still we have this story all day long,
'Close them, boys, and shear them well!' and this is all their song.

Sheep-shearing feasts were very big occasions a century or two ago; even in Shakespeare's time, as we know from *The Winter's Tale*, they were one of the important country holidays. Although the shearers in this village were not 'three-man song-men all, and very good ones' they seem to have enjoyed their singing, and the shearing frolic is still remembered by the older people.

Harry Mason, a Coddenham shepherd who was born a year or so before Robert Savage, recalls many of the sheep-shearing frolics in Blaxhall. He also remembers the actual work at the shearing and the way they opened the fleece: 'You trimmed the sheep's body first, and you opened the front right up to the neck just as though you were unbuttoning a shart or a weskit. Then you cut down the back legs where the wool hangs over; and you did the same for the front. Do you leave it till later you wouldn't get at the wool that lay just there. Then you set the sheep on its backside and you clipped up one side, just over the backbone. You next twizzled the sheep round and set into your work where you left off. *Bellying*— trimming the front—was the first job they gave the young "colts", the beginners; and the old 'uns would have to finish off.' Harry Mason also gave an interesting note on the shearing platform: 'Using the old hand-shears you *had* to hev a platform. If you hadn't a board, you couldn't set the heel o' your shears down: it would cetch in the ground. So you'd allus hev to set into your work askew, and you couldn't make a right straight job of it. It's different with the machine-shears: you can clip a sheep on the ground quite easily with them.'

Hand-clipping was displaced by machinery about forty years ago; but for some time many farmers still engaged the hand-clippers because they maintained that unless the machine-shearer had a very good knowledge of his trade, he could easily do more damage to a sheep than ever the old hand-shearers would. Moreover, in spite of the captain's admonition in the song to 'Shear them close, boys!' the hand-shearer rarely stripped to the skin as the machine does. He left an *undervest* of wool to shelter the sheep, and there were little ridges in this which *weather-boarded* or protected the sheep against the wind and the rain.

The sheep-shearers in Blaxhall often used their shears out of season as well. There was no full-time barber in the village at that time, just as there is none today. One of the shearers, Aaron Ling, used to cut hair and shave, chiefly at week-ends. Sometimes he would have as many as twenty customers at his house on a Sunday morning. On those of his customers who wanted a hair-cut he first used the sheep shears, to 'take off the rough'; afterwards he 'trimmed them up' with the scissors. Aaron Ling's son, Abraham—now retired and over seventy—is the village hair-cutter today. But he no longer uses the shears, having long ago been converted to the use of the modern hair-cutting machine or *clippers*.

Sheep Shearing

Each sheep-shearer, when he was out on a job, carried two or three shears in a long canvas bag slung on his back. As shears are sprung to the *open* position, they were shut for ease of carrying with a piece of wool tied tightly round the end of the blades. When he reached home the shearer's wife stripped the wool from the shears, substituting a piece of rag or cord, then washed it and put it away. When she had saved enough wool she used it for filling a pillow or a cushion.

One custom, called elsewhere *transhumance*, was yearly practised in this village. This is analogous to the custom, which is still prevalent in Wales, whereby the shepherd moves his flock from their winter-quarters in the valleys onto the hill pastures and moorlands. Here the sheep were taken down to the low marshes bordering the coast. After the lambs had been sold and the sheep had been *shackin'*—stubble-feeding on the fields that had already been harvested—Robert Savage used to take them down to the *saltings*. It was a break for a shepherd for he had nothing much to do except to watch out for the fly and the gentils, as Tusser called them, and to examine the sheep for foot-rot. He would be helped in his job by the *marshman*, a worker who was employed permanently on the marshes to count all the stock every morning and evening to see if any beast had fallen into the dykes. There were *drinkways* made here and there to enable the sheep or cattle to get to the water, but occasionally one would fall into a steep part of the dyke and be unable to get out by its own efforts.

The salt in the water and the pasture caused the sheep to *scour* at first; but after a few days they would settle down. They fed on the *roan* grass, the second crop of grass after the hay had been taken. The salt grazing did the ewes a lot of good and helped them to 'renew their blood afore the rams were turned in with them about October time. Ewes fare to breed much better after being down on the marshes.'

Here on the marshes the shepherd used his particular method of counting. In this parish the shepherd counted in scores, as shepherds have done from very early times. He placed his hurdle

so that there was enough room for two sheep—and two only—
to go through at a time. As each pair went through he would
mutter to himself: "Yew and yar partner; yew and yar partner,'
—ten times. Then he would let drop into his pocket a small
pebble, a handful of which he kept for tally-stones. Each pebble
he dropped would represent a score.

The return from the marshes marked a term in the shepherd's
year. Very soon afterwards the rams would be put to the ewes,
and the same round of birth and tending, shearing, lamb-sales
and temporary migration would start all over again—a rhythm
in the slow, steady pulse of the rural year. Perhaps it is this
element of permanence in the pattern of the shepherd's life that
has given him such a place in the literature of the past and has
not excluded him from that of the present day. The old ploughman and the broadcast sower have passed away as vital symbols
of the undying processes of seed, growth and endeavour; but the
shepherd's life is basically the same as it was in biblical times;
and, one supposes, as it always will be. Yet shepherds, from the
Greek poet Theocritus's time right up to the Elizabethans, and
even to the present, have been looked at with eyes a little
clouded by the supposed idyllic nature of their calling. But, as
our old shepherd has said, shepherding is a hard, lonely life,
a twenty-four hours a day job when a man can afford to have
nothing in his 'hid' but sheep. Yet, in spite of this, something
remains about a shepherd's life that appeals: perhaps it is that
the life is more selfless than most, more in tune with nature and
human kind. Whatever it is, shepherding undoubtedly seems to
bring out a quality which is best suggested by the words of the
old shepherd's toast:

> *If I had store*
> *By sheep and fold,*
> *I'd give you gold;*
> *But, since I'm poor,*
> *By crook and bell,*
> *I wish you well.*

PART TWO

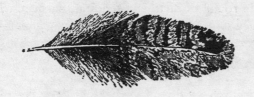

PRISCILLA SAVAGE

4 Bread

Priscilla Savage—or Prissy, as she is known—Robert Savage's wife, has had a life typical of that of a woman married to a farm-worker who had to bring up a large family on low wages. She sometimes complained with a humorous resentment about her husband: 'He knew little of it, because he was always looking after his precious sheep: most of my babies were born in the spring, and, of course, he was a-seeing to his precious lambs!' After she left school Priscilla Savage went as kitchen girl to one of the big farms in this parish. Later she 'went away foreign'— to service in a doctor's house in Essex; but after a few years there she returned and got married. She and Robert Savage first set up house on twelve shillings a week.

With so little money few things could be bought in the shops and people rarely went out to buy things in the town; the village was almost entirely self-supporting, most families living on what they grew or reared on their *yards* or allotments. There was no butcher, no baker or public bakery, and most households brewed their own beer. The Three B's—Bread, Bacon and Beer—were the staple articles of diet.

Bread was made at home from flour ground at the village mill; and the wheat in many families had been grown on the *common yard*, or had been given by the farmer as part of the harvest allowances. (This will be discussed in a later chapter.) Many of the old brick ovens in which the bread was baked are still in existence in this village, but none of them is used now. In most cottages the brick oven is in the kitchen; but behind a group of cottages in one part of the village there is a small outhouse containing a large brick oven, *a two-pail* copper and a *six-pail* copper, used for baking, the cooking of pig-products, and brewing respectively. This outhouse was at one time undoubtedly used by more than one of the cottages. The brick oven is beautifully constructed of a domed arch of bricks; and the skill of the old bricklayers must have been considerable, so perfectly do the bricks form the pattern of the arch, and so well has it survived its numerous firings.

Prissy's family of ten had two bakes a week, using altogether five stones of flour. The flour was often mixed with the whey left after making butter or cream cheese at the farm. The yeast was saved from the last brewing of beer; it was called *barm* and was kept in a cool earthenware jar on the floor of the larder. It would keep up to six months without going sour. But before Prissy mixed the dough she had to make sure she had plenty of fuel to heat her oven. This had to be heated by burning the fuel inside it. Apart from the door there is no outlet in a brick oven: the chimney is at the front just outside the oven-door and when the fuel is burning the oven-door is left open and the smoke escapes through that. The fuel used was most commonly *whin* faggots—the *bones* of *sere* or dry gorse—bound with elm withes. The process of making them was described by Prissy: 'You tied the whin faggots with green ellum withes. You put your foot on the bottom of a withe then you could rave the top of it like an S.' Broom was sometimes used for fuel: so also was heather. The heather was first stacked and pressed into bundles: it was preferred by some folk because, they said, it gave more heat. The fuel was thrust into the oven with a long-handled fork kept specially for the purpose. This fork was also used to stir up the embers until they burned completely out, leaving no smoke at all. It took about an hour for a brick-oven to become properly heated for the dough. The bricks would change in colour from black to red as they got hotter; and when a handful of flour, thrown lightly against the side of the oven, burned up with a blaze of sparks, the housewife knew that her oven was hot enough for baking.

But before the dough went in the oven the ash would be scraped out and stowed in a hole beneath the oven. This was done with an ordinary garden-hoe or with the *peel*, a long-handled spade-like tool used to slide in the tins of dough. While the oven was being heated the dough would have been rising in an earthenware pan covered with a cloth, and placed near the oven. Just before the oven was ready the dough was placed into tins or kneaded into the shape of cottage loaves which were baked on the actual floor of the oven.

The actual placing of the dough into the oven was called *a-settin' in*. It was a job that had to be done quickly and smoothly so that the oven-door was open for as little time as possible. When the housewife was *a-settin' in* everything else had to wait; even the doctor calling to examine one of the children would have to see the oven door closed before he could get her attention.

The bread would be done in about an hour. Often, however, the housewife took advantage of the heated oven to bake other things, risking the fact that by opening the door the bread might go *dumpy* or flat. One housewife in this village cooked her weekly joint of meat in the same oven as the bread. The meat, which took about two hours to cook, was placed at the back of the oven; then came the bread; and in front of the bread, at the edge of the oven, she placed two or three tins of Suffolk rusks which were done in about ten minutes and could quickly be withdrawn.

Small pieces of charcoal—the embers left from the fuel—often adhered to the loaves of bread that had not been baked in tins. These bits of charcoal gave an extra flavour to the bread according to the old people who are generally very critical of modern shop-bread. They say that no bread has the flavour of the home-baked bread. It was made from stone-ground flour with all the goodness of the wheat grains left in it; and, therefore, it was much more sustaining than the present day bread. It needed to be, for a meal in these days would often consist—apart from a hunk of cheese—almost entirely of bread, and before the coming of breakfast cereals many country children started their day with a 'mess of bread and hot skimmed milk'.

The mill in this village was burned down at the end of the last century; but the millstones are still to be seen, forming the doorsteps of three nearby cottages: a complete circle of stone for one cottage, and two half-circles for the others.

At the beginning of the present century Aaron Ling, Prissy's father, used to spend most of his time making whin faggots on the Heath. He charged one shilling for making twenty faggots and one shilling for carting them. But as the entries, later quoted (chap. 18), from the accounts of the overseers of the poor show, the use of gorse or broom as fuel was a very old practice. It is even much older than these eighteenth-century documents indicate. The closed type of oven was known in biblical times, as is shown by a verse in *Matthew* (Chapter vi): ' . . . the grass of the field which today is and tomorrow is cast into the oven' — a verse which could be puzzling were it not realized that grass in this context meant that it was used as a fuel. But closed ovens similar in principle to the ones existing here are still used in Egypt and parts of the Middle East.

One old implement is worth mentioning in connection with home-baking. This is the *salamander*—a thick disc of iron with a long handle—a kind of small portable girdle which was thrust into the fire until it was red-hot and then held over pastry, omelettes and so on to give them a *finished* surface. The salamander, as with many old tools, developed a secondary use: in some districts it served, long after its use in the kitchen was discontinued, for burning paint off doors and windows prior to redecoration.

It may also be noted that after the bread had been baked and removed from the brick-oven feathers and *dum* (down) that had recently been plucked from fowls were placed in the oven while it was still hot. Baking the feathers killed all the insects that might be in them, and also ensured that they would be dry and

not *mat* when they were used. After they had been baked the
dum and feathers could be stored for years before being used in
pillows and mattresses. In addition to the small feathers, *clip-
pings* obtained from the larger ones when they were being
shaped into quill-pens, were also treated in the same way.

Another use for the brick-oven was to bake a ham. If a family
was lucky enough to keep a ham for a special occasion—for
Christmas or for a wedding—it was often baked in the following way. First, the ham was washed and then it was covered
with a thick layer of dough. This dough was made from the
coarsest of flours. In the Suffolk village of Gosbeck the miller's
wife used the *middlings*, the coarse meal that was usually fed to
cattle. For the family did not eat the dough-crust: it was peeled
away from the cooked ham and fed to the pigs: it had served
its purpose, which was 'to keep all the goodness in the ham'
while it was being baked. This is a very old method of preparing a ham, and brings to mind Hamlet's 'funeral bak'd meats';
but it is practised in at least one village (Needham Market)
even today. The flavour of a ham cooked in this way is said to
be outstanding.

But the ham did not have a special baking; it was placed in
the oven during the weekly family bake. About a hundred
faggots a year was the usual estimate of fuel needed for a cottage
or a small farmhouse—two for each bake; and little allowance
was made for any special bakes. Faggots for heating the brick-
oven were an important part of the household economy, and
had carefully to be budgeted for. On many farms, those workers
with the extra skills and responsibilities—the head horseman,
the shepherd and the stockman—were supplied with faggots as
part of their perquisites.

5   Beer

Beer was the usual drink in most households in this parish
right up to the beginning of this century. Tea was drunk as
well, but the tea-drinking habit took root later, perhaps, in this
part of Britain than elsewhere. Tea, moreover, was expensive,
in the early nineteenth century: even tea that was smuggled was
much too expensive for the ordinary family. In 1777 Parson
Woodforde paid a smuggler 10s. 6d. a pound for tea and it did
not get much cheaper for many years. But it is understandable
that beer would be much used in a great barley growing district like this, especially as fresh malt would be easily obtainable
from a maltings just outside the village.

Prissy Savage regularly brewed beer for her own family, but
the First World War seems to have killed the practice in most
households in this village. The process used in each household
varied in small details but Prissy's method is more or less typical
of them all. On the day before the brewing started she cleaned
all the utensils and sterilized them with boiling water. For
cleaning the casks an old piece of chain was kept; this was inserted in the bung-hole and the cask was shaken and rolled about
until all the solid matter adhering to the inside was loosened.
The chain was then removed and the cask cleaned out and swilled
with boiling water. On some of the nearby farms enough beer
was brewed for all the men; and there was usually a big brew
just before harvest. The horseman, for some reason, was tradi-

tionally the man to take charge of the brewing. He had to see that the hogsheads—the great barrels, holding over fifty gallons —were cleaned out. He often placed the backhouse boy in the barrel to scrape it out and limewash it. Before the boy was lowered the brewer would test the air with a candle, in the same way as a well is tested before a man descends it: a candle is lighted, placed at the bottom of a bucket and lowered. If the flame continues to burn brightly no foul air is present.

The utensils used in the brewing were, with one exception, all made of wood. They were: a brewing-tub or *keeler*, made of wood and banded with metal, for steeping and mashing the malt; an *underdeck*—sometimes called an underback—another large wooden tub; a *beer-stool* or wooden stand for holding the barrels; *a horse-hair sieve* for straining; sometimes called a hop-sieve from its use in holding the small hop-seeds and preventing them from entering the finished beer; a funnel, called in this district a *tunnel*, for pouring the beer into the casks—one specimen here was cut out of one piece of wood; a rack or *tongs* on which the sieve rested during the straining process (ideally this was a rectangular frame, but a fork of a small sapling was often used for this purpose); a handcup or *jet*, a scooped-out wooden ladle; *a wilch* (or wilsh), a bottle-shaped appliance made of wicker (the wilsh was a filter used when straining off the liquid or *wort* from the *mash* of steeped malt. In Essex it was referred to as a tap-hose: this is a good name for it, as it fitted over the tap, on the inside of the tub, like a sock); taps or *faucets* usually made of wood, but a very old one, with a key, all made of brass, exists in this village; a *six-pail* copper which would be a fixture in the house, usually built not far from the brick-oven. The ingredients of the average cottage brew were: one bushel of malt, costing about 14s.; one pound of hops worth about 1s.; one pint of yeast passed on from a neighbour's brew.

There were usually two brewings every year: one just before harvest and another in time for Christmas. Each brewing took one whole day and a night. The housewife took charge; and all other jobs went by the board on this occasion as so much depended on the brew going well. The children were kept home from school to do the odd jobs about the house as more than one entry in the old log-book belonging to Blaxhall School shows:

August 11th, 1871: Great many absentees; required at home for brewing.

The wife, after first lighting the copper, set the brewing tub on the stool and placed the wilsh over the tap on the inside of the tub. She then poured two pails full of cold water into the tub, followed by one pail of boiling water. Into the water she poured the bushel of malt—on the side of the tub away from the tap. She then scrubbed and thoroughly cleaned her hands and proceeded to draw the malt from one side of the tub to the other. This was done four or five times until every kernel of malt was wet. To get the malt grain out of the wilsh and to enable the wort to run freely she opened the tap and drew off half a bucket of the liquid which she then poured back into the tub. Then she got half a bucket of hot water to rinse round the top of the tub and the wilsh to ensure that not one particle of malt was left dry. If there were, this would spoil the brew. The rack was placed across the tub which was covered with a cloth and sacks to keep in the *spirit* of the malt. The steeped malt was left for fifteen minutes.

After this time had elapsed five pails of boiling water were taken out of the copper and poured onto the malt. The resulting mash was stirred up for about ten minutes; covered up and allowed to stand for four hours—no longer. The wilsh was then cleared in the same manner as before. All the liquid or wort (called *watt* here) would then be drawn off into the underdeck which as the names implies would be at a lower level than the keeler. There would be five or six pails of wort in the underdeck after this process.

In the meantime the copper had been filled with four pails of water. When this water boiled it was poured into the mash left in the tub to make the *second wort*. The second wort stood for four hours as did the first.

Beer

The first wort was then taken from the underdeck, poured into the copper and ¾lb of hops were added to it. This was boiled up with the hops until the second wort was ready to be drained off. The first wort was next drained through the hair-sieve into the underdeck. The second wort was drained off from the mash and then boiled in the copper for four hours, exactly as the first wort. The hops were used for a second time with ¼lb of unused hops added to it. Before the hops had been added to the wort this was known here as *sweet watt* and was much sought after by the children who would be allowed just to taste it.

After the wilsh had been taken out of the brewing tub, also the remaining drains of malt, the second wort was then strained off into it to cool. The second wort gave mild or small beer; the first wort—if kept separate—strong beer. But in many cottages in our village the two worts were mixed together to give nine or ten pails—about twenty gallons—of beer.

One pint of home-brewed yeast was obtained from a neighbour. Each household would arrange this beforehand. There was a *yeast-chain* in the village, and the wife would know before she started to brew which of her neighbours had brewed last and would have the freshest yeast. Prissy remembers being sent out by her mother to 'borrow some barm'. Borrow was a word used advisedly for after the brew the debt could be paid back with interest. The yeast was added to the beer when it was milk-warm. A couple of clean corks, or a slice of toasted bread, were then placed on top of the beer; the yeast was poured in and as it began to work it collected round the corks. When once she saw this process beginning and the pleasant sight of the mushroom of yeast starting to form round the corks, the wife knew that the beer could now be left to itself. She would say: 'Everything is all right now; the beer is a-smiling!' or 'We are all right; the beer is on the smile!' and after covering the tub with a white cloth, off she would go to bed.

The next morning she strained off the yeast into an earthenware bowl. She got the funnel and the hand-cup and ladled the beer into the casks. These she left uncorked, and by the next day a little yeast would have worked out of the bung-hole. This yeast was skimmed off carefully, and the same process repeated for three or four days. The casks were then bunged down.

The beer was then left for at least a week before being drunk; although people who liked *young beer* often tapped the casks before the lapse of this period. As a variation on the above process some housewives reserved three or four pails of the first wort and placed two handfuls of clean wheat into the cask with the beer. This would keep for a year, as all the time the beer would be *feeding on the wheat*.

As has already been stated the home-brewing was an important event, demanding the utmost care and vigilance; for there would be a great loss to the household if the brew went wrong. Moreover, beer at that time was recognized as an essential part of the farm-worker's diet; and during times of extra work on the farm allowances of hops and malt were made by the farmer to his men. Robert Savage, for instance, got a *lambing 'lowance* of two bushels of malt and two pounds of hops so that Prissy often made two brews during the lambing season.

One lady from a nearby village remembers how, as a child, she hurried down with her brothers and sisters on the morning after the brewing to see whether the crown of yeast had spread all over the top of the beer. The children knew that if they saw the welcome froth of yeast the brew had been successful; and they were glad. The children's interest in the brew was chiefly theoretical—if they were good they might be given a glass of mild beer as a special treat with their Sunday dinner—but they rejoiced to the greater glory of the household. The largest amount of beer was naturally consumed by the father; and the good man in most households worked hard enough to deserve it.

The old community had many terms connected with beer which are worth passing note: *dew beer* was the beer bought with the shilling earnest money given by the farmer to each worker when the harvest contract was signed. With the dew beer the workers *wetted the sickle*, by filling a ceremonial cup to the success of the harvest. *Trailing beer* was bought out of the fines paid

Beer

to the Lord of the Harvest by anyone who had trampled down the standing corn or hay, thus making it more difficult for it to be cut. The farmer's wife at one of the Blaxhall farms once had to pay trailing beer money to the Lord of the Harvest because she had allowed her hens to stray into a field of uncut corn. *Key beer* was the strongest beer of all, so-called because for reasons of policy it was kept under lock and key.

But home-brewed beer had other uses in addition to its legitimate one. Thick beer was often used to help cure hams; also many women here believed that beer was the ideal hair-wash; it was supposed to make the hair shine. Another use for it was the staining of furniture. This was before the invention, or at least the widespread marketing, of furniture polish. Beeswax was much too costly to use on cottage furniture, and was kept chiefly for the manufacture of candles for churches and the bigger houses. The chair on which Robert Savage spent most of his last days is a golden brown in colour—acquired through frequent stainings with beer. It is possible that this custom of staining chairs with beer derives from a practice that used to be prevalent in the brewery which was built on the site of Shakespeare's Globe Theatre in Southwark: in the old days the customers, it is reported, poured some beer on to their chairs and sat on it in their leather-breeches. If a customer stuck to the chair he knew that the beer was of good quality.

Although beer is no longer brewed at home in this district, the custom is still kept up by half a dozen families in the Capel St Mary and Little Wenham district of Suffolk. Not so long ago the second prize in the horse class in a furrow-drawing match was two bushels of malt; and some of the home-brewers competed for this prize. Brewing is done exactly as it was by the old people fifty years ago, except that—inevitably—the modern home brewer has to have a licence. But this licence is free to the applicant who is the occupier of a house of an annual value of £8 or less, and who undertakes 'to brew during the currency of the licence a quantity not exceeding four bushels of malt or equivalent thereof for his own use'.

6 Bacon & Ham Curing

Prior to the First World War most of the meat eaten in this village was pork or bacon: mutton and beef were eaten only on special occasions such as harvest time or at the *frolics*. Most families kept their own pigs; and each owned the complete pig-killing equipment—the pig-stool; the steel-yards (*still-yards*) or weighing device; the *bucker* to help hang up the carcass; the knives and so on. Each also had a large earthenware pot, glazed on the inside. This was the ham-pot in which some of the pig-meat was cured.

Curing was done in a way that seems peculiar to Suffolk. The ham was first given a dry salt-bath; salt was rubbed into it and it was left in the pot, covered with salt, for seven days. At the end of this period the ham was taken out; the ham-pot was emptied of the salt and a *sweet pickle* was made in it. This consisted of two pounds of *real* black treacle; two pounds of *real* dark brown sugar; one quart of thick beer or stout—this, at least, was Prissy Savage's formula. The beer or stout was heated and then poured over the sugar and treacle. After the ham had been thoroughly drained of the salt it would be placed in the pot and the mixture poured over it and then rubbed well into it. A big stone was then placed on top of the ham so that every part of it would be covered by the pickle. It was left in the pickle or *sweet brine* for about six weeks; but every day it would be turned—flesh side up one day, skin side the next. When the six weeks were up it

Bacon and Ham Curing

was taken out, branded with the owner's initials—a blacksmith-made iron was usually the implement—and sent off to be dried.

In the big farmhouses the hams and bacon were often dried in the huge backhouse chimney. Some distance up many of these old chimneys iron girders can still be seen running across them. From these the hams and bacon were hung. In a farmhouse in the village of Tunstall a farmer used an *eighteen* or *twenty stave* ladder to climb up the chimney to hang his pig-meat. If one pig had been killed two hams and two *chaps*—the sides of the head—would be hanging from the girders drying in the wood-smoke. For only wood was burned in the backhouse fire when meat was drying.

But in Blaxhall most of the cottagers sent their hams to be dried to the next village of Tunstall. Here the wheelwright had built himself a special drying house. This was quite a small building with brick walls and a chimney but no fireplace. The hams and the bacon were hung on iron girders running across the drying house, about six or seven feet from the floor. Along the bottom of the wall on one side, the wheelwright would place sawdust and wood chippings left over after he had made a wheel or cart out of oak wood. He lighted a small fire and when it had caught he dampened the sawdust to stop it burning too quickly, also to make the fire give more smoke. Here, in this particular drying house, two or three pigs could be smoked at a time. Sawdust would be fed onto the fire each day; and the bacon would be left there for a period of a fortnight or three weeks. The children used to call this drying house *Smoky House*; and it is worth noting that Thomas Tusser used the same term to describe such a building nearly four hundred years ago.

Prissy Savage also had a method of *wind-drying* her bacon. After it had been pickled in the sweet brine it was wrapped in muslin and hung under the eaves to dry. It would then be eaten in the *green state*. The practice of hanging out shallots and onions under the eaves is quite common in this part of Suffolk, though nowadays one rarely sees bacon hanging there: a similar method of drying and keeping vegetables is used, it seems, across the North Sea in Friesland.

7 Cheese Making and Other Domestic Crafts

Cheese-making was a very necessary skill for country house-wives in the old days; as cheese, when meat was so dear, was one of the main items of the farmworker's diet. In Blaxhall a cream cheese seemed to have been the speciality. Prissy Savage made her cheese in the following way: Two gallons of milk were obtained, if possible straight from the cow. If the milk was cold it was first warmed to blood heat. It was then strained into a *butter-killer* (or keeler) and two spoonfuls of rennet were added. The milk was left to curdle and then the curds were hung up in a muslin bag to drain off the whey. After this the curds were placed in a basin and salted to taste; it was then placed in the cheese press. The cheese-making was synchronised with the bread-making so that the whey could be used for making the dough, another example, of the perfect dovetailing of the economy of the old community. About a hundred and forty years ago cream cheese in this area was made according to this recipe: 'The curd is broken up in the whey, which is poured off as soon as the former has subsided. The remainder with the curd is put into a coarse strainer, left to cool, and is then pressed as tightly as possible. After this it is put into the vat and set in a press to discharge the remaining whey: the curd is then taken out, broken again as finely as possible, salted, and returned to the press.'

At one time the cheese of this part of the country was famous. Camden, an Elizabethan writer, said: 'Great store of Suffolk cheeses were made and vended into all parts of England, nay, Germany, France and Spain'. But by the end of the eighteenth century a writer was able to record that the general quality of Suffolk cheese was known to be remarkably bad. And he gave the reason: butter-making had replaced cheese-making; 'and they who make good butter must of course make bad cheese'. In fact, there is little tradition of cheese-making left in this village; perhaps it is because there is comparatively little pasture in the light, sandy land of this parish; and it is interesting to note that Prissy's recipe for cream cheese came from 'the farmer's wife who used to be at Fir Tree: she wor a fine cheese-maker—a *heavy-land* woman she wor'.

The poor reputation gained by Suffolk cheese was thus understandable. The cream of the milk was taken for butter-making and the cheese was made from what was left over—milk 'three times skimmed sky blue'. It was called *flet* milk, milk that had been fleeted or skimmed with a *fleeter*, a shallow scollop-shaped ladle perforated to allow the milk to run through. The cheese made from this skimmed milk was called Suffolk *bang*—an onomatopoeic, dialect word that conveys its quality. Bang became the subject of many jokes; and old sayings tell us what people thought about it: 'Hunger will break through stone walls and anything except a Suffolk cheese.' Bloomfield, the Suffolk poet who wrote the *Farmer's Boy*, says:

> *It, like the oaken shelf in which 'tis laid,*
> *Defies the effort of the bending blade;*
> *Or in the hog-trough lies with perfect spite,*
> *Too big to swallow and too hard to bite.*

Someone joked that it was only fit for making door-latches and quoted the old saying:

> *Those that made me were uncivil,*
> *For they made me harder than the devil:*
> *Knives won't cut me; fire won't sweat me;*
> *Dogs bark at me, but can't eat me.*

It was made in farmhouses, chiefly to be eaten by the unmarried workers who *lived in* and slept in the farmhouse attic. But if bang was as hard as it was supposed to be, how could it be eaten? An old farmer has told how it was prepared and eaten with profit: 'Now I will tell you how I have seen it made eatable in an old Suffolk farmhouse. The old lady used to make eight or ten every spring: they were about the size of a barrow wheel and a good foot through when dried. They were kept in the drying room until well into the winter months. When the mornings were cold and dark, a cheese would be fetched down from the chamber, cut in half—cross-wise, not down—stood in a pan in front of a big fire until it was so roasted that it could be scraped with a knife. And now, here comes your breakfast! Cut two rounds of bread about an inch thick each one. Take your knife and cover one piece of bread with hot cheese. On the other piece of bread you would put two or three slices of fat pork that had been in salt for two or three months—as red as a cherry. Then *clap* the two together; and there you have a sandwich fit for a worker, and one that would stick to your chest all the morning.'

Butter was made in most of the farms of this parish until before the last war. In one farm it is still made occasionally now. At the Grove, Robert Savage recalled, no new milk was sold at all: it was all kept for cream to make butter. New milk was only sold as a special favour—if, for instance, someone was sick. The milk was fleeted in the morning, and the cream was placed in another bowl. This milk was then sold at one penny a pint. The cream which had risen to the top again was once more fleeted off and the milk that was left was sold at a halfpenny a pint. This *real* skim milk was much used for bread-making. The butter made in the farm was weighed into a pound and half-pound quantities, marked with a mould which stamped the name of the farmer and his farm on the top, and then sold to the local shop or taken to the market.

Until the coming of electricity to this village a few years ago, the lighting of cottages in the long winter evenings was always a problem; and it was one that had to be met as cheaply as possible. Until about the beginning of the last century most country cottages used rushlights. These were made from green rushes. First the rind or the skin of a green rush was peeled away from the pith, leaving a strip of skin equal to about a fifth of the way round the rush. The purpose of this was to hold the pith together all the way along its eighteen inches, which was the usual length for a rush. Then grease, specially kept for the purpose, was heated in a long pan. After the grease had melted, the rush was dipped into it, and held in it sufficiently long to soak. Then it was taken out and laid on a bit of bark until ready for use. Holders to fix the rushlight while it burned were made specially by the village blacksmith. In some districts the grease used was the skimmings of the bacon-pot. Here, a big sheep-rearing village as we have seen, mutton fat was used almost entirely. Mutton fat was considered the best because it dried hardest and burned the clearest. A little beeswax, if it could be obtained, when added to the mutton fat caused it to burn brighter still.

Rush candles were also burned. These were made in exactly the same way as the rushlights; but the rush was dipped several times into the grease, each time the previous coat of grease being allowed to harden. Cotton wicks later took the place of rushes; and the grease was poured into candle-moulds after the wicks had been fixed down their centres. Two kinds of mould for candles have been found in this village: a single mould about fourteen inches long; (this was made of iron); and a later one made of tin, enabling the housewife to make six candles at once. A cylindrical tin candle box is still to be seen in some old cottages, usually hanging by the fireplace, a reminder of the time when candle-making was a home-craft.

Wine-making is still practised by one or two of the old generation here—bullace wine, elderberry, parsnip and blackcurrant. Recently George Messenger, an old widower, brewed a quantity of wine but was not quite certain about one or two steps in the process. He went along to Prissy and told her: 'I want you to hev a look at my wine, gel; I ain't sure about it.' Prissy went

71

to the old man's house and her verdict was instantaneous: 'You want to take that there mould off the top right quick, you dew! Thet will spoil it. Thet at the bottom's all right—thet's the sediment; thet's the *mother o' the wine*; thet'll help. The wine will feed on thet. Thet's why it's called the mother! But take the mould off of it right quick!'

8 Clothes Washing

The following deposition by one of Prissy's forebears gives an insight into the domestic arrangements at the Grove Farm. The occasion is an inquest on May 21st, 1833:

'Letitia, the wife of David Ling of Blaxhall, the aforesaid labourer, upon her oath said as follows: "I have known James Smith for five or six and thirty year. I have been in the habit of washing for Mrs Ann Pope of Blaxhall, aforesaid widow, for the last year and upward. James Smith was in the habit of coming to doll for us. On Sunday last, the 19th inst., I went to sleep at Mrs Pope's in order that I might be up early in the morning. I got up at twenty five minutes past one. I and Mrs Pope's two maids kept wondering why Smith did not come as he was very punctual in general. In the course of the night there was a thunderstorm and about half past one it was most violent. We waited for Smith till a little after three o'clock and then we opened the door to see if we could see him. One of the maids called me to look at something under the tree right opposite the backhouse door. The backhouse boy said he would go down the path and see what it was when I said I would go with him—we both went together. The boy went into the road and picked up his hat and said, 'Poor old Jimmy is asleep!' I then went up and laid my hand on his shoulder and felt of him, when I found he was dead. He was sitting on an empty wine pipe and his head lay over the wall. We called John Hammond, who was a servant in

Ann Pope's house, and he got up directly and came to Smith and took off his handkerchief from his neck. We were all convinced that he was quite dead and supposed he had been struck by lightning. The tempest was so violent that Mrs Pope's men had been up several times to see that no accident had happened.

' "I have since seen the body again, and have no doubt whatever but that he was killed by lightning."

X 'The Mark of Letitia Ling'

Dollying clothes has not altogether died out, though it is not now practised in this district. The old wooden *dolly* is not yet purely a museum object; nor is the *posser*, the bell-shaped implement, made of copper or brass, which was used in the same way as the dolly. About the time the above incident took place potash was much used in the household for cleaning and washing purposes. This was obtained from wood-ash and a century or so ago making potash was a trade or craft on its own. This craft is later on referred to indirectly in an eighteenth-century newspaper advertising 'a very useful CART, fit—among other uses—for an *ashman*'. Traces of the craft are sometimes found in field names: a group of cottages outside a nearby village is still known as The Potash. Robert Savage, in describing the two milking-pails which he used to hand to the cowman every morning when he was a backhouse boy, stated that they were made by the cooper from Tunstall out of wood, with three metal bands each to strengthen them. The pails were kept spotlessly clean and the metal bands were scoured once a week with wood-ash.

9 Stone Picking

Although stone-picking takes us well away from the household it is included here because it was the province of the woman of the house and her children. Stone-picking, in the days of large families and low wages, was a family activity and children of all ages were pressed to it—often against their will—as it was one important means of getting money for an essential family need—usually boots for the children's own use. Many middle-aged people in this village remember the time they spent stone-picking with distaste, if not with bitterness; and a short time ago, when it was necessary to pick stones off a newly-set playing-field here, this feeling came to the surface again.

Arthur Young, at the end of the eighteenth century, records an experiment that was conducted on some of the flint-ridden land of East Suffolk; in order to come at the truth of whether corn did better on land that had been cleared of stones or not, an amount was sown over a known area of land that had been cleared of stones; and alongside it a like amount of seed was sown on an equal area of land that had not been 'stone-picked'. The yield from the land that had been left untouched was greater than that of the patch that had been cleared of its stones. In spite of this experiment stone-picking seems to have gone on during most of the nineteenth century. But it is likely that the practice was continued not only because of its supposed benefit to the land; for stone-picking was also bound up with the maintenance of the parish roads. Until the Local Government Act of 1888 the parish was still responsible for the upkeep of its roads and it was the duty of a parish officer, the Highways Surveyor, to see that the parish's liability in this respect was discharged. He was usually a farmer; and in this district where there is little stone, apart from the flints of the field, stone-picking was carried on as the only means of procuring adequate road-metalling. Even after the Act of 1888, when the County Councils took over the entire liability for the upkeep of the highways, the old system still prevailed in Blaxhall; and stone-picking did not stop until about thirty years ago when improvements in road transport enabled road-metalling to be brought easily from other areas and to be distributed around the various outlying parishes. At the present time no stones are picked from the fields here; and the yields of corn are at least as high as they were at any time during the nineteenth century.

Robert and Priscilla Savage, as parents of a large family, had great experience of stone-picking, and they have related how the practice was carried on. Stones were taken off the fields when the corn was about two inches high. The men raked some of the land overnight in order to loosen the stones so that the women and children could pick them the more easily the next day. The tool they used for this was the *daisy-rake* which was designed in the first place for raking clover. It was a wooden rake with six inch nails, closely set together, serving as *tines* or prongs. The farmer would allocate a field to one family, and Robert Savage remembered Church Walk, a field near the church, best of all. 'It was a whoolly good field for stoon-picking. It wor like a shingle-beach: you could hear the old plough a-grinding through the stoons as it turned it over!'

Each picker took an ordinary two-gallon pail which could hold about a peck of stones. The pails were filled and the stones were dumped in a heap in the furrow: each heap had to be twenty bushels, or a *load*; and since there are four pecks in a bushel eighty pails of stones were required to make up a load. To calculate how many pails the family carried the mother dug a small

Stone Picking

hole near the heap, and into this hole she would drop a small pebble for each pail of stones added. These were the *tally stones*, and Prissy recalls: 'If you weren't some careful the mischieful boys would keep a-dropping stoons into the hole on the sly so that they get done the sooner; but it wor no use, the farmer would know when he came to measure up the load if there wor some pails missing from it.' The boys often had to pick two or three buckets of stones before going to school in the morning.

Treading down the young corn was said to benefit it, but when it had reached a certain stage in its growth, stone-picking would have to finish. The heaps were left in the furrows—in every other furrow between the *stetches* or rigs—and the farmer or the bailiff inspected the heaps. He could tell fairly accurately how much each family had picked and he was accustomed to give the mother a little of the money *on account*. When the harvest had been gathered in the stones were carted across the stubble when the ground was hard and could 'take no harm'. But the heaps were first measured. This was done as the cart was loaded, the cart being first measured by the farmer's men. They used a bushel *hod* for doing this—a big tin, like a refuse-container. They filled twenty hods of stones into the cart and then levelled the stones off. Nails were then knocked into the side of the cart to mark the height each succeeding load would have to reach.

The stones were taken and dumped at the side of the road where the roadman wanted them. Humpy Sam was the roadman about fifty years ago; but it was only a part-time job, and he 'filled in' by working on the farms. The pickers were paid about three shillings a load for their stones, which works out less than halfpenny a pail. Whatever their wages amounted to they went to pay the *shummacker's* bill shortly after the harvest.

Robert Savage has provided a coda to the old practice: 'You had to pick stoons at that time o'day if you wanted to keep the children tidy. Some of the children today don't know they're alive—they don't pick stoons or nawthen. But they stopped taking the stoons a good few years back. They could git them cheaper from up the *Sheres* (shires) somewhere. They used to come up the river in barges—grut big ol' stoons as big as this lil' ol' burd-cage.'

This reference to the Sheres is worth a note. If one has not had the good fortune to have been born in one of the Three Counties —Norfolk, Suffolk or Essex—one comes from the Sheres, a term that seems to embrace the rest of England, not to say Scotland and Wales as well. It used to be the worst judgment one could pass on the working qualities of a horse to say that he had 'a bit of the Sheres in him'. A similar judgment was given recently by an old native upon a marriage that had turned out badly; the girl was born here and except for a brief period during the war had lived here all her life; but the man—well: 'He came from the Sheres'! And all was explained, since all products of the Sheres turned out no better than they were expected to, whether they were men, horses or merely 'grut big ol' stoons'.

But this division into the Three Counties and the rest of England has, in fact, some sort of historical sanction. Domesday Book, the 1086 survey, was originally produced in two volumes: the smaller volume was entirely devoted to Essex, Norfolk and Suffolk. Moreover the descriptions in this volume are very much more detailed than those of the larger one.

PART THREE

GEORGE ROPE: 1814–1912
JOHN GODDARD: 1855–1953

10   Two Old Farmers

George Rope farmed at the Grove where Robert Savage spent most of his working life; and although he has been dead for over forty years he is still talked about by the older people of the village. They refer to him as *Old George* or the *Old Gentleman*. In addition to being remembered on grounds of personal affection he seems to have become, in the minds of the older generation, a symbol of the old community that has gone irrevocably. His life almost spanned the nineteenth century; and he saw farming brought out of a state where ancient and mediaeval survivals and usages were a commonplace, right to the threshold of the modern era. Some of his memories of his early days have been recorded but even in George Rope's life methods of farming were changing slowly compared with our time—the age of the internal combustion engine—and his observations on the changes in agriculture are scanty when put side by side with the other changes he recalled.

But George Rope was first in business with his uncle at Orford, the old port and 'pocket borough' about six miles from this village. The firm had a fleet of nine vessels that sailed regularly between Orford and Newcastle and Orford and London: they took corn to London and brought back general merchandise and when there was no corn to carry they went to Newcastle *in ballast* for coal. The firm also carted this coal to villages for miles around: they drew the corn from a radius of twenty miles of the port. They had a quay and warehouse at Iken Cliff on the nearby inlet: here two vessels a day were loaded during the autumn, each vessel taking between one and two thousand *coombs* of corn. The business practically came to an end when the railways opened up the district towards the middle of the century; though George Rope continued to trade in corn and coal—as well as to farm—right into the present century.

Old George however, recorded—not long before he died—one memory of his early days that throws light on the overall change in farming during the century he had lived through. He remembered when bullocks were regularly used on the plough. The Devon breed was the kind most used; and it was not unusual at that time to see the bull of the farm, if he was a Shorthorn, harnessed to the plough. It kept the bull quiet. The harness of the bullock was roughly similar to that of the horse except that the bullock required a much larger collar. This was open at the top and fastened with a buckle and strap. The cost of feeding a bullock was much less than the cost of feeding a horse; as the bullock only needed a *skep* of turnips and some marsh hay or straw; while a horse would need corn and *stover*—clover, trefoil, sainfoin used as winter fodder. After a few years' work the bullock was grazed and came to a great weight of beef; but even with this advantage it was found that bullocks did not pay and they gradually went out of use. A bullock could not do much more than half the work a horse would do in a day; and was not suitable for all purposes. It was on light land, such as we have in our parish, that bullocks were last used in this district. The last field cultivated by bullocks—as related to Robert Savage by his grandfather—is at the east end of the parish and is now under the trees of the Forestry Commission.

But what is more important for our purpose, George Rope preserved nearly every document he handled as corn factor and farmer; and these have proved invaluable as evidence of the state of farming at various times during the last century and a half. They have also helped to annotate some of the farming practices carried on in this district, as the following account of an eighteenth-century farm sale shows. It is dated August 1774 and is headed VALUATION OF AN ESTATE IN BLAX-HALL late in the occupation of Mr JOHN POPE, deceased:

The Mansion House of the Estate is a Timber and Tiled building, the Walls rough-cast & in decent Repair. It consists of a Kitchen, Parlour, Backhouse, Dairy, two Butteries, with indifferent Chambers and without Garretts.

The Hog-house and Sty are in ruinous condition and must be rebuilt.

The Barn belonging to these premises is a timber thatched building. The thatch wants to be repaired, the Great Doors to be new, also a New Barn Floore.

The Stable is a timber and thatch building much out of repair.

The Cowhouse is a timber and thatch building wants repair.

The Carthouse, timber and thatch, wants repair.

Which by moderate Computation to put the whole Premises in Tenantable Repair will take not less than £80.

The Land of the Estate consists of Meadows and Arable, the Arable being of a Gravelly, Light Soil is forced by Clay and other Manure, being old Plough'd, will not answer mending to Produce the Corn as it has done heretofore.

The Meadows or Marshes are but of an indifferent Ouze, some part thereof are much hurt by the tide flowing thereon. The Ditches and Drains are well opened, drawn and Bottomfyde and kept in a Neat Manner by the Industry and good Management of a very neat Occupier, which really makes them appear to be much better than they really are.

There's no wood upon these Prem''cs for Kindling, Oven or Milk Copper: a Shilling in the Pound is the common and annual Allowance for Firing in such cases.

Annual Rent of the Farm: £90. 0. 0.

The actual acreage of the farm is not given, but it is believed to be one of about 250 acres. If it is this farm, the meadows are still of indifferent *Ouze* and the tide still flows over them on occasions. Evidence of the former practice of *forcing* the land with dressings of clay or marl is still to be seen in the number of pits scattered about the parish. These pits can easily be picked out on the aerial photographs of Blaxhall. At one time there must have been a pit in nearly every field, but many of them have been gradually filled in, surviving only as steepish hollows which the tractor driver has to look out for when ploughing. Marl or clay was dug out of these pits and scattered on the land as manure. 'The other manure' referred to might well have included *crag*. Crag is composed of an immense mass of comminuted sea-shell coloured by oxide of iron; and it used to be the custom here to spread it on the land to prevent it becoming exhausted by frequent corn-cropping. Arthur Young, writing about twenty years after the above valuation, gives details of the practice:

'In a part of the maritime sand district called the Sandlings which are south of Woodbridge, Orford and Saxmundham they formerly made a great improvement by spreading shell-marl on the black, ling heaths which with all that tract was covered. But as the marl, called there *crag*, is all dry powdered shells like running sand without any principle of adhesion, the effect was good only for once; for after cultivating those heaths, on trying the crag a second time it was found to do little or no good, and in some instances, even to make the sand blow more. It seems, therefore, to have acted in this respect like lime which has been frequently found to have great effect on first application upon land long in a state of nature, but on repetition that effect has been found to be lost.'

11 *Taking The Harvest*

One of the most interesting documents left by old George Rope concerns the harvest. Under the old community the harvest was the climax of the rural year, not merely an incident in the more mechanical and depersonalised round on the farm as it has become today. The whole village was involved and there was a carefully laid down ritual which had long roots far back in mediaeval times. The first step was known as *Taking the Harvest*. This meant that the men on each farm, with the addition of certain seasonal workers like the company of sheep-shearers, agreed with the farmer to bring in the harvest on 'piecework'— so much per acre of crops; or perhaps they would contract to get the harvest in during the period of a month from the time they started; or instead of a month some agreements would state *Twenty Four Fine Days*.

Here is an actual contract for 'taking the harvest': it was drawn up at Grove Farm by old George Rope some time during the last quarter of the nineteenth century. The confusion of person in the first sentence is understandable as the contract was written out in Old George's hand; and as the sole contracting party on one side it was easier for him to write *my* than the more impersonal, if more accurate, *the master's* or some other third person equivalent.

We the undermentioned agree to cut and secure all the corn

grown on the farm in a workmanlike manner to my satisfaction; make bottoms of stacks; cover up when required; hoe the turnips twice and turn or lift the barley once; turn the pease once—each man to find a gaveller. Should any man lose any time through sickness he is to throw back 2s. per day to the Company and receive account at harvest. Should any man lose any time through drunkenness he is to forfeit 5s. to the Company.

Joe Levett
Jas. Hammond
R. French
Jn Keable
Joe Row
Samuel Ling

Allowances to each man:

    1 Coomb of Wheat at 20s.

    3 Bushels of Malt—gift

    1 lb of Mutton to each man instead of dinner

    $2\frac{1}{2}$ lbs of Mutton at 4d a lb every Friday

David Ling, lad: To receive half as much as the other men make in their harvest and half their allowances

Boy Woodbridge: $\frac{1}{2}$ Bushel of Malt: 2/6 a week during harvest

Boy Leggett: 3s a week during harvest. 1 Bushel of Malt

    92 acres at 6s. 6d   £29. 18 0

                                 2. 0

                              £30 0. 0

If, instead of 'piecework', the men contracted to get the harvest in by the end of a month, it meant that should they finish before that time they could then go to other jobs on the farm, drawing their usual wage whilst doing so. If, however, they were unlucky enough to meet wet weather the harvest extended itself over the stated month, then they might well find themselves working in the fifth week without drawing any extra money. But if the farmer had agreed to insert the phrase 'Twenty Four Fine Days' in the contract instead of one month, the contract would operate on fine days only: on wet days the men would do their usual tasks about the farm, drawing their usual wage for those particular days.

According to the above agreement the six men, the lad and the two boys worked for £30. Estimating that the harvest would take about a month to gather, this worked out that each man averaged about £1 4s a week in wages; but out of this he would have to pay his gaveller. Yet even when she had been paid he would still have about double his normal wage—ten shillings, or even less in this village when the contract was drawn up about eighty years ago; and there were the allowances in addition. The harvest worker certainly earned this double pay as he started working at five o'clock in the morning and finished at dusk.

Many of the terms in the contract need comment; a coomb is equivalent to four bushels; 'to make bottoms of stacks' refers to the practice of building the stack off the ground on a low, iron or wooden platform to prevent vermin from getting into the corn. The *gavellers* were usually women, wives of the harvest workers. Their job was to rake the mown corn into *gavels* or rows ready for carting. Corn that was not bound into *shuffs* (sheafs) was said to be *on the gavel*. 'Barley,' as Arthur Young noted, 'is everywhere in Suffolk mown and left loose, the neater method of binding in sheaves is not practised. The stubbles are *dew-raked* by men drawing a long iron-toothed rake.' A tool called a *shack-fork*—a fork with curved tines and an iron bow at the shoulder was used to gather the swathes of barley into gavels ready for pitching on to the wagons. A gaveller worked behind each wagon feeding the corn to two men—one on each side of the wagon—who did the *pitching* while another two men on top of the load received the corn and arranged it evenly. The man paid the gaveller about a shilling a day: if she had a young child to look after at the same time she would have to manage as best she could. Priscilla Savage remembers her mother telling her that she was placed down in the shade between two bundles of corn in an angle of the harvest field, and she was fed during the brief intervals her mother won from the gavelling.

The phrase 'hoe the turnips twice' gives a clue to the old method of sowing turnips before they were drilled. They were sown broadcast, or *fleet* on the ground; at the first half of the century by the broadcast sower, later by a machine—the *seed barrow* or broadcast seed-drill. When the seed was sown by hand the sower had a small seed-bowl on his chest: this was secured by a leather band which went round his neck. He took the small seed between his finger and thumb and sowed *in step;* that is, as his left foot came up, his left hand dipped into the seed-bowl and scattered the seed. It was a skilled job to sow with both hands and keep in step as the rhythm could very easily be broken. If this happened the sower would have to stop and start again, as a break in the rhythm meant a *blank patch* in the sowing. Few men, too, could judge the amount of seed to sow at each *pinch* of the thumb and the forefinger: turnip seed was sown at the rate of half a pint an acre and if the sower dug too deeply into his bowl with his thumb and forefinger he would not make his seed last. Not more than one or two men on each farm could sow at the necessary rate with two hands. Most men were only able to sow with one. This was necessarily slower, but the sower who used one hand only was able to carry a *seed-hod*—a bigger container—on one side of his body. Clover and mustard were sown in the same way as turnips.

When the turnips came up it would be some time during the harvest; and the men would be set to hoe in the early morning before breakfast when the *dag* or dew would still be on the corn. They would likewise hoe turnips when a damp or wet day compelled them to make a break in the harvesting. It was a hard job hoeing plants that grew from broadcast seed, and they would have to hoe twice; the second time to cut out the *knots* or concentration of plants and the weeds that had grown since the first hoeing. If the harvest had not been taken on contract, the men received half as much for the second hoeing as they did for

the first. When, later, seeds were drilled the second hoeing was
not necessary.

What was the difference between a boy and a lad? It can be
seen from the contract that the lad got more money than the
boys: he was, in fact, older and would not be called a lad until
he had left school. While he was still at school he was a boy. At
the time of the contract a boy left school when he was between
ten and twelve years of age. From that time until he was seventeen or eighteen he would be called a lad. A lad who had not
long left school would be taken on at harvest time as a *half-
man*—that is, he received half a man's wages. He did very light
jobs during the harvest: taking the loaded wagons to the stack
yard; or *drag-work*, leading a horse with the drag-rake. The
horses he handled would be the staid old *jobbing* horses that had
lost all their sprightliness after long years of hard ploughing.
When a lad was sixteen or seventeen he was taken on at harvest
as a *three-quarter man*, getting three-quarters of a man's wage.
He did all the jobs a *full man* did except *pitching*, the handling of
the sheaves of corn from the ground on to the wagon—the
heaviest job of all. A three-quarter man was usually stationed
on top of the load.

Boys and girls who were still at school were often taken on at
fixed wages. They had various jobs: they helped with the turnip
hoeing; they carried the *elevenses* and *fourses*—the men's snacks
at eleven in the morning and four in the afternoon—into the
fields; some of the boys would lead the wagon horses and both
boys and girls would be employed as *bind-* (or *band*) *pullers*.
The bind-puller worked with a tier-up, the man or the woman
who came after the reaper and tied the corn into sheaves. When
the *cradle* or *horns* attachment was used with the scythe it would
leave the wheat or oats, that had been cut, leaning against the
standing corn; the tier-up put his foot underneath a bunch of
corn to help him to lift it into his arms. The boy or girl who was
acting as his bind-puller would in the meantime have pulled out
three or four ears of corn from a bunch lying somewhere near
and would be ready to hand these to the tier when he was ready

to make his knot. The type of knot varied from village to village, and some of the old people here can still demonstrate the knot they used when they tied the hand-cut corn.

One of the reasons why lads and boys were included in the contract is that they were taken on to *make up the harvest*—to bring the company up to the requisite strength. For, necessarily, two men on the farm—the stockman and the horseman—would not be included in the contract; and boys were taken on to avoid bringing in a stranger into the team and possibly hindering its smooth working. Boys, moreover, meant a lower wage-bill.

The allowances—*'lowances* in the dialect—were an usual item in the harvest contract. The wheat, along with the wheat won at the gleaning, went to the local miller who ground it into flour, keeping a proportion of the flour in payment. The malt, as we have seen, was for the home-brewing of beer. At the Grove, where Robert Savage spent many years as shepherd, he used to kill a sheep every Friday in order to supply the men with their mutton allowance.

When the harvest contract was signed there would be a supper at the house of the farmer. All the company would be invited and after the business of the harvest had been settled there would be songs and general merriment. There were two of these *Frolics*, as they were called, at harvest time: one at the signing of the agreement and the other when the harvest had been gathered in. This was the real *horkey*, or harvest frolic—the *Largesse Spending* or Supper as it was also called in Suffolk.

The man who actually treated with the farmer about the terms of the contract was called the Lord of the Harvest. He was generally the foreman on the farm and would be elected by the men to command the company during the term of the harvest. The farmer would, for this period, be on a slightly different footing from the rest of the year; and once the contract had been signed he would be a little in the background. The man next in authority to the Lord was called, strangely enough, the Lady. He was the second reaper and took the Lord's place at the head of the line if he were absent. Tusser recommended:

Taking the Harvest

Grant harvest lord more by a penie or twoo
to call on his fellowes the better to doo:
Give gloves to thy reapers a larges to crie,
and dailie to loiterers have a good eie.

The reapers used gloves to prevent their hands being pricked by
thistles as they curved them round the corn when using the serrated sickle. Gloves, judging from the above context, may also
have been a necessary adjunct to the ceremony of *crying largesse*.
This is a very old custom; any stranger who went past a harvest
field or any visitors who entered it would be asked to contribute
something, usually a shilling, to the harvest or largesse supper.
At the beginning of the last century the custom referred to by
Tusser was still practised in Suffolk. It was called *Hollering* (*or*
crying) *Largesse*. The reapers gathered in a ring, holding each
other's hands and bending their heads to the centre. One of the
party, the Coryphee or caller, standing a few yards apart called
out loudly three times: 'Holla Lar! Holla Lar! Holla Larg-
jees!' At the last long syllable he would lower his voice. Those
in the ring would cry: 'O. O. O. O. O' with a low, full
note; at last throwing up their heads and shouting a loud
'Aaah!' This was repeated three times and at last the caller
shouted: 'Thank, Mr . . . for his largesse.'

The Lord made it his duty to gather largesse; and in later
days when the above custom had died out, the Lord and his Lady
visited tradesmen in the nearby towns—anyone who had done
business with the farmer: the miller, the corn-factor, the saddler
and the grocer—to ask them for largesse. All rabbits, also, that
were caught on the fields while the corn was being cut were sold
and the money went to swell the largesse fund. But the Lord's
most important job was to lead the men in the reaping: to set the
rate at which they were to use their scythes, to determine when
they were to stop for a break and, most important of all, to de-
cide which way they were to cut—along the stetches or strips
marked out by the plough, or across them. The Lord went off in
front at the head of the line, 'And pity help anyone who got too

near him!' as Henry Puttock (see Part Four), who often formed one of a harvest company, remarked.

A description of the reaper's tools is probably the best substitute for a picture of him at work. His scythe attachment was called a *cradle* or *horns* in this village. Its purpose was to lay the corn neatly so that the tier-up could easily gather it into a sheaf. Each man made his own cradle and for that reason the cradles varied a little in pattern from one another. The *horn* part of the cradle was made either from wood or iron. In some districts a length of hessian was tacked to a large bow to form a similar attachment to the scythe: this served the same purpose. The pattern of the scythe handle or *stick* also differed; like the cradle each man made the stick to suit his own style of work. The bend in the stick was obtained in the following manner: a piece of green ash was placed across the beams of an old shed or barn. Where the bend was required in the stick a weight was hung. After a time the stick would be tied to preserve the resulting bend; it was then left to season. The two scythe grips are called *tacks* in this village. To sharpen his scythe the reaper carried a sandstone *rub*. He kept this in a *rub-bag*, a small leather pouch attached to his belt and hanging at his hip. He also wore a strap beneath each knee to keep his trousers loose at the knee-joints, thus enabling him to bend more easily. The straps were called *elijahs* in Blaxhall. As well as his *horn drinking-mug* each reaper carried a certain number of 'spares' in his pocket in case of breakages to his scythe and cradle in the field. These were chiefly: a *grass-nail*, the iron attachment which fixed the scythe blade to the stick; a couple of *worrells*, the metal ring at the top of the stick into which the hook at the end of the blade fitted; and a length or two of *thong*, in case the leather thong steadying the cradle were to break. Thus equipped, and with his beer and his food, his *beaver* and his *bait*, brought out to him during the day the reaper stayed in the field until his work was finished.

After the corn was cut and carted it was stored in the big eighteenth-century wooden barns. Many of these barns are older than this but still in good preservation. Most have now been converted into storage places for farm implements and machinery, and on some farms into cowsheds. They are rarely used today for the storage of corn. The big doorway in the centre of the barn was built high enough to allow the full wagon of corn to enter. It is easy to recognize this type of barn, which is very common in this district, by the big double doors extending beyond the eaves with the smaller door in the opposite wall. The space between the doors was the *middlestead* of the barn. Here stood the loaded wagon while the corn was stored in the spaces on each side: these were called the *goafstead*. Here the *goaf—gove*, in Tusser's time—the mow or rick of corn in the straw, was placed ready for threshing. In order to pack as much corn as possible in these two confined spaces, the oldest and therefore the quietest horse on the farm was used to trample it down as it was unloaded from the wagon. A boy got on the horse's back and rode him round and round treading down the corn. This was known as 'riding the goaf'. As the wagons were unloaded, the corn in the goafstead would mount higher and higher until the boy would find it impossible to ride or even lead the horse with any freedom. The horse would then be secured by a long rope expertly fixed around him. The end of the rope was thrown over one of the stout beams of the roof and the men below gently helped the old horse to regain the floor.

The middlestead of the barn was always kept clear, for here the threshing was done later in the year when it was too wet or cold for outside jobs. The floor of the middlestead was paved with *clay-daub* (dab)—clay beaten down until it became as hard as concrete. The threshing was done with a flail, a *frail*, or a *stick-and-half* as it was called in Suffolk. The *half* part of the flail was called the *swingel*, and was made of very tough wood like holly or blackthorn; the handle was made of ash. The handle had a swivel on its top; and the swingel was attached to it by thongs of snake- or eelskin, the underside of a horse's tail or sometimes just pigskin. The knot was of a special design peculiar to each district. In this part of East Anglia a number of *eel-pritches* or *glaves*—fork-like implements for spearing eels—are still to be found. They indicate that eel-catching was once more frequently practised than it is now. The eel was as much prized for its skin as for its edible qualities; and farmers were always ready to buy eelskins for the making and repair of flail knots, for they regarded eelskin as the best and toughest *leather* for tieing the swingel of the flail to the handles.

When using the flail the thresher swung the handle over his shoulder and brought down the swingel across the straw just below the ears so that the grain of corn were shaken out without being bruised. An illustration in the Luttrell Psalter brings out this point. Skill was needed to handle a flail; and it was easier for a beginner to hit himself at the back of the neck with the swingel than to get it to fall neatly across the corn. George Messenger, an old Blaxhall man, said: 'When I fust used the *frail* I hit myself sich a clout at the back o' the hid! It whoolly hurt: the wood was some hard! But the ol' boy along o' me said: "Niver you mind, you'll git one or two of those afore you git used to it. But you'll soon git the swing on it!" And I did, and I used to thrash the corn I growed on my *common yara* for many years arter that.'

While the threshing was going on the big double doors were pinned back; as also was the smaller one in the opposite wall. The through-draught thus set up helped to carry away the dust. After the threshing came the sieving: the sievers separated the cavings, called *colder* in Suffolk, from the grain and chaff (or *chobs*). Then the grain was piled at one side of the middlestead and thrown with a *scuppit*, or wooden casting-shovel, high into the air. The heavy grains would fall furthest away, while the lighter and inferior ones would drop short, thus forming a kind of tail. These inferior grains, which were often fed to cattle, were in fact called *tailings*. The through draught was often assisted by an artificial draught set up by a hand-turned wheel with sacks fixed on its arms. There was also a *hand-winnowing* machine, a *fyeing* machine as it was known or more descriptively, a *blower*, for getting rid of the chaff.

Barley was treated to an extra process after the threshing.

Taking the Harvest

To remove the awns or beards, *havels* in Suffolk, a *hummeller* or *haveller* was rolled over the grain as it lay on the threshing floor. This was an implement very like a lawn-mower in design: except that the *blades* were set parallel and were blunt, taking off the awns with a chopping action. Another type of haveller, a flat grid in appearance, was fitted to a wooden handle and used with a chopping action. Havellers can sometimes be spotted doing service as foot-scrapers alongside the entrance of farmhouses. As far as barley is concerned the old traditional song, *The Barley Mow*, gives an accurate summary of the processes described above:

> *Here's a health to the barley mow;*
> *Here's a health to the man*
> *Who very well can*
> *Both harrow and plough and sow.*
> *When it is well sown,*
> *See it is well mown;*
> *Both raked and gavelled clean;*
> *And a barn to lay it in.*
> *Here's a health to the man*
> *Who very well can*
> *Both thrash and fan it clean.*

Threshing and *dressing* (or *fyeing*) the corn was monotonous work, often lonely work as well. In a later chapter a thresher is described looking out through the barn door as he takes a rest from his work. Time passed slowly, and to mark the hours the men cut notches in the side of the barn; and the sunlight streaming in oblique winter rays through the doors or a crack in the timbers reached these marks and told them how the day was going and what time they could stop for their meals.

It is worth noting here that the chaff obtained from threshing oats was often used for making beds. They were called *oat-flight* beds. Oat-chaff was too light to be fed to cattle as it got into their nostrils: '*Things* (animals) won't eat it unless it is dampened fust and mixed with other sorts of chaff.'

Most of the old harvest customs and the old implements went out after the introduction of machinery. With machines the old team-work, highly organized and ruled according to immemorial custom, is not as necessary; the time taken over the actual harvest is shorter; and latterly, since the introduction of the combine-harvester, much of the corn is not even stacked. But there are one or two flails still surviving in our village; and a number of the older men know how to use them. Flails, in fact, went out much later than one would expect. There appear to be many reasons for this: farmers retained the use of the flail because it helped to solve the problem of what to do with their workers in the winter season when outside work on the farm was impossible. They put the men to thresh beans for feeding to their horses or beans for keeping as seed. Again, for a long time after the introduction of the threshing machine, a flail was used if the straw was wanted for thatching. But it is likely that the flail was seen last of all—at least serving its ancient purpose—on the *common yards* or allotments of small cottagers who used to thresh the wheat they had grown to add to their winter store.

Rider Haggard, writing at the beginning of this century, gives some indication of the rate of threshing with the flail: 'At Kelsale, on a farm belonging to Mr Flick, we saw his bailiff, Philip Woodward, a fine old man who said that he had been sixty years in farming. As a boy he had started on sixpence a week; and as a young man was paid tenpence a coomb for thrashing with a flail with which instrument he knocked out something like three and a half coomb a day.'

If, however, all that has already been stated about threshing gives the impression that there was something colourful or romantic about using the flail, we have the testimony of an old Suffolk farm-worker, who is still living, to disprove it. He was paid at the rate of 3s. a coomb for threshing; and he had no two thoughts about it: 'Threshing was real, downright slavery.'

But if a company of men was threshing, the work was much easier, simply because they were together at a shared task. They also had certain devices for relieving the monotony. If the

Taking the Harvest

company was all bell-ringers they stood round the threshing-floor, which was usually made of elm, and they rang the changes with the flail, in exactly the same rhythm as they did in the steeple with the bells, all coming in their proper turn, and changing and changing about at a signal from a leader. From a distance this rhythmic beating of the elm floor made an attractive simulation of the bells.

Another device to brighten the occasion was to hold a kind of competition. Each member of the company took a piece of straw. The pieces were all of the same length—-about six inches. The game was to hold the straw in the mouth as they were threshing: each time they leaned forward and brought the flail down on the corn they let the swingel brush against the short straw. An old man from another village had seen this game and reported: 'I dursn't try it myself! I saw many a young 'un very nigh crack his skull with a blow from the swingel when he were a-trying this caper. But the old timers could swing it within a quarter of an inch of where they wanted to—they were so steady and accurate.'

12   *After the Harvest*

In the old days, before the corn was taken into the barn the parson would have collected his share of it. Henry Puttock remembered his father telling him what used to happen at the beginning of the last century. The parson took every tenth sheaf of corn and had his own wagon to cart it; and he stored it in a barn specially built for the purpose—the tithe-barn as it was called. In some parts of Suffolk the turnips had also to be set in heaps for the parson to tithe.

The tithe is a church tax, and very early in the history of the church in every European country a tenth part of the produce of the land was claimed. The church based its right to do so on references in the Old Testament; but it is probable that the tithe is a vestige of the old Roman tribute of one tenth. Up to the beginning of the last century most tithes were paid in kind; but after the Tithe Act of 1836 a rent-charge was substituted. When the tithe was paid in kind there was endless friction between farmers and clergy and when payment in kind was changed into a rent-charge much of the friction was removed—but by no means entirely. After the First World War there was a recrudescence of the movement against payment of tithes and there were many *seizures*—appropriation of the goods and stock of farmers who refused to pay. There was a seizure in the Suffolk village of Elmsett which had an interesting sequel: a farmer living there lost his farm and stock and later emigrated to New Zealand. But before he left he recorded the incident in the permanent form of an eight-foot concrete block, taking care first to buy the land on which the memorial was erected. It reads:

1935

TITHE
MEMORIAL
1934
To Commemerate (sic) the Tithe
Seizure at Elmsett Hall
Of Furniture Including
Baby's Bed & Blankets
Herd of Dairy Cows
Eight Corn & Seed Stacks
Valued at £1,200 for
Tithe Valued at £385.

After the corn had been gathered in from the field the gleaning started. In this parish there was a definite pattern for the gleaning. First of all, the gleaners—usually women and children —were allowed to operate only within the bounds of the parish. There is an entry in the Blaxhall Churchwardens' Book during the late eighteenth century recording that the sexton was paid 4s. extra for ringing the bell at harvest time. This bell was rung for the gleaners, first at eight o'clock in the morning and again at seven in the evening.

At eight o'clock the gleaners gathered outside the field to be gleaned. The farmer indicated what fields he had finished by leaving them bare of sheaves. If one sheaf remained standing in the field the gleaners would not enter because they knew that the farmer had not gathered all the corn—perhaps one of his men had still to go over it with the hand drag-rake. As the eight o'clock bell tolled the gleaners flocked onto the field and began picking up the wisps of corn that had been left by the harvesters. They carried on gleaning until the ringing of the seven o'clock evening bell gave them the signal to stop. Boys, it seemed, were not as popular on the gleaning fields as girls: they were too *mischieful*. Sometimes the farmer stopped them from entering the fields; but it was not unknown for a boy to be dressed up as a girl and so escape the farmer's eye in this way.

An old poem written in the Suffolk dialect gives an excellent picture of a rather harassed mother setting off to the fields with her numerous children on a gleaning expedition. It is called *Gleaning Time in Suffolk*, and its author hid his identity under the pseudonym *Quill:* many a man would have been proud to put his own name to it:

> *Why, listen yow—be quiet bo'!—the bell is tolling eight—*
> *Why don't yow mind what yow're about?—We're allers kind o'*
> * late!*
> *Now, Mary, get that mawther dressed—oh dear! how slow yow*
> * fare—*
> *There come a lot o' gleaners now.—Maw', don't stand gawkin'*
> * there!*
>
> *Now, Janie, goo get that 'ere coach, an' put them pillars in—*
> *Oh! won't I give it yow, my dear, if I do once begin!*
> *Get that 'ere bottle, too—ah, yow may well stand there an' sneer;*
> *What will yowr father say, d'ye think, if we don't taak his beer?*
>
> *Come, Willie!—Jane, where is he gone? Goo yow an' fetch that*
> * child*
> *If yow don't move them legs of yow'rn, yow'll maak me kind o'*
> * riled!*
> *There, lock the door, an' lay the key behind that 'ere old plate;*
> *An' Jemmy, yow run on afore, and ope the whatefeld gate.*
>
> *We'll here we be at last—oh, dear! how fast my heart do beat!*
> *Now, Jane, set yow by this 'ere coach, an' don't yow leave yowr*
> * seat*
> *Till that 'ere precious child's asleep; then bring yow that 'ere sack*
> *An' see if yow can't try today to kin' o' bend yowr back!*
> *Yow'll all wish, when the winter come, and yow ha'en't got no*
> * bread,*
> *That for all drawlin' about so, yow'd harder wrought instead;*

After the Harvest

For all yowr father 'arn most goo old Skin'em's rent to pay,
And Mister Last, the shoemaker; so work yow hard, I pray.

*   *   *

Dear me! there goo the bell agin—'tis seven, I declare;
An' we don't 'pear to have got none;—the gleanin' now don't fare
To be worth nothin'; but I think—as far as I can tell—
We'll try a coomb, somehow, to scratch, if we be 'live an' well.

Maw' or *mawther* in the first verse is the dialect word for a girl
—*mother* in Tusser's time. *Coach* is also dialect for a home-made
perambulator, or go-cart. The body and the wheels were
roughly made of wood, as Priscilla Savage remembers it, and the
wheels were given iron tyres by the blacksmith.

After the harvest was all gathered and the gleaning finished
the Largesse Spending or Harvest Frolic was held. But first
there was a meeting of the company of men at the farmhouse to
'settle up' and if it had been so arranged the Frolic took place
there immediately afterwards. This rejoicing at the bringing in
of the harvest is a very old custom and is mentioned in the Old
Testament:

'Thou shalt observe the feast of the tabernacles seven days,
after that thou hast gathered in thy corn and thy wine. And thou
shalt rejoice in thy feast, thou, and thy son, and thy daughter and
thy manservant, and thy maidservant, and the Levite, the
stranger, and the fatherless, and the widow that are within thy
gates.'

In the farmhouse all sat down in the big kitchen to partake of
the supper. There was roast beef and vegetables followed by
quantities of plum-pudding to eat, and home-brewed beer to
drink. The Lord and Lady of the Harvest presided at the supper;
and it was the Lord who proposed the toasts. The Lord, in fact,
sat at the head of the table. After the supper the wives and the
children were asked to the 'best parlour' and the men were left
to their merry-making and the singing of the traditional harvest
songs. A detailed description of a Suffolk harvest frolic is given
by Cobbold in his novel *Margaret Catchpole* (1845).

101

Sometimes in this village the supper was held in the village inn, or in the largest of the cottages owned by the farmworkers. If it was held in one of the cottages the tables were set up outside the cottage-door; and after the supper had been eaten there was merriment both inside and outside the house. Thomas Tusser had long ago advised:

> *In harvest-time, harvest-folk servants and all*
> *should make all together good cheer in the hall;*
> *And fill out the black bowl of blythe to their song,*
> *and let them be merry all harvest-time long.*

But the harvesters wanted little encouragement to natural fun and fooling; and they could heartily agree with him when he said: ''Tis merry in hall, Where beards wag all'. The form that one piece of fooling took during the Frolic has come down to us:

One of the men would stalk into the midst of the company shouting provocatively:

> *I am the Duke of Norfolk*
> *Just come into Suffolk:*
> *Say, shall I be attended,*
> *Or no, no, no?*

One of those present would instantly answer in soothing tones:

> *Good Duke, be not offended,*
> *And you shall be attended:*
> *You shall be attended*
> *Now, now, now!*

And some of the company would hasten to conduct the 'Duke' to the best chair, at the same time crowning him with an inverted pillow, while one of their number was filling up a jug of beer for him to drink. This at last he would offer to the 'Duke', kneeling with great ceremony as though he were doing service to a king.

The real Dukes of Norfolk—the Howards—had owned great estates in Suffolk from early times; and this old harvest custom seems to have been an ironic reference to their importance.

13   The Revolution in Farming

A few years ago John Goddard, a farmer in the next parish of Tunstall, died at the age of ninety-eight. He had been farming up to six months before his death—a continuous period of seventy-six years as a farmer in the county of Suffolk. He had lived through the death of an old era and had witnessed the birth of a new; and his life-story illustrates the revolution that has taken place in British farming in the course of the last hundred years.

Until he was twelve years of age John Goddard went to school at Framlingham in Suffolk. After leaving school he worked on his father's farm; but when he was twenty-two his father set him up on a sixty-acre farm near his home. At that time it was hard for a young man to make a start because the land was nearly all tied up with the big estates. Young Goddard had to pay £2 an acre rent for his farm, plus tithe charges. Stock and gear were also expensive: it was impossible, for example, to get a useful horse under £50. He soon found out that he could not work the farm while paying such a rent; and he was on the point of emigrating. He stayed in this country, however, and undertook the jobs of Parish Overseer of the Poor and Surveyor of the Highways in his village. These two offices brought him in about £20 yearly, and helped to keep his farm going. His landlord, too, was reasonable and let him have some land, which he did not farm himself, without charging any additional rent.

George Rope—John Goddard

Two or three years later came a disastrous year. This was the notorious *Black '79*, the memory of which lived long among the old farmers. 'It was the worst of a succession of wet seasons and the winter of 1880–81 was one of the severest ever known. The land, saturated and chilled, produced coarse herbage since the finer grasses languished and were destroyed. Fodder and grain were imperfectly matured, mould and ergot were prevalent amongst the plants and fluke produced liver-rot amongst live-stock. In 1879 three million sheep died or were sacrificed for rot in England and Wales. Besides this great calamity the year was distinguished by one of the worst harvests of the century; by outbreaks of foot and mouth disease and of pleuro-pneumonia.'

John Goddard knew that if he could only hang on over this disastrous period rent and prices would come down and he could then carry on. He weathered the storm and stayed in that parti-cular farm for twelve years. Then a 300-acre farm on the estate of Lord Rendlesham became vacant. At that time the Rendle-sham estate was highly preserved for game; there was a small army of keepers, all dressed in a livery of blue velvet with but-tons bearing their master's coat-of-arms, parading about the countryside. This was hardly an inducement to a hard-working farmer to hire the land. But he took the farm and made it pay; and later he bought nearby farms until at one time he was farm-ing, with the help of his son, over 2,000 acres of land—nearly all arable.

A little while before his death this old farmer said: 'I'm an agriculturist of the old school. Although I have kept my methods up to the present I believe in the old Norfolk four-course system —but I can see that the new ways have surpassed it. I could see, too, the need for using artificial manure on a large scale long before it was actually used to any great extent. There has been a complete revolution in agriculture during my day: the internal combustion engine has changed the whole science. But, do you know, all that has happened has been so gradual as almost not to be noticeable. Yet when I compare the beginning of my career with the end I realize how amazing the revolution has been.

The Revolution in Farming

Take one instance—threshing. At one time the farmer did not go to the stack: the stack, in a manner of speaking, was brought into the barn. I remember them using the *stick-and-a-half* in the barns to beat out the corn from the straw; and they had been using that since the days of the Bible. They had fans, too, to get rid of the *chobs*, the chaff as they call it now; they tried all sorts of contrivances to separate the chaff from the corn. But today there's little talk of barns: with the combine-harvester they've even done away with the stacks!'

Before the coming of mechanical power John Goddard needed thirty horses to work his land. But he wanted more power and he was the first to experiment with the old steam ploughs. He was one of the earliest buyers of the *Suffolk Punch*—a steam engine and plough-set made by Garretts of Leiston, a famous firm of agricultural engineers. The usual form of the steam-plough equipment consisted of a combined engine and haulage drum at one end of the field, and a self-propelling anchor and pulley at the opposite end or *headland;* the plough was hauled up and down the land in between by an endless wire-rope. The *Suffolk Punch* was designed to plough six furrows; and it cost £700. But John Goddard found it too expensive to work: he ploughed twenty acres with it and then scrapped it. He carried on with horses, and much later changed over to motor-tractors.

The Norfolk four-course system on which Goddard set so much store was evolved by *Turnip* Townshend and Coke of Holkham. It consisted of a rotation of crops in four groups. About the time John Goddard started farming the rotation on the heavy land district of Suffolk was: *first year;* fallow—either clean fallow tares, beet or turnips: *second year:* barley: *third year*, half clover, half peas or beans, alternatively: *fourth year*, wheat. The course on the light land districts was: fallow, swedes, white turnips, mangel-wurzels or carrots in the first year; followed by barley; then by seeds in the third year; and wheat last of all. But there was, naturally, much variation in the order of cropping, especially among the smaller farmers.

But one of the crops that John Goddard grew successfully, a

crop that helped to make his farming prosper, was clover—
White or Dutch Clover grown for seed. He made the marketing
of clover seed an art; and the process is typical of the care that
went into the old farming. It is described by Thomas Frost,
Goddard's son-in-law—also a farmer for over fifty years.

'The clover was cut and carted during the late evening or very
early morning. Nothing was done to it while the sun was up
because if the crop was moved when it was dry, much of the *cobs*
(the husks containing the seed) would be lost. After carting it
was threshed: first of all to get the cobs off the small stalks;
then it was threshed a second time to get the seed out of the
cobs. Then it was sieved repeatedly to get the pieces of stalk,
leaf and so on out of the seed. But on John Goddard's farm an
extra bit was added: after the seed was sieved it was *spooned*:
I never saw this only at his place.

'The clover seed was put in a measure and shaken about till all
the stringy bits, still left in after sieving, came to the surface of
the seed. These bits were then taken off carefully with a spoon.
A man could do about a sack a day; therefore each sack cost 2s. 6d
extra, allowing that much a day for the man's wages. But it was
worth it because when John Goddard took the samples to show
the dealers, they would pay pounds more for his clover-seed
than for the seed of the other growers.

'The seed of Dutch clover is very small and it's golden in colour. When it was *guinea-gold* you got a good price for it. Some
years, owing to the weather, it would be brown in colour and
you wouldn't get as much for it then. But clover seed was expensive to grow and not many farmers had the patience to cultivate
it for seed. It had to be mown, first of all—there were few *clippers* (cutting machines) about at that time o' day. Then you had
to have special tools to harvest it: *daisy rakes* for instance, rakes
with six-inch nails or special metal tines instead of the usual
wooden ones. Again, clover for seed took up a field for a whole
year. It was sown in with wheat—three or four pounds to the
acre—in early spring; and it was not ready for harvesting until
the next July twelvemonth. If you were lucky and it wasn't too

dry a season you might be able to sow a crop of turnips on that particular field—but that was rarely possible. Then there was the dressing of it: men were in the barn for days and weeks in the winter spooning the clover seed. But, all in all, it paid because the seed would fetch a wonderful price—often as much as £1 for a pound of it, a lot of money in those days. It was good farming, in a sense, too; because it gave something for the men to do in a slack season. Before this the men used to be employed in the barn a-thrashing of the corn—I've thrashed beans myself but you only did this occasionally, not on the same scale as the corn —and when the thrashing machines came in there was nothing for the men to do. Spooning the clover seed and getting it ready for market was a winter task for the men which kept them in the barn during the bad weather. Another point was that so much was lost in the harvesting, in spite of all the precautions, that the crop would often come again, and give two crops from one sowing.'

14   *The Worth of the Old Farming Methods*

The impression may have been given in the last chapters that, now we have reached the age of soil analysis, the combine-harvester, and chemical fertilizers, farming has become *rationalized* completely and that science has given a kind of laboratory surety to most modern farming practices. Such an impression, however, would be false; for in spite of its advances farming is only partially scientific; it is still very much an art, depending to a large extent not so much on a body of generalized rules—the precepts of modern agricultural science—as on their application to a particular farm or district. Farming, in this respect, is like medicine: the modern doctor has his encyclopaedic knowledge, his drugs, his specifics, and his up-to-date equipment but in the last resort he still cannot treat by rote; each patient has to be regarded not only according to the dictates of general practice concerning one disease or another, but just as much as an example of the disease's particular and individual manifestation. In the same way the farmer knows that his job does not entail simply the mechanical application of a set of text-book rules: each farm, each field, in fact, is different; and like a patient demands to be treated with the sympathetic understanding born of long experience.

This long experience—the accumulated wisdom of generations of practical farmers—has by no means been supplanted; and it would be wrong to suppose that science has made ana-

The Worth of the Old Farming Methods

chronisms of all the old traditional practices. It would be wrong, too, to assume that farmers in the old days did not know what they were about and cultivated the soil without any science at all. They did have a science although it was not as organized and effective as it is today. A body of very valuable farming knowledge was handed down from generation to generation; and in some branches of farming recent scientific advances have been chiefly concerned with improving and bringing this knowledge into some sort of system. Long before the beginning of modern science, farming was carried out in a way that showed at least the germ of scientific practice.

The rotation of crops—to give an example—is assumed by many to have first been discovered and applied in the eighteenth century by Townshend and Coke: apart from the fact that Sir Richard Weston had experimented with turnips and clover in the first half of the previous century, many well-known Roman writers like Cato and Varro had given their minds to the improvement of farming; and the Romans had a rough system of crop rotation in very early times. This is evident from *The Georgics*, Virgil's long poem about agriculture. In this the poet states that certain crops, oats for instance, exhaust—*burn up*, he calls it—the land; and that by alternating corn with leguminous crops, such as beans, the land is given a chance to recover.

The Romans even invented a reaping machine. It was a kind of cart with two wheels; and it was pushed through the standing corn by an ox. In front of the cart a kind of comb was fixed; the teeth of this comb closed round the corn and tore off the ears which fell back into the cart. But this machine was only suitable for use in flat lands. It was used chiefly in Gaul, the modern France, and was described by the elder Pliny, a Roman writer who perished in the great eruption of Vesuvius in A.D. 79.

The mention of Pliny recalls another instance of the wisdom of the old farming practices—this time taken from Britain. In recent times the truth that frequent application of lime to light land improves its fertility has been rediscovered; but farmers in East Anglia have been, for centuries, applying lime, in some form or other, to their land. The numerous marl-pits in this district have already been mentioned: marl—clay with an admixture of chalk or lime—was taken out of these pits and spread on the field like cattle manure. The old farmers knew that this clay improved their crops: they did not perhaps realize that it was the lime in the clay that chiefly helped the soil to produce more; but they persisted in the practice because it gave results. Only when it was dropped did the land become sour and sterile. Pliny states that the Britons marled their land in pre-Roman times, and sank pits over a hundred feet deep to get at the material. Chaucer mentions a marl pit in his *Canterbury Tales;* but marling went out of use in early mediaeval times. It was revived by Townshend who marled the light land of Norfolk with spectacular results which helped to give currency to the proverb:

> *He who marls sand*
> *May buy the land;*
> *He that marls moss*
> *Suffers no loss*
> *He that marls clay*
> *Throws all away.*

Then marling once again went out of favour, perhaps due to Arthur Young's reservations about the practice; but the application of lime to light land is now in full favour again and has the blessing of the agricultural scientists.

The use of crag or shell-marl also shows how science confirms an old practice. Crag, it has been discovered, contains phosphates and nitrates, two of the most important compounds in modern fertilizers; although the eighteenth-century farmers were ignorant of its chemical constituents, they knew from experience that scattering it on the land improved their crops.

Another instance of the wisdom of old traditional practices is shown by the rearing of pigs. It has recently been found that young pigs often do much better in the low, stuffy and apparently unhealthy pigsties of cottagers and smallholders who keep pigs as a side-line than in the roomy, specially constructed modern piggeries. These are usually excellently planned, well lighted, easy to clean and to all appearances ideal for breeding and rearing healthy pigs. But it was found that there was a rather high death-rate among the young ones. In planning these piggeries the architects had overlooked the fact that a young pig needs warmth before anything else. This had been the old pig-breeder's first concern: the rough pigsty with its low roof and poor ventilation was much nearer the ideal for the young pig, as in the wild state it would spend its first weeks in a warm *nest* that its mother had made for it in dense well-protected under-growth.

In most localities, there are, too, various methods of farming which have been tried over the centuries; and it would be a rash man—even though a scientist, a demi-god of the modern age—who would brush aside these local beliefs without first giving them very careful consideration. Some of these local beliefs and practices may appear to be simple superstition; but it must not be forgotten that superstition is often a primitive attempt at science and sometimes has the germ of an important truth under-lying it. Agriculturists meet this sort of thing when opening up new areas to the plough: they ignore the old practices to their cost. Sir James Scott-Watson, the well known farming scientist, stated not very long ago that he believed there has been so much soil erosion in the Middle West of the United States—The Dust Bowl Area—chiefly because methods of farming that had been found suitable in Western Europe had been applied here uncritically. A new approach altogether was needed, and a clue to this might be found in the old traditional practice of the natives.

Sir James gives another instance. He writes:

'A colleague, Mr. T. E. Miller, relates that when he took up his first post as Adviser in the East Riding of Yorkshire, he encountered what seemed to him to be a mistaken notion. This was in the days of strict four-course farming, with wheat follow-ing clover. But there was the old bugbear of clover sickness, and it appeared to him that a ryegrass-clover mixture would, as elsewhere, be a useful measure of insurance against a complete failure of the "seeds". But the farmers were not to be convinced; ryegrass was a bad preparation for wheat. Miller consulted his chief, Professor Seton, who advised silence; and eventually it transpired that the farmers were right. Both ryegrass and wheat are among the hosts of the frit fly, and in autumn, when a ryegrass ley is ploughed, the maggots migrate from the grass to the wheat seedlings, often with devastating results.'

In this connection the mediaeval open-field system may be mentioned. Most school history books go out of their way to attack this old method of farming, and on ground on which many of the historians are little qualified to do combat. It is likely that the open field went out of use more because of the rigidity of the social organization connected with it than for its technical insufficiencies as a method of farming. The eighteenth century damned the old system so effectively that it implanted a prejudice against it that has lasted to the present. Yet there must have been some health in this method of farming for examples of it to survive into the twentieth century. Laxton in Nottinghamshire, the most complete example of the old system still working, has to this day its three open fields, its common grazings and its manorial court. The old mediaeval three-course rotation—spring corn, fallow, and winter corn—is still followed and the court leet of the manor still governs the actual farming as it did in mediaeval times. The Laxton farmers are satisfied with their system because it still works; and one can hazard a guess that when the Ministry of Agriculture and Fisheries purchased, three years ago, the 1,758 acres of the Laxton estate from the Earl of Manvers the transaction did not spring altogether from a sentimental regard for this example of ancient farming organization.

The open field system, however, is not likely to return; nor is the less remote past so bemoaned by an old farm worker in this village. In bewailing present-day methods of farming, he said: 'It's the machines! They'll hev to come back to hosses yet. Two ton of iron (the tractor) going over the land don't do it no good:

The Worth of the Old Farming Methods

it stands to reason!—You git the roller on the land, it's true; but too much of thet ain't no use. It's inways and sideways: thet's how they go on with the land today. It's not done. It's got over!'

Robert H. Sherwood, who farms at Blaxhall, has given a specific example of the re-discovery of the old practice of marling or liming in comparatively recent times: 'When I came to Lime Tree Farm, nearly forty years ago, I was warned that certain fields on this farm were unsound for sheep when they were heavy in lamb; and on no account were sheep to be folded in these fields. This was quite correct, as the fields were sour with megbeg, sorrel etc. Yet after the fields were chalked—nobody knew about this fifty years ago—the weeds disappeared, and all these fields were then quite sound for sheep in lamb.'

Robert Sherwood was born two or three miles from Blaxhall at Snape Croft where his father, S. H. (Sam) Sherwood farmed. Sam Sherwood was among the foremost Suffolk farmers of his day, and was one of the deputation who met Rider Haggard when he visited this part of Suffolk while he was making his famous survey of English farming at the opening of the present century. Farming was at a very low ebb at this time. Many of the better workers had left the land, and there was little spirit left for experiment or improvement. It was not until the necessities of the First World War compelled the country to give more attention to its farming that the industry started to revive. More machinery and new methods were introduced; and at the same time some of the older methods, such as liming, were re-assessed and used again.

15   Common Yards and Old Farm Implements

During most of the nineteenth century and for a good deal of the present one the farm worker's lot was hard. He rarely earned enough to keep his family; and his wife and children were forced to work on the fields to get enough money to keep the family together. The system whereby women and children worked on the land in poorly paid gangs was widespread. Children of a very young age were often seen in the fields, but in 1873 an Act was passed making it illegal to employ a child under eight. Three years later, the age below which a child might not be employed was raised to ten. But these enactments did nothing to improve the family budget: about this time, it was said, families stole turnips from the field for food; and every other man was a poacher. It is not surprising that Joseph Arch's ironic grace had a wide currency at this time:

> *O Heavenly Father bless us,*
> *And keep us all alive;*
> *There are ten of us to dinner*
> *And food for only five.*

Parish relief was common; and rarely did a worker manage to bring up a family without at some stage making application for it. If he did manage this almost impossible feat, he had the rather dubious satisfaction of being granted an award certificate issued by one of the societies formed on the pattern of 'The Royal Association for Improving the Condition of the Labouring Classes'. One of these certificates was given (in 1874) to a Blaxhall man for bringing up a large family without parish relief.

But there was little real improvement of the condition of the rural worker until the attempt to form the agricultural unions. In 1872 the movement called 'The Revolt of the Field' started in Warwickshire. Joseph Arch, a well-known figure in this county—a champion hedge-cutter and Methodist lay preacher—formed a union of local farm workers. In March of that year the first strike of rural workers occurred, and wages rose immediately. But when the union movement began to spread farmers retaliated by issuing notices to all men who had joined a union. By 1874 the farmers in East Anglia had formed an association at Newmarket. Suffolk farmers, particularly, showed great hostility and when in that year the farmers reached a decision to give their men notices, a great part of Suffolk was included in the *lock-out*.

This temporary defeat slowed down the union movement. But it was a pyrrhic victory for the farmers; and British agriculture received a blow from which it took years to recover. Many of the men, rather than continue working under the old conditions, either emigrated or moved into the towns. This movement into the towns, however, caused another attempt fifteen years later to encourage unions among the rural workers. The town unions realized that unless the rural worker was organized they would always suffer from the danger of his deserting agriculture and selling his labour in the towns at whatever price he could get.

In 1889 the Van Movement began. Itinerant lecturers were sent round the countryside in caravans; they stopped at country villages and talked to the men about matters that affected them. The English Land Restoration League, which advocated Henry George's single tax on land as the means of settling the land question for the benefit of the country as a whole, was invited by the Eastern Counties Labour Federation to send their Red Vans into Suffolk. That there was plenty of work for them to do here was early apparent to the lecturers; and confirmation came from an unusual quarter:

'Friendly gypsies fraternizing with the Red Vanners and assuming that they had something to' sell would tell them that Suffolk, where wages were low, was a poor county for trade, and that better business was to be done in the fenlands.'

There is no record of one of the vans stopping in this village; but Robert Savage remembered his father telling him that Joseph Arch once spoke on the *Knoll*—the small triangle of green near the village inn. Joseph Row recorded that his uncle, who worked at the Grove Farm, Blaxhall, was asked by Old George Rope sometime in 1874 whether he was a member of the union. He made a non-committal reply but did not return to the farm after the Great Lock-out of that year.

When wages were at starvation level any method to increase the family income—in money or in kind—was welcomed. Not the least important was the *common yard* or allotment. It was usually about a quarter of an acre in extent; but one man sometimes made shift to cultivate more than one allotment; and grew, in addition to the usual vegetables, a patch of corn for his fowls or even for his family's own use. He cultivated his yard as best he could: if he was fortunate he might borrow one of the farmer's horses. Should he manage to get a horse from the farmer in order to prepare the ground for his pototo crop, it would be lent on a Good Friday, and only then with the stipulation that 'the horse would be back in the stable by *church-time*'—eleven on Good Friday morning. Most farmers, however, would not lend their horses for the ploughing up of yards, and the men had to manage as best they could, putting in an hour's digging with the spade at any opportunity. But many devices were tried to avoid the task of digging a whole yard. Aaron Ling, Priscilla Savage's father, owned a small plough and a donkey; but the donkey could not—or would not—manage the plough by himself; therefore Aaron trained an old sow to pull along with the donkey. The sow was a quiet animal, and was harnessed to the plough in the same manner as that used on bullocks—the *cradle* harness. The sow walked on the *land* and the donkey in the furrow. 'She wor a big ol' sow, and when the donkey wor in the furrow you couldn't tell no difference: the sow wor as big as him.' Later Aaron Ling acquired a pony, and he went with him around the village ploughing up common yards on contract.

One interesting feature of these allotments is that the old implements, which were discarded on the introduction of the new farming machinery, were still used for a long time afterwards for the cultivation of the common yards and for the harvesting of crops grown upon them. Many of these old tools have been found in this village in the old sheds that are often attached to or at least associated with allotments.

One of the oldest implements found here is a *corn sickle*. The sickle was in use for cutting corn as early as history is recorded; and it is said the earliest type of sickle was a crescent shaped flint, or several pieces of flint fitted with a bone or wooden handle. The Romans used an iron sickle similar to the ones illustrated in many mediaeval manuscripts. The blade of the sickle found here is serrated up to about two inches from its point. The point is blunt, as it was used not to cut but to divide the corn. The reaper grasped a bundle of corn in one hand and curved the sickle round it with the other; then he drew the sickle towards him, cutting the corn with a sawing action.

After the sickle, in the evolution of corn-reaping tools, came the *swap-hook* or *swab* as it is known in this village. With a swap hook the reaper used a slashing action. In his free hand he carried a short crook, made of wood or iron, to hold back the stalks.

Interesting facts concerning the history of the sickle and the swap-hook were gathered when the director of a long-established Sheffield firm of tool-makers recently recognized a swap-hook owned by Harry Keble, an old man in this village, as one that had been made by his ancestor and founder of the firm. The hook has the stamp J. H. impressed upon it, and dates from the early years of the nineteenth century when John Harrison of

Dronfield used to bring his tools into Norfolk and Suffolk on pack-horses. This firm used to make serrated sickles until about forty years ago: after the sickle had been beaten out a worker held it between his knees, both of which had been padded on the inside with leather, and made the small serrations with a cold chisel and hammer. This process was called *tedding*, and the worker received three-halfpence for every dozen sickles he completed. But sickles are still made by another Sheffield firm— Thomas Stanniforth of Severquick Works—for export to Asia and the Middle East where methods of farming have not changed since biblical times.

The scythe was in use before the end of the fifteenth century. Illustrations show that the early scythes had straight *sticks* or handles; and a similar stick was used in Blaxhall in recent years. To the scythe the reaper often attached the *cradle, rake* or *horns* (page 92); but when he was harvesting barley he used a metal bow in the shape of a query-mark. This is called a barley-*bale* or -*bow*. It was mounted on the scythe when barley was being mown: the *nail* at the top of the bow was inserted into the *worrell*, the ring at the top of the scythe handle; and the bottom of the bow was fixed to the stick. Sometimes the barley-bow was merely a piece of bent hazel twig: whatever the material from which it was made, its use left the barley in neat swathes ready for the gavellers.

If a reaper had not made his own scythe-stick he would have it made by the local wheelwright who allowed him to handle likely pieces of wood until he found one, which for size and weight, was most fitted to his style of work. About a hundred years ago it was estimated that during a ten-hour day a man could reap at the following rates:

Wheat:	2.3 acres with a scythe
	1.1 acres with a hook
	1.0 acre with a sickle
Barley and Oats:	4.0 acres with a scythe
	2.2 acres with a hook
	2.0 acres with a sickle

Common Yards and Old Farm Implements

Many cottagers in this village also owned a pitchfork, a two-tined fork that has not changed its shape for centuries. Many also have dibbling irons or *dibbers*, called *debblers* in some parts of Suffolk where they are still used even today. Holes were made in the ground with these and the seeds were dropped in carefully and covered up with the harrow. Arthur Young describes the process graphically: 'The ground being rolled with a light barley roller, a man walking backwards on the *flag*—as the furrow slice is called—with a dibber of iron, the handle about three feet long, in each hand strikes two rows of holes about four inches from one row to another, on each flag; and he is followed by three or four children to drop the grains—three or four in each hole. A bush-harrow follows to cover it.' There is a Suffolk rhyme describing the children's part in the process:

> *Four seeds in a hole:*
> *One for the rook, one for the crow,*
> *One to rot and one to grow.*

Beans as well as corn were dibbled. After wheat was dibbled it was well hoed by hand. This hand-hoeing was done in the spring. An old lady in Blaxhall recalls that an aunt of hers, born near the middle of the last century, remembered being told by her mother that on the day she was born—sometime in March—the women were out hoeing wheat. In such families as this, with their long memories of past events, the old implements are kept and treasured as things that are closely woven into the pattern of family history.

Another implement often adapted for ordinary gardening jobs is a *bush-draining tool*. It was used to take out the bottom *spit* or spade-depth of a bush-drain, the channel cut across land to take off the surplus water. The process of making a bush-drain consisted of cutting out a fairly wide channel—the width of a spade, for instance, and a spit in depth; another smaller channel was then cut at the bottom with the above tool so that a wedge-shaped channel or drain resulted. At the bottom of this, hawthorn or blackthorn bushes were packed tightly and then the channel was filled in. The water on the land would thus be able to percolate through the tightly packed bush, as through a mesh, emerging at the outlet of the drain which was in the wall of the ditch at the side of the field. No vermin would penetrate into this small channel to block it up; and the field could be cultivated for many years without the drain being renewed. Bush-draining was practised in pre-Roman times, and the bush-draining tool is still in use in Suffolk. At the beginning of this century it was used extensively. Rider Haggard wrote in 1902:

'At his farm in Acton (Suffolk) Mr Cady kept fifteen score of ewes . . . . He told me that all the land about there wanted draining. This they did with bushes, as the cost of pipes was greater than the state of affairs would warrant.'

The *hand-drill* was the next stage in development to the dibbling iron and the dibbling *frame*—a frame with wooden *teeth* which would dibble four more rows at a time, at intervals that could be varied by shifting the teeth. A broadcast seed-drill or *seed-barrow* for sowing small seeds broadcast on the land is still in use on a Blaxhall farm. These seed-barrows were first made about a hundred and thirty years ago. Few of the old seed-*maunds* or baskets, used by the sower when he broadcast seed by hand, still survive: where they do they are used for scattering fertilizers on the land.

Thomas Tusser wrote:

> *In May get a weed-hook, a crotch and a glove,*
> *and weed out such weeds as the corn do not love.*
> *For weeding of winter corn now it is best;*
> *but June is the better for weeding the rest.*

There are at least half a dozen old *weed-hooks*, of a pattern very similar to the mediaeval ones illustrated in the Luttrell Psalter, still left in our village. The weed-hook or little sickle was fitted to a long wooden handle, and was used with a forked stick or *crotch* as Tusser called it. The weed was held firmly with the forked stick and was cut off with the hook well below the ground.

Common Yards and Old Farm Implements

Weed-hooks are not used here for their original purpose but like many of the old tools they developed a secondary use: up to a few years ago women and children took weed-hooks with them on blackberrying expeditions and they used a hook to draw the branches of the bramble towards them.

Another old weeding tool, the thistle *spud* or *grubber*, sometimes called a *dock-chisel*, is still in use. The thistle was a bad enemy of the farmer a few centuries ago; and few went about their farms without a thistle spud in their hand like a walking-stick. This was the time when it was considered that: 'The best dung for the soil is the master's foot, and him walking over it daily.' Tusser hints that June is the best month for weeding, and farmers were warned not to cut thistle before St John's Day (June 24th) because if they did, each root would be likely to sprout three or four fresh plants. There is a rhyme which confirms this:

> *Thistles cut in May*
> *Come again next day.*
> *Thistles cut in June*
> *Come up again soon.*
> *Cut them in July,*
> *They'll be sure to die.*

Under *December's Husbandrie* Tusser states:

> *When frost will not suffer to dike and to hedge*
> *then get thee a heat with thy beetle and wedge.*

A *beetle* and *wedges* are still used for splitting timber in Suffolk. A beetle is a heavy banded wooden mallet, its striking surfaces studded with nails. It was made from an *ellum tod*, the twisted knotted growth often found on an elm tree. The sight and the feel of a beetle admirably explains Shakespeare's phrase for a nit-wit—*beetle-headed*. Some of the draining tools mentioned by Tusser:

> *a* didall *and* crome
> *For draining of ditches that noyes thee at home.*

And again:

A scuppatt *and* scavell *that marshmen allow.*

are still used for the draining of ditches, an occupation which
seems to run in families in this village. A *didall* is a triangular
spade with sharp edges for cutting the sides of a drain; a *crome*
(cf. muck-crome) is a tool with a long handle and long metal
teeth or tines, hooked for raking loose the bottom of ditches. A
scuppatt is a wooden shovel made all in one piece like a malt-
scuppit; but a mud-scuppit for use in ditching had a leather
apron· at the top of the blade to prevent the soft mud from
slipping back as the scuppit was used.

There are many more of the old tools still surviving, too
numerous to be listed here; but in passing them by the old farm-
wagons must not be forgotten. In this village they were made by
the wheelwright and the blacksmith who had their shop and
forge next door to one another. The forge still exists, as also
does the old saw-pit and the shed which housed the wheelwright's shop. It was in this shop—so the village story goes—
that they once made a wagon that was too big to be wheeled out
of the shop: it had to be taken down again and re-assembled outside. Some of these old wagons were made at the end of the last
century or the beginning of this. They are still being used and
seem good for another fifty years or so yet.

A rather rare old farm-tool has recently come to light, recall-
ing an early type of reaping machine that was used in Blaxhall.
The tool is a rack-engine rake, and Robert Savage once described its use: 'A rack-engine were an old horse-drawn grass-
cutter that had been fitted up to cut corn. One man drove it,
and another sat on a special seat holding a rake. As the knife
cut the corn the man raked it together onto a platform just under
him. When he'd got enough corn to make a *shuff* he pressed a
lever with his foot. The platform then tilted, and off went the
corn; and the women and children then came along to tie it up.'

16   Fairs and Occasions

Mention is made later (page 136) of a village called Dunningworth, once situated on the outskirts of this parish. With its church it has long since fallen into decay. Yet the name is often heard here, although the village itself is no more than a folk-memory. A well-known horse-fair, dating—it is believed—from the time of the old village was held near the site of the former church right up to the end of the last century. The date of this fair is still referred to at least once every year. It fell on the eleventh and twelfth of August; and the older generation still commemorate it because they know the first day—*Dunnifer Fair Day*—as the date on which they must sow their spring-cabbage seed.

The fair used to be held on a strip of ground in front of a farmhouse called Dunningworth, reputed to be the site of a royal hunting-lodge. But the farmer objected to having it so near his house and one year planted trees on the strip of land to prevent its return. The trees are still standing. The fair continued to be held, however, in a field a little further removed from the farmhouse. This is known today as Fair Field. Later it shifted towards the village of Snape where it seems to have petered out in an ordinary amusement fair of swings and roundabouts.

There is a memory of the old horse-fair in the Savage family. Robert Savage described how horse-dealers from all over the country used to attend it. The Suffolk horse or the Suffolk Punch, as it is generally known, was naturally the chief breed of horse sold at this fair. One of the most outstanding qualities of the Suffolk Punch is his pulling power. He was, therefore, in great demand by City flour merchants who wanted a reliable draught horse to pull their heavily loaded wagons from the docks to their warehouses. Crowds of horse-dealers from London attended Dunningworth Fair. The dealers used to test a horse in two ways: they first got the owner to hitch his horse to a fallen tree, and then they watched the horse's pulling or *drawing* power. The horse would not be expected to shift the tree, which was usually of a fair size; but if in his efforts to move it he got down almost on to his knees in the approved Suffolk Punch manner, the dealer was satisfied that the horse had the quality he was looking for. The second test meant harnessing the horse in a tumbril, and *backing* him for some distance. Some horses—presumably those who had been bred to the plough—could not bear the feel of the breeches-strap against their haunches as they backed. If a horse could not back, the dealers would not look at him, in spite of his strength; for as a shaft horse working in a town he would frequently be called upon to do this.

Since the coming of the tractor most of the farms here have lost many of their horses; and the term 'eight- or twelve-horse farm' marks a phase of agriculture which is now history. But two or three Suffolks are still to be seen on every farm in this village. They are used for carting for harrowing and drilling and sometimes for ploughing the *headlands*, the strip around the outside of a field that has been ploughed in the main by a tractor.

The Suffolk, with his beautiful chestnut colour and rounded lines, was a popular breed not only in his home county, but all over Britain; and he was not unknown in Australia, New Zealand and South America. He is a compact horse, called *Punch* because like Mr Punch he is short-legged and barrel-bodied, in fact a short fat fellow. His hardy build, his determination, his long working life and his quickness at starting, and his ability to go for long hours without feeding, have made him the ideal horse for the plough. Two horses were normally used with the plough: a *land* horse and a *furrow* horse. The furrow horse, as the name implies, walked in the furrows; and it is interesting to note how he developed the pigeon-toed action noticeable in some Suffolks: he put his forefeet down one in front of the other, thus enabling himself to walk steadily in the furrow without swaying and faltering.

But it is for his *drawing* power that the Suffolk Punch has been most famed. He will, in fact, get down on to his knees before he gives up pulling. This attitude is shown in an old manuscript, *The Luttrell Psalter*: it depicts the leading horse of a team crouched down to put his full strength into the pull. The horses shown are probably ancestors of the Punch; though 'every animal of his breed now in existence traces his descent in the direct male line in one unbroken chain to a horse foaled in 1760'.

The Suffolk horse's ability at a *dead-pull*, or pulling of a dead weight, was often the subject of wagers in the eighteenth century. Arthur Young wrote: 'They (the Suffolk horses) are all taught with very great care to draw in concert, and many farmers are so attentive to this point that they have teams, every horse of which will fall on his knees at the word of command twenty times running in the full drawing attitude, and all at the same moment; but without exerting any strength till a variation in the word orders them to give all their strength; and then they will carry amazing weights. It is common to draw team against team for high wagers.'

An earlier eighteenth century Suffolk writer, the Reverend Sir John Cullum, whose history of his parish of Hawstead has a deservedly wide reputation reaching far beyond his native county, also gives us a picture of a *drawing match*. He quotes an advertisement from a newspaper of 1724:

'On Thursday, July 29th, there will be a Drawing at Ixworth Pickarel for a piece of plate 45 shillings value, and they that will bring five horses or mares may put in for it; and they that can draw 20 of the best and fairest pulls with their reins up, and they that can carry the greatest weight over the block with fewest pulls shall have the said plate, by such judges as the masters of the teams shall choose. You are to meet at 12 o'clock and put in your name (or else be debarred from drawing it) and subscribe half-a-crown a piece to be paid to the second best team.' He also explains: 'The trial is made with a wagon loaded with sand, the wheels sunk a little into the ground, with blocks of wood laid before them to increase the difficulty. The first efforts are made with the reins fastened, as usual to the collar; but the animals cannot, when so confined, put out their full strength; the reins are therefore afterwards thrown loose on their necks, when they can exert their utmost powers, which they usually do by falling on their knees, and drawing in that attitude. That they may not break their knees by this operation, the area on which they draw is strewn with soft sand.'

So much for the eighteenth century drawing match which was in effect a proof of the strength and *bottom* of a Suffolk horse. Drawing matches are still held in Suffolk, but they are a very different thing from the old matches just described. The modern ones should be more properly called *furrow-drawing* matches as they are held to discover the ploughman who can *draw* or plough the straightest furrow. Suffolk appears to be the only county that makes the distinction between a furrow-drawing match and a ploughing match. In the first, a single furrow is drawn, and the ploughman who has the straightest is the winner; whereas in a ploughing match a whole *stetch* or *rig*, perhaps twelve furrows, has to be ploughed before the prize is taken.

These furrow-drawing matches are one of the important occasions in this area. There are always two *classes* in them—horse-ploughs and tractors. The horses are decked out in the old style for these matches, sometimes with hounces, more often with red tassels and green and red croupers. The ploughing and especially the judging is worth watching. As soon as the furrow has been drawn, the judges or *stickers* plant square white sticks, about eighteen inches long, at each end of the furrow. They are first plumbed with a spirit level to ensure that they have been placed in the ground upright. The sticks are placed flush against the coulter-cut, the smooth vertical cut in the furrow. Then the stickers, one at each end, start to shout their instructions to their helpers to assist them to find 'the worst place in the furrow'—the point in it most out of the straight. These instructions have an attractive, but obscure, music of their own, for instance: 'Put your top downhill, Walter.—It will bear to go in a little more—No, prove it where you are.—There! It's a little the worst. There! just front on you.'

The stickers, lying prone, judge by the eye, sighting along the two end sticks. Once the *worst place* has been found they tell their helpers to place in two more sticks at that point—the true stick, in dead line with the two end ones, and alongside it a stick placed upright in the bent furrow. A helper measures the distance between the two sticks, and this tells how much the furrow is out of the straight: this measurement is known as *the deviation*. The deviation is rarely more than two or three inches; and winners of furrow-drawing matches have drawn furrows in which the stickers have been unable to find any deviation worth measuring.

But why a straight furrow at all? We know that drawing a straight furrow has become proverbial for the man who sees a job through to the end, a job over which he has bent all his strength and given the full measure of his integrity. And a furrow drawing match is a rural occasion that brings out the healthy emulation of ploughman against ploughman, preserving —at least in spirit—something of the country contests of the past. Yet is a straight furrow essential in working the land; especially as the furrow is so quickly harrowed and flattened out immediately afterwards? If one asked a ploughman this question a tolerant smile would probably be his first reaction; then he would perhaps say after a pause which he would need to reflect on a question he never thought could be put: 'A straight furrow! You got to have a straight furrow to make your stetch come out square. Of course you got to have a straight furrow. It wouldn't be right if you didn't. Besides, there's the drill: if your furrow isn't straight, your stetches will be wrong; and how are you going to fare when you get the drill going? I mean, you got to have a straight furrow!' Good practical reasons, forcibly put, would be forthcoming; and yet after watching a furrow drawing or a ploughing match one has the feeling that the most cogent reason is rarely stated. To the ploughman the straight furrow is an end in itself, calling for all a man's skill, a kind of quest after the mathematically unattainable: skill and craft carried to the point where the straight furrow becomes utility's tribute to art. The ploughman aims at a straight furrow because it looks right; and because it gives him the craftsman's satisfaction of a self-set standard; of doing a job as he feels it should be done, without need of praise except his own self's approval—which is not far from the aim of the dedicated artist. All of this would probably make our ploughman smile again; but a smile is as good a measure as any of the *weight* of the imponderable.

PART FOUR

HENRY PUTTOCK
(1871–1955)

17 *The Church*

Henry Puttock was our first real link with the past of the village: 'If you want to know anything about the olden times, Harry Puttock's your man—he's got a book, too.' This turned out to be one of White's Suffolk directories dating from the middle of the last century; but its owner was able to start many more lines of thought than the book. He was in his eighty-third year when he died recently. All his working life had been spent on the land, and he had always lived in this village as did his father before him. He was tall and thin with the quiet manner and high domed forehead of a scholar—which he might well have been in other circumstances. It was he, who by recounting an old legend, led us to consider the shape of the village and why it is situated where it is (see Appendix).

Henry Puttock lived in one of the nearest cottages to the church; and this building, especially the bell-tower, was his centre of interest throughout his life. Through long conversations with former rectors he gained a great deal of knowledge about the history of the church fabric, information that was rarely written down and which he, alone in the village, possessed. He recalled that his father told him how, before the restoration of the church in 1863 and the installing of an organ, the music for services was supplied by a flute, violin, and 'cello, the musicians sitting in the gallery. He remembered this gallery being used as a class-room during Sunday school; and he gave a picture of one of the old teachers who served there. He was called James Smith but he was usually known by his nickname of *Handky*. He was so named because in an accident with a chaff-cutting machine he had lost all his fingers except one. This was the index finger on his right hand. On his left wrist he wore a webbing strap and a buckle. By placing tools and implements under the webbing he made shift to use this hand with remarkable skill. He was accounted the best mole-catcher in the district; and in 1879 he was reputed to have caught 654 moles in thirty-two days. This was the time when mole-skin waistcoats were in fashion! He was also employed as a warrener, making snares and setting traps as well as anyone with ten fingers. For many years he was Parish Clerk, managing to use a pen by curling his one finger around it. This one finger, too, did great service in the gallery during Sunday school, when it was his custom to correct the more high-spirited boys by leaning over and tapping them with a long cane. It is in this role that he is best remembered.

The church in our village is not outstanding for the beauty of its fabric, but the nave dates from the fourteenth century; and the building has an interesting history like the most modest of the old churches which were once the real centres of village life. There is a fine fifteenth-century font big enough to take a young baby in it. That is, in fact, what happened at the time the font was made: the baby was not simply christened, or sprinkled with water, it was totally immersed; and the hammer-beam roof must have rung with its cries of protest. There are also remains of the rood-stairs which once led to the rood-loft where the rood or great cross stood, reaching up into the chancel-arch. The rood was taken down and destroyed in most churches during the time of Edward VI, son of Henry VIII, who made the final break with the old religion. The pulpit is of dark oak and was erected in the late sixteenth century. It is fairly high, and the height is a sure sign that the congregation once sat in horsebox pews—high pews complete with doors to keep out draughts; this was at a time when church heating was unheard of. Great attention was paid to pulpits during the eighteenth century and many were made very high and elaborate. One of the carpenters who built such a pulpit has recorded his opinion in a bit of concealed carving on the pulpit itself:

> *A proud parson and a simple squire*
> *Bade me build this pulpit higher.*

But there were no seats at all in churches before about the year 1400. The reason is that the church was put to many more uses than it is today. It was a community centre in the true sense of the word: all sorts of occasions were celebrated in the church. It was even used for dancing; and in turbulent times often served as a kind of fortress or keep and a food store-house for the district. A Tudor merchant of Aldeburgh, a nearby town, stated in his will: 'My ships *Christopher*, belonging to the havyn or port of Aldeburgh, *Erasmus* and *Thomas* shall be proclaimed a sale in the church.'

The memorials in a church are always worth attention. The most interesting in Blaxhall church is to a former rector who died in 1652. A wooden board on the wall under the tower explains why. It has the following inscription painted upon it:

'Thomas Garthwayte, clerk formerly Rector of Blaxhall, and Elizabeth his wife gave by their will a Messuage situate in Woodbridge and known by the Name of Red Cross and now in Occupation of John Harris and rented at 12 Pounds a Year. Which said Sum after necessary Repairs are discharged is to be employed for the clothing of the poor Men and Women and Children of Blaxhall: nor shall it in any wise be a Means or Occasion to lessen or abate any Sum or Sums of Money which ought to be assessed and collected for the necessary Relief of the Poor of the said Parish. And as a Memorial of the above this was erected in 1762.'

It may seem a little puzzling that after a lapse of a hundred and ten years it was necessary to put up this memorial, and the amount and terms of the charity. But about this time many charities were being appropriated, and it is likely that the parson and his churchwardens went to the trouble and expense of having the purpose and terms of the charity permanently set down in order to forestall any attempt to annex it. The danger came from the Overseers of the Poor. As their name suggests, their job was to look after the poor and provide for them at the parish's expense. This expense was met by a rate which was levied on property in the parish. As the Overseers were usually chosen from the land-owners—two were chosen to serve for each year —it was in their own interest to fix the rate as low as possible. In many parishes the Overseers had argued that as all charities went to the poor it was quite in order to take them over to help the poor-rate which they were responsible for fixing and collecting. They, therefore, annexed the charities to save themselves the expense of a high poor-rate. But Garthwayte's eighteenth-century friends were too vigilant to allow this to be done and the charity still survives. The Red Cross, the property the old rector left, later became an inn, which it still is. About fifty years ago the trustees of the charity found that repairs to the house were leaving little money over for distribution; therefore they sold it and invested the money in government stock. The interest on the sum invested is paid out each year to the parishioners who apply for it. The gift is now usually granted to those who do not own any property. Between sixty and seventy gifts have been distributed annually during recent years out of a fixed income of £70 14s. The gifts once took the form of varying lengths of calico which were distributed from the church as Henry Puttock recalled. But in the eighteenth century the charity was given out in cloth other than calico as is seen from this section of a list of those who received it in 1728:

Coats Disposed of as followeth:

Will Smith a coat	4yds ½
Thomas Wilson a coat	4 yds
Dame Blos A peticoat	3 yds
Dame Greenleafe A peticoat	3 yds

Within living memory sheets of unbleached calico were given out in the church porch. Priscilla Savage said: "The church-wardens used to have a table in the porch and they cut the sheets of calico from a big roll—one sheet for each family; two if the family was a big one. The sheets lasted a whoolly long time. I got one now as good as new and washed nearly white. If you didn't want the calico for sheets you could make shirts, knickers and short *slops* from it. Mr Gibson's stuff—he was the village shopkeeper—was the best, good brown calico. The trustees, the churchwardens and so on, were supposed to see that the people who had the gift wore the calico or used it themselves. It wasn't right to sell it.

'But after they sold the Cross Inn instead of giving out calico you had vouchers to spend in certain shops, the same as you do now. But you were not allowed to buy finery with the vouchers at that time o' day—no hats, no ribbons, no feathers or knit lace. And the bills were sent back to the trustees to see that you kept to the rule. But they don't go on like that today. Buy what you like it is today!'

Before the Cross Inn was sold it was naturally favoured by Blaxhall men when they went to the town. 'When the wagons went to Woodbridge, the men allus used to say: "Let's have a drink in the Cross, boys. We must support the Cross!".'

Many churches display a list of priests who served in the church. This church is no exception. The list starts in 1320. Like most lists of this kind it has one or two points of general interest. In one part it reads:

> 1341   Joseph de Colesworth
> 1349   Joseph de Hardleston

The Black Death swept across England in the years 1348–9; and it has been calculated that a third, or possibly half, of the inhabitants of the kingdom died from this sickness. Whole villages were wiped out and became deserted; and crops stood rotting in the fields because there was no one to gather them. The first Joseph on the list was very probably a victim of the plague which hit the village very badly if village tradition can be believed.

In passing it may be stated that the Black Death has been blamed for more disturbances than can rightly be attributed to it. There has always been a tendency to attribute events in the past to some spectacular cause: a deserted cottage, or even more so a decayed village, invites the dramatic explanation; and there is hardly a castle whose ruins have not been blamed on Cromwell's cannon. This village might well have suffered temporary desertion owing to the plague: on the other hand its desertion might well have been due to less spectacular but, in the long run, even stronger agencies. Throughout the fourteenth and fifteenth centuries many villages all over England were abandoned because of the changes in farming. Arable land was being put down to grass for grazing sheep: the result was depopulation as sheep required less labour to tend them; and huge tracts of country became a green desert peopled only by the occasional shepherd. Contemporary literature is full of references to this tendency: the passage in Thomas More's *Utopia* is well known, and a lesser known writer of the time complained in something of the same manner:

> *Sheep have eaten up our meadows and our downs,*
> *Our corn, our wood, whole villages and towns.*

There are sites of two decayed or *lost* villages on the boundaries of this parish. They are both named in the Domesday Survey. One was called Beversham and had one and a half plough teams listed against it. No trace now remains of this village except its name, which has descended to a railway crossing near the supposed site, and a field-name nearby which is suggestive of a settlement. The other village was called Dunningworth. A decayed chapel survived on this site until the latter half of the eighteenth century. A farmhouse now bears the name, and some of the old people can say that a field quite near it once bore the name *Chapel Field*.

The most outstanding name on the list of rectors is one who entered this church in 1550. His name was William Bulleyn, known as the author of one of the first English herbals, *The Book of Simples*. Bulleyn had an unusual life for someone who was the rector of a quiet country parish. But times were disturbed when he held the living: Mary Tudor became queen of England and

proceeded to restore the country to Catholicism. She acted with
zeal and Bulleyn, who was a Protestant, thought it best to keep
out of her way. He, therefore, went north to Tynemouth near
Newcastle. Sir Thomas Hilton, the governor of Tynemouth, was
his patron. But Sir Thomas died of a fever while he was under
Bulleyn's care; and William Hilton, his brother, accused Bulleyn
of murdering him. He was imprisoned, and although he easily
cleared himself of the charge he was still kept in prison for not
paying a debt. While he was there he wrote most of his medical
books. He gave an account of this chapter of his life in *The Book
of Simples*:

'I was accused by William Hilton of no lesse crime then of
most cruell murder of his own brother which died of a fever—
sent only of God—emong his own friendes, finishyng his life in
the Christen faith. But this William Hilton causing me to be
arrayned before that noble prince, the Duke's Grace of Norfolke
for the same; to this end to have me died shamefully. But his
wicked practice was wisely espied, and finally I was with justice
delivered.'

Later, when he was released from prison, William Bulleyn
married the wife of his late patron.

One of Bulleyn's chief remedies against sickness, if we can
judge by his *Dialogue Against the Fever Pestilence*, seems to have
been a merry tale; and he ends a chapter of this book by saying
in the character of *Medicus*:

'Therefore, sir, to conclude: plucke up that weake harte;
rejoyce and cast awaie all care, I warrant you.'
—advice that has a modern therapeutic ring.

Bulleyn's name was well remembered in learned circles for
many years after his death by reason of a statement he made in
one of his books, *A Bulwark of Defence against all Sickness* (1562):

'In the year of our salvation 1555, in a place called Orford in
Suffolk, between the haven and the main sea, where never plowe
came, nor natural earth was, but stones only, there did Pease
grow, whose roots were more than ij. fadomes long; and the
coddes (pods) did grow upon clusters like the Kaies of ashtrees,

bigger than fitches (vetches) and lesse than the field Peason. Very sweet to sate upon, and served many poore people, dwelling there at hande, which els would have perished from hunger; the skarce of bread that yere was so great, insomuch that the plain poore people did make very much of akornes, and a sickness of strong fever did sore molest them that yere, as none was ever heard of there. Now whether the occasion of these peason, and providence of God came through some shipwrake in mocke misery or els by miracle, I am not able to determine thereof, but sowen by man's hand they were not.'

It is known that a blight ruined the harvest in 1555, but it is unlikely that Bulleyn could have visited Orford and seen the peas in that year, as he had given up the rectorship of Blaxhall and had gone north the year before.

The suggestion that there was a miracle was taken up by later writers. Conrad Gesner mentioned the tale in his *Historia Animalium;* then Camden took it up; and later Thomas Johnson in a 1633 edition of *Gerardes Herbal.* But John Ray, a seventeenth botanist appears to have acted with commendable scientific thoroughness: he visited the site and investigated the sea-pea himself. His verdict was:

'that these pease did then spring up miraculously for the relief of the poor, I believe not: that there might be then, Providence so ordering it, an extraordinary crop of them I readily grant. Yet do they not grow among the bare stones but spread their roots in the sand below the stones wherewith there may also be some owze mixt and are nourished by the sea-water.'

The peas, which are reputed to be rare, still grow on this spot in the way that John Ray has described. And this summer (1955) four hundred years after the abundant, providential harvest recorded by Bulleyn, there is another fine crop. But there can be little controversy about the cause of this year's abundance: the rabbits which formerly ate the peas were last year wiped out by the myxomatosis plague, and the plants have been allowed to grow unmolested.

Little evidence of Bulleyn's stay in this neighbourhood can

now be found; but the following, taken from an old newspaper of March 1776, may have some connection with it:

'This to forewarn all People in this publick Manner not to give me, Richard Flatt of Blaxhall, any Physics or Powder or any other Medicine whatsoever or any Drinke as they have done for some time. For it has been of great Detriment to all circumstances of Life as well as Business.'

From this we get a picture of an old gentleman of rather indifferent health and indifferent state of mind hobbling about the village and being plied with various remedies and cures by sympathetic and obliging neighbours; many, possibly, of the Physics and Powders being Bulleyn's *simples* handed down by generations of local folk and being recommended as certain cures for all the ills the flesh is heir to.

18 Bell Ringing

Henry Puttock took part in a practice ring three weeks before he died. He started ringing at the age of sixteen and kept up his single-minded devotion to the bells right to the end. During his lifetime he travelled all over the Eastern Counties on bell-ringing expeditions; and in a little black notebook kept a record of every church he visited, the number of bells in the tower, the height of it and the peal rung on each occasion. His list dates from the year 1888 and gives the names of over two hundred churches he visited. He rang more than one peal in some churches and his list would have been much longer if these second and third visits had been recorded. In the early days the ringers rarely travelled far from their parish: wherever they went they had to walk or use pony and trap. But later on after the coming of the railway, then of buses, they could travel much further in a day; and they visited churches that up to that time had been merely names to them.

When he visited a church Henry Puttock was not content with ringing the bells: he wanted to see them; to examine the way they were hung and to read the inscriptions on them. He was so steeped in the history and art of bell-ringing that he knew by heart details of bells and peals rung in churches he visited more than half a century ago. He knew everything connected with the bells in his own steeple—the inscriptions on them when they were first hung, when recast and the names of the churchwardens who supervised the hanging. The third and fourth bells each have the inscription: *John Brend made me. 1655.* The sixth or tenor bell was also made by the same bell-founder, but it was re-cast in 1902 and has two inscriptions:

> *Laudet Dominum Omnis Sonus*
> *Vivat Edward VII*

This John Brend was a member of a famous Norfolk family of bell-founders. Bell-founding appears to be an enterprise in which competition was very rugged; and it was the custom among bell-founders to record their sharp rivalries in the permanent form of bell-metal. The Brend family were no exception and were involved in a dispute with a Colchester founder called Miles Graye. John Brend, with his brother-in-law Thomas Draper, formed a little *ring* to keep out their rival. There was 'a mighty pretty quarrel' and a trace of it is still to be seen on the bells of a church not very far from our own: one of these bells has the inscription:

> *The monument of Graie*
> *Is passed away:*
> *In place of it doth stand*
> *The name of John Brend: 1657.*

We also learned something of the history of campanology from talks with the old bell-ringer, and from a few visits to the bell-tower. Bell-metal, from which the bells are made, is a mixture of copper and tin, usually in the proportion of four to one. It is believed that the musical sound that can be obtained by striking metal was first discovered in the Bronze Age, and that the earliest bells were saucer-like in shape. Our modern bells are really descended from this type. At first the note was produced by striking the bell with a hammer: later the inside *clapper* was developed. The clapper was first operated by being pulled sharply against the stationary bell. Next the bell was hung on a *headstock*, a block of oak-wood moving on a horizontal axis. To the headstock was fixed a lever and the bell was rung by pulling a rope tied to the end of the lever. An ancient bell at Manningford Abbots, Wiltshire, shows this stage of development. Later a wooden half-wheel was attached to the headstock, then a three-quarter wheel; and from this developed the present-day method of bell-hanging. Now a full wheel is fixed to the headstock, the rope being fastened to the wheel and running in a groove on its circumference. The advantage of the full wheel or *half-pull* system is that the bell is better balanced and, most important of all, that the ringer gets *fore* and *back* strokes, as they are called: that is, only half as much labour is required to ring the bell under the modern system as under the old-fashioned *whole-pull* system in which the bell swung back of itself after each pull.

When a bell is rung, she—a bell, like a ship, is always a *she*—is first pulled, or *upset*, being held in this position by a stay. Then as the ringing begins, she is first pulled off with a fore or handstroke. In this the hands are on the *sally*, the tufted handgrip a few feet from the rope's lower end. Then comes the backstroke, with the hands on the lower end of the rope, since at the previous pull the rope has coiled itself three-quarters of the way round the grooved wheel's circumference; and the sally consequently has ascended towards the bell-floor. At each pull the bell describes almost a full circle until she is back to the upright position: therefore, once the bell is moving, and as long as it is well-balanced and running smoothly, she requires not so much force to strike her as a proper sense of the exact moment to exert the pull and of the exact amount of power necessary to apply to it. When a bell is *chimed* as distinct from being *rung*, she sways just far enough for the clapper to strike one of the sides.

The most straightforward way of ringing bells is in *rounds*. Here the treble bell leads; the second bell follows—and so on to the tenor, the biggest and last bell. *Change-ringing* is a much more complicated method. It was invented in England at the beginning of the seventeenth century—not, it is believed, by any one ringer; the possibility of ringing a number of variations on a group of bells occurring to several ringers at about the same time. The art—or science, as it is called by its adherents—is

Bell Ringing

practised in England more than in any other country. *Change* in this connection means a patterned changing of the order in which the bells are rung. It is possible, for instance, to ring three bells in six changes, each bell altering its position in the sequence by one place at the time:

$$1, 2, 3$$
$$2, 1, 3$$
$$2, 3, 1$$
$$3, 2, 1$$
$$3, 1, 2$$
$$1, 3, 2$$

Four bells could be rung in twenty-four changes ($1 \times 2 \times 3 \times 4$); five bells in one hundred and twenty changes ($1 \times 2 \times 3 \times 4 \times 5$); and so on.

It is not possible for a bell to alter its position by more than one place in the sequence for the following reason: when a bell is *upset* or upright, the ringer cannot hold it, or retard the swinging, longer than it takes for one bell to precede him in the sequence. Change-ringing on five bells is called Doubles; on six a Minor—and so on to twelve bells which is called a Maximus, the limit. A peal consists of at least 5,040 changes. Change-ringing has been called musical mathematics, and it takes long years of apprenticeship to master the more complicated systems.

The *method* as our bell-ringer called the science of change-ringing is something of a mystery to the layman. The ringers stand round in a circle, each with his rope before him, and the conductor gives the signal. To the uninitiated the movement of the ropes appears to be haphazard; but this is not so and it is these movements that the ringer watches most closely. By the position of the gaily coloured sally on each of his colleagues' ropes he knows his own place in the sequence, the moment when he must strike with perfect accuracy of timing and physical endeavour. 'It's all right once you get *rope-sight*,' one old ringer confided. But one is not so sure if that is all there is to it, especially when the conductor calls out a sharp and urgent 'BOB!', an exclamation, it appears, as pregnant in meaning as the 'OM' of the eastern mystics.

An Ipswich bell has the inscription: *Ars Incognita Imperitis Contemnitur:* An unknown art is despised by those who do not practise it—and this seems to sum up the general attitude towards change-ringing. It is not an art that can be picked up lightly, just for a few hours' amusement: it requires a long discipline, and a life-time of application if not of dedication. Another old inscription, this time taken from the belfry walls in a Somerset church, gives in pithy form the qualifications for the true bell-ringer:

> *Who rings this belle*
> *Let him loke welle*
> *To honde and hedde and herte:*
> *Ye honde for werke,*
> *Ye hedde for wytte*
> *Ye herte for worshyppe.*

(The rhythm of this old verse is perhaps best brought out by making the word 'worshyppe' a tri-syllable; the final 'e' being a distinct syllable as often in Chaucer).

'Ye herte', as far as bell ringing is concerned, is the member most in need of looking to: 'If your heart is not in it, you'll get nowhere!' The heart it is which gives the stamina needed to master change-ringing. This is the moral of a story recently told by one of the bell-ringers here. He says: 'We went over to . . . Church for a tidy spell a-larning on 'em the method. After seven weeks they told us they didn't want us no more. They said they were going to carry on with the *call-changes.*' He made no further comment, but a later elucidation of the term call-changes showed that comment was unnecessary. Call-changes are: 'Changes rung in an unscientific and monotonous manner by which one ringer at intervals of his own choice directs the others in what order their bells are to strike; each change being repeated several times till a fresh change is called for.' The devotees of the 'method' in this village refer, with a good-humoured contempt, to call-changes as *Turkey Driving* or *Churchyard Bob*.

'Wytte' is still needed as well as the 'herte', especially since the more complicated systems of change-ringing have been evolved; but the 'werke of the honde' is not as strenuous as it used to be. In the old days the ringers had to be strong because the crude methods of hanging the bell and the imperfect frames that contained them often made ringing a feat both of strength and endurance. In those days the proportion of brains to brawn possessed by a Bullcalf was undoubtedly the best equipment for a ringer. Bullcalf, it will be remembered, was 'a likely fellow' —at least to look at—who tried to excuse himself from doing 'national service' by pleading:

'A whoreson cold, sir—a cough, sir—what I caught with ringing in the king's affairs upon his coronation day, sir.'

At the present time, with the full wheel and the bells balanced with all the skill that modern engineering can bring to the task, no great physical exertion is necessary for ringing a peal. In fact, women are often members of ringing teams: in our own village two young girls are now being coached to follow on the tradition. And this tradition is very important: for once it dies out in a village it is extremely difficult to start it up again; chiefly because the coaching and quiet bringing along of two novices is a very different matter from starting from scratch with a team almost entirely made up of beginners.

This falling away of the tradition of bell-ringing appears to have been going on for some time in villages near this one. Henry Puttock recalled that in the year 1908 he thought he would like to ring the bells at Campsey Ash, an adjoining village. They had not been rung within living memory. 'And it was a pity,' as he said, 'because they were four good bells and the steeple stands up straight and well.' So he asked his rector and permission was obtained, and he took the Blaxhall team over: 'When we got the bells up down came a shower of dust and stoons, enough to cover us; but we enjoyed ourselves—they were good bells—and the sexton gave us five shillings afterwards to take away some of the effects of the dust. But the bells have never been rung since.' Another nearby village has a set of very old bells with a fine tenor-bell dated 1589; but they have never been rung, 'as far back as anyone can recollect'.

It goes without saying that a company of ringers is an asset to any village; and it is a great loss when the tradition of ringing is broken. Apart from the pleasure the actual sound of the bells gives to the rest of the village, the object of the team is a praiseworthy one; and the companionship and the loyalty to one another of a good company of ringers is something of positive worth. A notice recently written by the captain of the ringers upon the death of one of the company gives a glimpse of this quality:

'As a tribute and respect to Edward Smy who after a short illness was taken at the age of twenty-seven, being a member of the Blaxhall Company of Ringers and the Suffolk Guild, also a sidesman and clerk of the parish church; whose funeral service took place Saturday 29th Jan. 1955, after which, with clappers half muffled, touches of Oxford Treble Bob were rung by the following band and friends:

'Gordon Keble, Frank Shaw, Aldeman G. Ling, Aldeman Ling, Arthur Smith, E. Steward, Henry Puttock, G. Berry, H. Hall, A. Pipe and L. Carter.'

Clappers half-muffled, refers to the practice on these occasions of attaching *buffs* or *mufflers*—leather pads—to the striking sides of the clappers. When fixed to both sides, the bells are said to be fully muffled; when one side only they are half-muffled. *Bob* is the 'call' made by the conductor to cause certain bells to make an alteration in their regular work. The process itself is also referred to as a *bob*.

The Blaxhall Ringers own a set of old hand-bells. Aldeman Ling—another old ringer, near contemporary of Henry Puttock —told how the party of ringers used to go round with the handbells on the eve of Christmas and the New Year. There were six ringers, and they tramped all round the parish on these occasions; sometimes as a special favour they went into part of the next parish where they have no ringers. No kind of bad weather deterred them and on more than one occasion they tramped through the snow of a traditional old Christmas. They used to be asked into the farms and big houses and were bidden to ring the bells for the delight of the occupants, either in the drawing-room or the big porch. An old lady who was a servant at one of these houses remembers the excitement with which they looked forward to the visit of the ringers. They were rather late in coming one Christmas Eve, and it was long past the usual bedtime before they actually arrived; but the mistress of the house, realizing that the maids would not settle down until the ringers had been, gave them permission to stay up. That night the ringers rang their bells in the big porch; and afterwards the maids took a great delight in serving them with coffee to which a strong dash of rum had quietly been added.

They rang, too, out of doors at certain points in the village. Robert Savage, the old shepherd, often went round with them. He carried the lamp, and when they halted he stood in the centre of the ringers, his lamp resting on his shepherd's crook which he carried for the purpose. Of these hand-bell excursions Aldeman Ling said: 'They spoiled my Christmas dinner many a year. Everywhere we went we had to have something to drink—gin, beer, home-made wine, rum, all sorts of drink you can think on!' On being asked what tunes they played on these occasions, the old ringer answered without any garnishing: 'No tunes. We allus rang the *method*, the same as we did in the steeples.' Which shows some of the temper of the old ringers, in that even in the midst of jollifications there were to be no concessions as far as their art was concerned—even after a twelve-mile walk with the 'hedde' not working at its best and the 'honde' flagging through fatigue the discipline must be remembered: it was the *method* or nothing at all.

19   *The Parish Chest*

Churches in the Middle Ages often had an amount of costly plate and fabric which it was necessary to keep in a safe place—usually in an ark or coffer, as the chest used to be called. The chest in Blaxhall church—as in most churches—is now kept in the vestry; but it is likely that it once stood by the north wall of the sanctuary, the priest's part of the church. As the sanctuary is the 'holy place' the chest was less likely to be interfered with there. In that position, too, it would offer a seat for the acolyte or priest's assistant.

The earliest form of parish chest is the *dug-out* type, made from a single block of wood in much the same fashion as a primitive dug-out canoe except that the latter was usually burned out whereas a chest was hollowed out of the tree-trunk with an adze. Such a chest was used for many purposes as the modern word trunk—a box for clothes—reminds us. The wood was usually oak and the centre of the log was crudely hollowed and its sides squared with an axe. This dug-out type of chest dates from Saxon and early Norman times. Later these trunks were skilfully made with rich carvings on the front and delicately fashioned locks and scutcheon plates.

Many parish chests had slots in the centre of the lids: into these coins were dropped in the times when the chest was used for collecting alms as well as for storing treasures and documents. Many chests also have a date inscribed on the lid; some have, in addition, the initials of the churchwardens for the year the chest was installed. In many churches a cubical iron box serves as a chest. This type frequently has the date 1813 inscribed on the lid.

The form of our own parish chest is not outstanding; but as in many instances the documents inside the chest are of much greater interest than the chest itself. The contents of the various parish chests vary a great deal: some are rich in old documents relating to the history of the church and the parish; some are poor. In all parish chests we find the parish registers. In these were once entered every wedding, christening and burial in the parish. One of Henry VIII's ministers, Thomas Cromwell, ordered that this should be done in every parish in the kingdom; and in addition the parish was to find a 'sure coffer' to keep the registers. The coffer was to have two locks, the parson having charge of one key, the churchwardens the other. At first the entries were made on paper; sometimes even on loose sheets; but sixty years later, in 1598, Queen Elizabeth ordered that each parish should buy a parchment register for the entries and that the older entries should be copied into it.

Very few, if any, parishes have a complete series of registers dating from this time. Many parishes, like our own, have lost their early registers altogether. But even where the actual registers have been preserved most of them have gaps during the seventeenth century when at the time of the Civil War entries were made in a very haphazard way. Apart for the historical information to be gained from these old registers, most of them have two or three entries of curious interest. Blaxhall registers are no exception, though it is chiefly for certain general trends that they are noteworthy: for instance, this parish always appears to have been rather isolated, keeping well to itself. This tendency seems to be confirmed by the frequency of the marriage entries where both parties are 'of this Parish'. Certainly, there is no entry comparable to the following, found in a Staffordshire register, in a child's handwriting, between two burial entries for the year 1657:

Henry Puttock

'Robert Stud and Tobey Dean born in nuting time. Sara dean his born in coucumber time. Joseph Dean is A very sober young man and mind the larming Bisnis. So that his father dotes him more than all his Ribbis and sayes he will buy him a litel horse and he shall ride up on doben tooe.'

From internal evidence one might say that it was Joseph Dean himself who made the entry: perhaps he was the parson's son. Whoever he was he knew how to give himself a good character and how to get the promises made to him put down on to paper; even if he was not such a brilliant speller. But they did not seem to have as many spelling rules in the old days, and there was much more scope for individuality; yet they were very particular about their full stops and commas if we can judge from the following advice, also taken from a seventeenth-century register:

'Obsarve when you lok in a ragester and kep your stops.'

According to an early law, one or both of the churchwardens had to be present when the parson made entries in the register; this he usually did after the Sunday service. It is not known when the office of churchwarden originated, but from the beginning his main duty seems to have been to look after the fabric of the church; to maintain it and keep it in good repair. The churchwardens had to keep a careful account of the money they spent; therefore we should expect to find their account books in the parish chests. These are worth study not only because they tell how the wardens spent the church money but also for other entries of a more general interest. In the parish chest here there are two churchwardens' books in which are recorded, as well as the accounts, the proceedings of the vestry or parish meeting. Here is an entry after the Easter meeting of the vestry in 1777:

'Whereas great Damage is done in this Parish by so great Number of Asses running at large and being of very little Service to the Owners of them, we whose names are under written do agree and are jointly determined to use all lawfull Means to prevent, for the future, Damage done by them. And every Subscriber in whose Premises they are found is desired to give

Notice of such Mishaps that proper Steps be taken for punishing
the Owners or Owner thereof.

> Wm. Brown, Rd. Taylor,
> Geo. Bates, Thos. Row,
> John Cole.'

It is assumed that the parish officers meant the breed of ass with
four legs: if so, it is worth noting that not one is now left in the
parish; although there were thirteen within living memory. In
fact many old donkey-bits and bridles have been found lying
about in sheds and outhouses. The donkey-bit is of a slightly
different design from a horse-bit; and, naturally, it is much
smaller.

The accounts of the overseers of the poor are also in the parish
chest; and these give a good glimpse into the way the poor lived
during the eighteenth century. Here are the disbursements or
payments made by an overseer called John Pope in the year 1749:

Pd to Goodwife Rackham	5.	0
To a woman for sitting one night with Mary Butcher		6
To 17 loads of Flags at 3/9 £5.	1.	3
To ½ load of Broom	4.	0
Pd the Draper's Bill	19.	6
Pd the Shoemaker's Bill	10.	6
Pd the Glover's Bill	6.	6
Pd for Stockings	3.	4

Flags are turf or peat, cut for cheap fuel, from the common.
It was burnt in open grates for heating and cooking. The poet
Crabbe, writing about the nearby town of Aldeburgh, throws
light on this entry:

> *Lo! where the heath with withering brake grown o'er*
> *Lends the light turf that warms the neighbouring poor.*

Brake, or brakes as the present-day form of the word is in this
village, was the bracken.

Poor people who were permanently on the charge of the parish
were housed in a cottage equipped by the overseers. A list of the

furniture and utensils owned by the parish also occurs in the overseers' books. The year is 1745:

'In the hands of ye Widow Freeman:

'One bed, 2 tables, a joint stool, 5 chairs, 2 cubboards, 2 Boxes, 3 Kielers, 2 Vessels, a pail, an Iron Pot, a Skillet, a Frying Pan, a warming pan, a pair of Tongs, a Firepan, a Hake, a pair of andirons, a Gridiron, a Flagiron, a Box Iron, a pair of Bellows, a Spinning Wheel, a Meal poke, a Kettle, a Spade, a Hook, 2 Candlesticks and a Tunnel.'

A kieler or keeler is a big wooden tub; a hake is a fire-crane, fixed to the chimneypiece so that from it an iron pot could be suspended over the fire, at a height determined by adjusting the crane and its chain on the end of which the pot was hung. A poke is a bag or sack; a tunnel is still the dialect for a funnel.

On the same page as the above list in the entry:

'A Town House and about 2 Roods of Land inhabited by John Rackham and Widow Woods above mentioned.'

Town House is a grand name for a cottage: it is still standing, but now privately owned. Yet the adjoining piece of land is still known as *Wukkus* (Workhouse) *Common*, preserving in unmistable accent the original purpose of the cottage and the stark name by which it was later known.

The children of parents who had died or who were too poor to keep them were looked after by the overseers. These children usually had a hard time because the overseers tried to get them off their hands so that they would no longer be chargeable to the parish; and often they were not too particular about where they went. The Blaxhall books give instances of children who were 'farmed out' in the parish:

'I do promise to provide for an maintain for the Term of one whole Year from the Date here set down the two Children of ye late Samuel Hillins for the Sume of Six Pounds Five Shillings.

'Written by my hand

X

The Mark of William Church

April 20th, 1731.'

Or again:

'Put ye boy Woods to Mr Rowe for one Year at Nine Shillings. Ye Parish to find ye said Boy with all wearing Apparels. Mr Rowe to pay ye Parish ye Nine Shillings for Wagges.

7 October 1751   John Rowe,
                              Griffiths Randall, Overseers.

Here are the accounts paid in the same year towards the upkeep of the same boy and his brother and sisters:

for ye weeskate for John Woods	3. 6
for making a shart for Jean Woods &	
cote and mentel for Ledey Woods	8
for bord for the girl Ledey Woods £1 17 6	
(25 weeks at one shilling and sixpence a week)	
pd for a coat for Boy Woods	6. 0
pd for a pair of gloves and stockings for same boy	3. 0

Some years before this time a law had been passed stating that every poor person and his wife and children 'should wear upon the shoulder of the right sleeve of the uppermost garment . . . in an open and visible manner . . . a large Roman P, together with the first letter of the name of the parish . . . in red or blue cloth'. Therefore it is likely that the Woods children's new clothes, listed above, were defaced by the letters PB.

But the practice of putting out poor children to employers living in their native parish was not such a bad one. It is true that it was open to abuse; but if a child was not well treated, local feeling could always be relied upon to be a safeguard. If, however, a child was sent away—separated from his parents and friends and unable to read or write—he was at the mercy of his new masters; and there is sufficient evidence in vestry records all over the country to show that the masters of many children apprenticed by the parish were of the type that no principle either of human decency or Christian charity would restrain. And the parish overseers were often to blame; for in their eagerness to take a burden off the rates they would pack off a pauper

child to whoever would take him. By the end of the eighteenth
century boys and girls of poor parents, unable to maintain them,
were being sent by the wagon-load to the mills in the North of
England; and once they had gone, the vestry and the overseers
who had sent them, would—except in very exceptional cases—
wash their hands of them, not wishing to hear about them again.
The overseers may have obtained favourable terms of employment for the boy—favourable on paper; but the agreement was
worthless if the boy had no one to turn to when he found that
his master did not keep to his part of the bargain.

Most parish chests have copies of apprentices' indentures.
The Blaxhall chest has one that takes the usual form. But it is
notable for two rather important little words that are left out.
Every indenture of this period had a great number of *nots* in it,
making clear to the boy what he must *not* do. Two of these nots
are left out in this particular copy—quite serious mistakes as
they gave the boy licence to 'play at Dice, Tables, Bowls or
any other unlawful games'; and to 'embezzle or waste or lend or
give to any Person or Persons the goods of his master'. But
these mistakes could not have caused much harm; even if the boy
had been shown a copy of his indentures, it is unlikely that he
would have been able to read them. The boy, William Saunders
of Blaxhall, was bound to Robert Scourfield, a shipowner of
County Durham, for a term of five years. The master agreed to:
'teach, learn and inform him, the said apprentice, or cause him
to be taught, learned and informed in the art, trade or business
of a Mariner or seaman with the circumstances thereunto belonging. And shall and will find him and provide for the said
apprentice sufficient meat, drink and lodging, and pay unto him
the sum of twelve shillings yearly during the said term in lieu
of washing; and also pay unto him the sum of forty five pounds
of lawful money current in Great Britain in manner of, allowing
—that is to say—Seven Pounds for the First Year; Eight
Pounds for the Second Year; Nine Pounds for the Third Year;
Ten Pounds for the Fourth Year and Eleven Pounds for the
Fifth and Last Year. The said William Saunders finding and

providing for himself all manner of Sea Bedding, Wearing Apparel and other necessaries'.

Many apprentices ran away before completing their term of indentures. We do not know what happened to William Saunders but the story of another apprentice from this parish can be inferred from an advertisement inserted in a newspaper. The year is 1771:

'This is to inform Robert Willson who absented himself from his master, Mr John Flatt of Blaxhall, bricklayer, that he is now by mutual agreement of his father-in-law, Mr John Cole and his said master John Flatt, fully discharged and freed from serving the Remainder of his apprenticeship; Mr Flatt's indentures being delivered into the Hands of his said father-in-law and discharge given to him in Writing before two of his Majesty's Justices of the Peace at their Session at Woodbridge on the 9th of April last past; and that his Mother is very uneasy at his long Absence and desires to see or hear from him as soon as possible. As witness my hand:

The X Mark of
Elizabeth Cole'

But one of the most interesting documents in the Blaxhall parish chest is a *Wool Book*. The part played by wool in helping to make Britain a European power has been widely recognized: the sheep, it is said, is the most important animal, apart from man, that has ever walked these islands. The wool was not only made into cloth but it was exported in its raw state to Flanders, the most important trading centre in Europe during the Middle Ages; and here in East Anglia the fine churches, built one might say on wool, are living witnesses to the wealth gained from its trading. But the wool trade did not always remain prosperous. By the end of the seventeenth century it had badly declined: Parliament therefore passed an Act to protect it. The export of raw wool was forbidden; and a law was introduced ordering that everyone who died should be buried in a woollen shroud.

In many parishes a new volume of the burial register was started in 1678. In this book the parson was constrained to make note of the burials and whether a certificate had been brought according to the law to show that it had been complied with. These registers are often referred to loosely as Wool Books; they are to be found in many parishes in the Eastern Counties. The first page of the Blaxhall Wool Book reads:

'The Widow Jaggard was buried May 1716
Zephaniah Eade, an Infant, was buried Aug. ye 18th, 1716
Sarah Randal was buried
John Randal was buried: Jan. ye 5th, 1717

Affidavits were brought in, according to law, of the persons above mentioned.

Zeph. Eade, Rector of Blaxhall,
April 29, 1717.'

It must have been a sad duty for the rector to record the death of his own child on the first page of the new book. The book was filled by 1785, with three entries on its last page. But the Act remained in force for nearly thirty more years; it was, however, not always obeyed as it is certain that there were many more deaths than there were entries in Wool Books. There were, however, fines if the Act was not complied with. A penalty of £5 was levied on the estate of the dead person if it became known that he was not buried in woollen. Half of the penalty was given to the poor of the parish and half to the informer. If a family decided to defy the Act, they would arrange for one of their members to inform: in that way they reduced the fine of £5 to half that sum. But the practice of burying in woollen must have been very widespread, and traces of it have survived even into the present century; for in parts of East Anglia, and notably in Wales, flannel up to a generation or so ago was the traditional material for a shroud. Flannel, incidentally, is a corruption of the Welsh word *gwlanen* meaning wool.

Our parish was once a well-known sheep-rearing district with a tradition of many generations of shepherd families. Yet a year or so ago it was impossible to find a shepherd's smock surviving in the parish: there was plenty of the old shepherds' equipment dating back a couple of hundred years: the short smock or *slop*, as it was called here, various types of crook, sheep-bells, a fold-pritch and other shepherd's tools but no smock with the traditional honeycombing on its front and sleeves. Priscilla Savage gave us the probable reason for this: Most of the shepherds in this village were buried in their smocks. At first the old lady did not want to talk about this custom because she hinted that it was done secretly so that the parson might never get to know of it. It may be that the shepherd families kept this old custom secret because they feared that the parson would object to what was very much like a pagan practice; or more likely, their secrecy was a survival of the attitude of former generations who knew they were breaking the law by burying the shepherd in his smock—a smock was made of *drabbet* (twilled linen) and they knew that it was the parson's duty to see that the shroud was made of wool.

But a handful of wool was in fact frequently buried with the old shepherds—a long established custom, followed for centuries before the passing of the Wool Burial Act. It is believed that its purpose was to enable the dead shepherd to produce the wool on the day of judgment, as an earnest that while he was on earth he followed that calling. He could not then be accused of the sin of not attending church on a Sunday and other holy days, as from the nature of his calling he would naturally be excused. In the light of this custom it might be considered that some such belief was behind the practice of burying the shepherd in his smock.

PART FIVE

KATHERINE MESSENGER

20　The School

An old lady died three years ago in this village at the age of eighty-three. Her name was Mrs Messenger: she had lived in the village all her life and was well-known for her quick and active intelligence. She had a remarkably wide and accurate memory; and provided some valuable facts that were used in the section on harvesting. A year before she died she recalled her school days: she remembered vividly the day she started school as Katie Ling, a little girl of three years of age:

Katie Ling entered school in the year 1873. Her mother was ill, and had a younger child in arms—also ill with bronchitis. To relieve the mother the schoolmistress offered to take Katie on the school 'roll'. During her first day at school the child sat on a small stool in front of the fire. She remembered this well because her mother had dressed her in a red petticoat which caused the other children to laugh at her.

Later on in her school life Katie became a monitress. There were at this time two monitors in the school: each received twopence a week and their main job was to clean out the building. The following tasks were allotted to them:

MORNINGS:	Lay and light the fires; whiten the hearth; dust the school and ring the school bell just before morning session.
AFTERNOONS:	Sweep out the whole school
WEEK-ENDS:	Scrub the lavatories; and scrub round the hearths.

Katherine Messenger

After Katie had been a monitress for some time, her companion fell out. No one could be found to take her place—not surprisingly. Therefore Katie had to do her share of the work as well. She cleaned the whole school by herself for some weeks; but during this period she was worried not so much by the amount of work as by the children who were kept in after school in the afternoon. These prevented her from getting on with her job.

When she had been working on her own for some weeks, the Rector called at the school and summoned Katie before the teacher's desk. He asked her whether she could manage to continue to do all the work on her own. Katie said that she preferred it that way, as then she could come and go as she pleased without having to wait on another girl's pleasure. The Rector then raised her wage to sixpence a week; and gave her half a crown for the additional work she had already done.

In addition to working at the school she also: fetched the schoolmistress's bread and milk (twopence a week); helped at the village shop on a Saturday, mainly scrubbing and cleaning (one shilling a week); she also ran errands for her neighbours. Her regular wage weekly thus amounted to one shilling and eightpence. Of this her mother kept one shilling and sixpence as Katie's contribution to the family's expenses. The remaining twopence a week was her pocket money. She remembered at one period saving this money until she had enough to buy her small sister a wooden doll. Its shoes and hair were painted in black on the wood.

At Christmas time, she recalled, the Rector made a Christmas tree at the school. The children sang carols; and their singing was worth hearing. Afterwards it was the Rector's delight to scatter nuts about the school and to watch the children scramble for them.

But life at the school must have been very varied at the time Katie Ling was a scholar. Here are two entries from the school log-book for the year before she entered: 'Two girls severely punished for wilfully burning one of the younger children with a red-hot poker.' 'Oral lesson *The Elephant* to the lower classes; children unsteady on account of the Treat.' And another entry for September two or three years before this: 'Eleven children ill; two dead.'

The school in this village was built over a hundred years ago; but before that time there was at least one school held in a cottage. The cottage is still occupied and lies at the edge of a field called *Schol'us* (school-house) *Walk*. A few years ago when the occupant was redecorating her living-room she discovered a large recess in the wall: it had been hidden by successive layers of wallpaper. The recess once served as a cupboard to keep books when the room was used as a class-room. This particular school was kept by a woman and was one of the type quite common in villages. It was called a dame school, and the pupils paid a small weekly fee to the dame or mistress. Attendance at the dame school was far from being regular; and it is unlikely that the children learned very much.

Some people held that it was not right to teach the children of the poor too much in case they would look upon laborious occupations such as farmwork or other manual work with disdain. In many schools, therefore, they were taught only to read; teaching them writing and arithmetic, it was believed, would tend to make them discontented with their station. Hannah More, a well-known educationalist and reformer, who did most of her work at the beginning of the nineteenth century, wrote in one of her letters:

'My plan of instruction is extremely simple and limited. They (the children) learn on week-days such coarse work as may fit them for servants. I allow of no writing for the poor. My object is not to make fanatics, but to train up the lower classes in habits of industry and piety.'

In the same letter she wrote:

'To teach the poor to read without providing them with *safe* books, has always appeared to me an improper measure.'

And Hannah More was considered in the van of progress during this period; her ideas were so new that they caused a lot of opposition. One person even claimed that her writings 'ought to be burned by the hands of the common hangman'.

The children of wealthy families were often taught by a specially engaged tutor or schoolmaster. These children learned reading, writing and arithmetic—but especially writing; as the beauty and correctness shown by a good pen were at that time considered to be the signs of proper education. It was necessary to write in a good legible hand in those days; for there were no mechanical writing machines or typewriters; and a fine writing hand was one of the first accomplishments of both a lady and a gentleman, as well as of anyone who wished to enter business or the professions.

Here is a receipted bill listing the services given, and their cost, by one of these tutors to a wealthy family of four children who lived in Blaxhall:

Mr T. Row: Debtor to J. Cole

1812.			
Education of Master J.		8.	6
Ditto of Master T.		7.	6
Ditto of Miss Betsy		7.	6
Ditto of Miss M.A.		5.	6
3 copy books for B.		2.	3
Copy book for J.		1.	0
Copy book for Thomas			9
Slate for James		1.	2
$\frac{1}{4}$ quire of writing paper			6
Pens and ink		3.	0
Firing		6.	0
	£2	3.	8

It is probable that six shillings for *firing* was for fuel needed to heat the school-room; unless under this head the tutor included the cost of means or measures taken to kindle zeal for learning in his pupils.

An old arithmetic text-book, published in 1767, gives the

tables and sums used in schools at this time. Here is one of the tables:

LONG MEASURE:

3 Barleycorns	make 1 Inch
4 Inches	make 1 Hand
12 Inches	make 1 Foot
3 Feet	make 1 Yard
6 Feet	make 1 Fathom
5 Yards & a Half	make 1 Rod, Pole or Perch
40 Poles	make 1 Furlong
8 Furlongs	make 1 Mile
3 Miles	make 1 League
60 Miles	make 1 Degree

The schoolmaster in a town or a big village would sometimes have an apprentice or a monitor, as he was called, to help him, perhaps in addition to an assistant. Some schoolmasters signed an agreement with their monitors as did other masters with their apprentices. Here is an indenture of this kind, shorter and more to the point than the usual ones:

'This Indenture witnesseth that Benjamin Moulton of Worlingworth in the County of Suffolk, of his own free will and with the Approbation and Consent of his Parents, doth put himself an Articled Assistant of John Godwin of Laxfield in the said County, Schoolmaster, for the term of three years from Christmas 1820, to be fully completed and ended; and the said John Godwin (in consideration of the sum of twenty two pounds, a firkin and a half of butter, eleven pounds of which is hereby paid this day and the remainder of the aforesaid sum to be paid when one half of the term shall be expired; and the firkin and a half of butter to be paid as follows vzt: ½ a firkin in each of the three years) shall use his endeavours to instruct and to get the said B. Moulton as forward in Learning as the time will admit; of finding unto the said Benjamin Moulton sufficient meat, drink and lodging (harvest and Christmas holidays excepted) during the said term. And for the performance of the said Agreement either of the said Parties above named to these Indentures interchangeably have

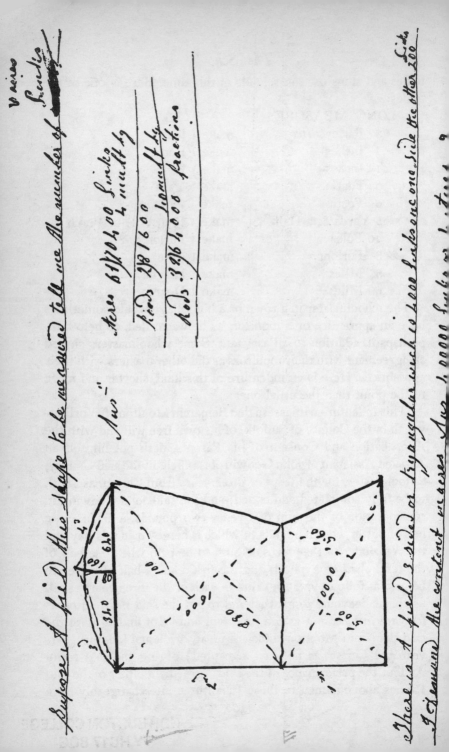

V new
Scotia

Suppose a field this shape to be measured tell me the number of

Acres 61,704.00 Links
4 multiply

Rods 278,600
Rods 3,896,000 fraction

Luo "

Suppose a field 3 sided or triangular with 1,000 Links on one side one side the other 200

I (sidewann) the content in acres Ans 1,00000 Links or 4 times 9

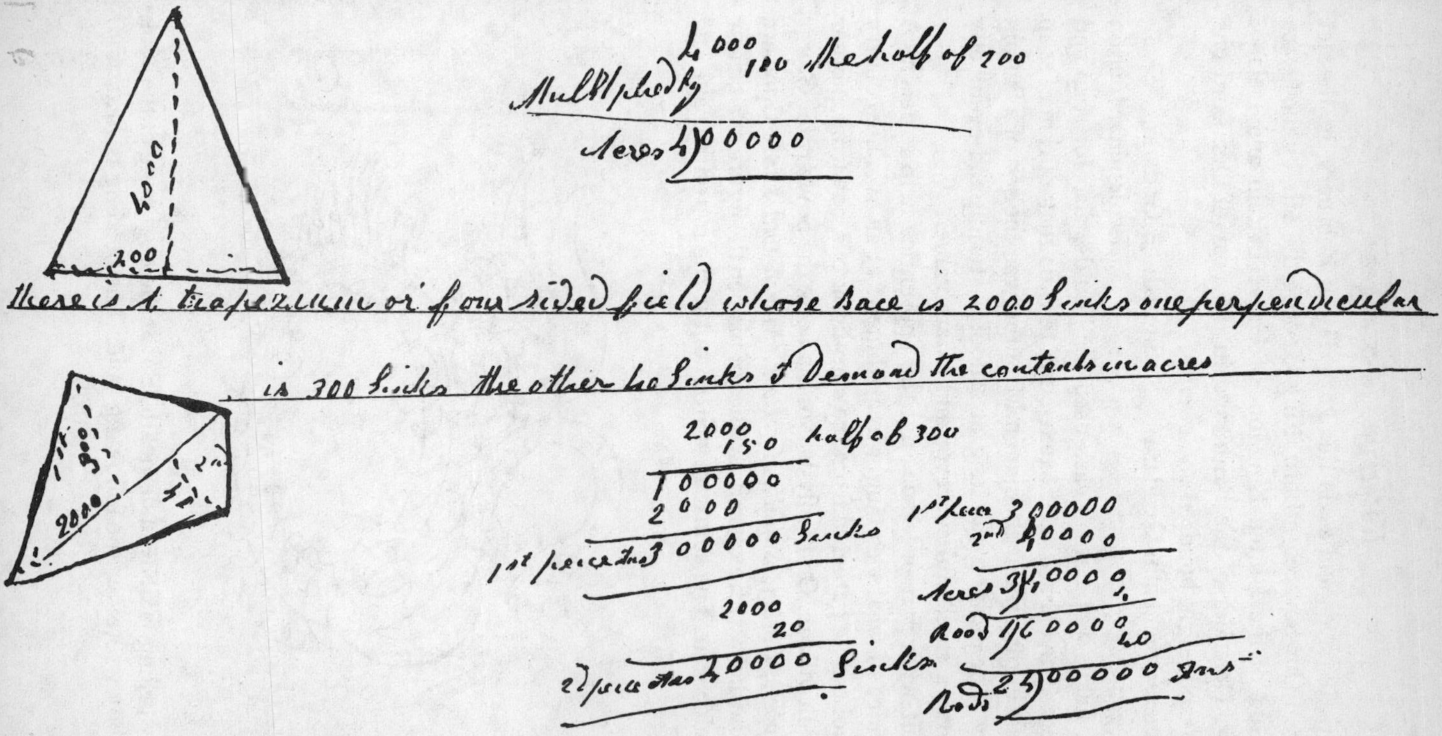

4000 100 the half of 200
Multiplied by
Acres 4)00000

there is A trapezium or four sided field whose base is 2000 links one perpendicular is 300 links the other 40 links I demand the contents in acres

2000 150 half of 300
100000
2000
1st piece has 300000 links
2000
20
2d piece has 40000 links
1st piece 300000
2nd 40000
Acres 3/4,0000
Rood 1/60000 40
Rods 2 4)00000 Ans

A PAGE FROM GEORGE KNAPPETT'S SUM BOOK

put their hands and seals this 25th day of February in the 1st year of Our Sovereign Lord, King George the 4th, by the Grace of God of the United Kingdom of Great Britain and Ireland, King, Defender of the Faith; and in the year of Our Lord one thousand, eight hundred and twenty.

Witness: Benjamin Goddard   Signed: J. Godwin,

                                            Benjamin Moulton

A firkin was a small cask used for liquids, also for soap and butter. The old arithmetic text-book tells us that a firkin of soap equals eight gallons. Benjamin Moulton was the son of a Suffolk farmer; he did not stay long at schoolmastering and eventually became a successful surveyor and estate valuer.

But what sort of lessons did the apprentice help to teach? A fair idea of what was taught in arithmetic at an average country school can be gathered from the sum-book of a boy from another Suffolk village. On the fly-leaf of his book the boy wrote: *George Knappett, Sutton, Suffolk. His Book. March 2nd 1851.* Opposite this he drew with expert flourishes of his pen the figure of a pen, or female swan. The sums are written out at the top of the page and

the working is done underneath. But at the beginning of the book the boy wrote out the following rule. The heading is *Reduction:*

The School

First of all, great are brought into small by multiplying with so many of the less as make one of the greater. Secondly, all small names are brought into great by dividing with so many of the less as make one of the greater.

Here are some of the earlier examples:

'How many Crowns, Shillings, Groats and Pence in 50 Pounds?

'How many ounces, pennyweights and grains are in 37 lb?

'How many inches are between London and Newcastle or in 273 miles?

'A merchant sends to his correspondent as much corn as comes to £1,575, to receive the same in Ducatoons at 6s 3½d each. How many Ducatoons ought he to receive?

'A corn factor sends to his correspondents in Spain 10,000 quarters of wheat and agreed at £8. 7s 6d per load; and he had received by several remittances £10,000. What is still due to him?

'How many furlongs, rods, yards, feet and inches and Barleycorns will reach round the Earth, supposing it according to the best calculation to be 25,020 miles?'

The boy, in a page of working, threw a girdle of 4,755 million barleycorns round the earth.

There are one or two examples in the book which the teacher must have given the boy to keep him engaged while he did some other tasks, perhaps teaching a younger group of boys in another class. They are worth quoting as they give some idea of the preoccupations of the time:

'A rich Nobleman has 5 villages, and in every village 3 streets, in every street 12 houses, in every house 5 rooms, in every room 2 Beaureaus, in every Beaureau 12 drawers, in every drawer 4 bags; every bag is valued at 150 guineas which he is going to exchange for £3. 12s pieces. How many must he receive?' The working of the sum takes up a whole page and forms a pyramid with the apex of one figure and a broad base of nine. There is another example of this kind:

'A general of an army consisting of 5,000 men after a very sharp engagement lost 2,380 men; but coming off victoriously he, for there valiant Behaviour, gave 1,000 guineas to be equally divided among them; and the Remaindor, if any, to be given to the little errand boy. How much did each man receive?'

In spite of the ominous 'if any' the little errand-boy received, according to George Knappett's calculation, four shillings—a very modest reward for doing service in such a bloody battle. But it seems that he treated the little errand boy at less than his deserts; for his reward, according to others' calculation, came to forty shillings—even more than the soldiers'. It is interesting to note that the spelling of the possessive *their* floored our schoolboy as it still does many today.

Throughout the book there is a strong rural bias to the examples. According to the best modern practice, the boy's teacher related his arithmetic to his everyday experience, sending him on occasional imaginary journeys into Spain, into battles or noblemen's houses only as a kind of relief from the honest-to-goodness work at home. As though to underline the real purpose of the boy's instruction the following is written at the end of the book in exemplary copper-plate:

Method of Ascertaining the Wheight of Cattle While Living

'This is of the utmost utility for all who are not experienced judges by the eye; and by following the directions the wheight can be ascertained within a mere trifle. Take a string; put it round the beast, standing square behind the shoulder-blade. Measure on a rule the feet and inches the animal is in circumference—this is called the girth—then with the string measure from the bone of the tail which plumbs the line with the hinder part of the buttocks. Direct the line along the back of the forepart of the shoulder-blade. Take the Dimensions on the footrule as before, wich is the length, and work the figures in the following manner: Girth of the bullock, 6 ft 4 ins; Length 5ft 3 ins, wich multiplied together make 31 superficial feet, that again multiplied by 23, the number of pounds allowed to each superficial foot of cattle measuring less than 7 and more than 5 feet in girth, make 713 pounds.'

And so on for sheep and pigs.

Yet there was a single and, at that time, up-to-date example in the book which fired the boy's imagination in spite of the schoolmaster's intentions:

'If the circumference of the driving wheel of a locomotive be 16½ feet, how many revolutions will it make between Bristol and Exeter, the distance being 75½ miles?'

The sum is meticulously worked out, the figuring more than usually careful, the lines faultlessly ruled, and at the end there is a proud flourish of lettering: ANSWER: 24,160 REVOLUTIONS.

It is probable that the boy had never seen a railway engine; but he had found his real interest; for records show that shortly after leaving school he travelled up to London where he remained for the rest of his life, working on the railways.

At the beginning of the last century people were becoming alive to the need for more widespread schooling. It is true that the old grammar and public schools were already taking a number of boys, chiefly the sons of well-to-do parents; and private individuals like Hannah More were doing a lot to bring schooling to numbers of boys and girls who had little chance of getting it in any other way. But at this time industry and commerce were growing very quickly, and it was soon realized that if the business of the country was not to suffer many more boys and girls would have to be literate. Therefore the opposition to educating the mass of boys and girls was gradually swept aside; and there was formed 'A National Society for Promoting the Education of the Poor in the Principles of the Established Church'. A little later another organization called 'The British and Foreign Society' was founded. The schools started by them became known as *National* (church) schools and *British* (nonconformist) schools. It was not until much later in the century (1870) that Parliament made itself responsible for educating the children of the country; and from this date parents were compelled to see that their children received regular schooling. But education was not yet free; and children had to take their twopences or pennies each week to help pay for their schooling.

When the school in this village opened in 1851 it was a

National or church school; but the cost of erecting it was met by the local landowner, Squire Shepherd. The log-book or school record book, in which the head teacher writes down everything of note each day, does not date from the opening; but we know that there were between 80 and 100 children attending school during the first few years. They were all taught in one long room, and were divided into groups managed by the headmistress, an assistant teacher and possibly a pupil teacher. The lowest class was called *The Babies:* this was an exact name for it for many of the infants were admitted when they were hardly out of the crawling stage.

The first existing log-book in this school was started in 1863; and from the early entries we get a good picture of how the school was run. The Gallery was a term much mentioned. This was a huge stair-like platform situated at one end of the long room and nearly reaching the ceiling. The whole school often had scripture lessons in the Gallery, with the little ones sitting on the steps near the floor, and the bigger ones looking down on the teacher from the top, while she talked about the life of Joseph, or many other such subjects recorded in the book.

On 25th October 1866 the mistress recorded: 'Gave the younger children a lesson, the Sin of Disobedience.' Next day she wrote: 'Children very quiet and orderly.' But the children were not always so. One afternoon about this time five boys played truant; and a little later there is the entry: 'Two monitors scolded severely for breaking up thoughtlessly some picture-boards, but forgiven on showing penitence.' But if a boy behaved himself very badly at school in those days, he was soon sent home and he did not come back except at the teacher's pleasure. Here is an instance:

'Tuesday 24th March 1868: Admitted Ambrose Livett, aged 10 years to the Third Standard.

'Wednes: 25th March 1868: The elder children attended church in the morning. Having heard that the boy Ambrose Livett bore a very bad character, and as he had spoken impertinently to the mistress and injured a little boy by throwing a stone he was sent away and his name erased from the books.'

Another entry reads: 'One boy removed from School, the rules being objected to.'

But the most interesting entries in the old log-book are those which tell us what the children did outside school rather than in it. They record the jobs children did on the farms when they were absent from school—sometimes with permission, quite as often without it. Until a few years before this, these boys and girls had worked all their time on the farms. Here is what a Suffolk farmer said in the years just before this school was opened: 'Boys come sometimes at 2d a day; little things that can hardly walk come with their fathers.' Another farmer stated that children sometimes go to work at six years of age: in most districts, however, nine or ten years was the usual age to begin work.

Here is another picture from about this time:

'If you lived in the country as I do, you would sometimes see a sight which would make your blood run cold, and yet it is so common a sight that we country people grow accustomed to it. You would see a great lumbering tumbril, weighing a ton or two with two wheels nearly six feet high, loaded with manure, drawn by a great Suffolk cart horse as big as an elephant; and conducted by a tiny thing of a boy who can hardly reach the horse's nose to take hold of the rein; and, even if he can, has neither the strength nor weight to make such a huge monster feel, much less obey. Some of these urchins are employed upon the highroad which is comparatively safe for them. It is when they come into the fields with deep wheel-tracks, as deep nearly as half their little legs, it is turning into gate spaces where the children are obliged to cling to the horse's bridle and stumble along tip-toes, that the danger is.'

But it was necessary for boys and girls to go to work very young as the wages their fathers got as farm-workers were often too low to keep the family; and the little bit of money the children earned was needed to help the family pay its way. And what the way was may be gathered from a few remarks made by

George Messenger, husband of Kate Messenger: 'My father brought up seven children on ten shillings a week. It was four rounds of bread each in a day—no more. And often it was a pinch of salt in a kittle of hot water and that was poured on the bread, and my mother would say "C'mon, there's a sop for you!" *Kittle-broth* we used to call it.'

In 1880 the farmers complained before a Royal Commission that the loss of the schoolchildren's labour had adversely affected their farming as they were unable to pay men's wages for the work the children had been accustomed to do. And even as late as 1901 people were still complaining in this county that: 'The primary cause of this (the unsatisfactory condition of the roads) I believe, is the doing away with the system of picking stones in the fields due to the advance of education.'

The farmers wanted cheap labour and the parents wanted money; and these two facts conspired to keep many children out of school when they should have been at their desks. In fact many of them must have spent as much time working on the land as they did at school. The third entry in the school log-book reads: 'Numbers low. Boys wanted for field work.' A few weeks later a number of children were away picking up potatoes; and at the end of October they were again absent gathering acorns as winter-fodder for pigs. About this time, too, but in the following year a number of children were absent harvesting beet—cattle beet or mangel-wurzels. In November the head teacher wrote: 'Forty five boys given permission to go out *brushing*.' The boys were away acting as brushers at a partridge shoot, beating the undergrowth with sticks to rouse the birds and drive them onto the guns. And so it went on all through the year. In January the teacher was worried because boys and girls were absent picking up stones and flint chips from the fields. They were paid for doing this by the farmers who carted away the stones, as already mentioned, to use as metalling for the roads.

In February and March they were often out of school employed in crow-keeping, bird-keeping or tending as the entries put it. That meant they were out scaring birds—rooks, crows, magpies and pigeons—keeping them away from the fields that had just been sown with spring corn. In many years they were out doing this again in the month of June, when the corn was just beginning to ripen. The children would be given a wooden rattle or clapper to scare the birds. Sometimes they made their own rattle by placing pebbles in a tin; sometimes they just had to keep shouting. In some districts there was a traditional form of shouting to scare the birds; and there were many rhymes or scaring songs which were sung in between the noise made by a wooden clapper:

> *We've ploughed our land, we've sown our seed,*
> *We've made all neat and gay;*
> *So take a bit and leave a bit:*
> *Away, birds, away!*

An old lady still living in the village used to scare crows for the whole of the harvest holidays: she was paid six shillings. She was given a wooden clapper and had to keep making a noise with it: if she once stopped and the clapper was silent, the man who hired her would look out of his house to see what she was doing.

The children (the old log-book tells us) were out *singing beet* at the beginning of July, working with hoes thinning out the rows of young mangel-wurzels. In June many boys would be absent at the sheep-shearing; in June, too, and at the beginning of July agricultural shows were held, as they still are today. There are two or three entries in the book showing that many of the children were away from school in order to attend these shows.

In the autumn they were sometimes absent picking acorns. It is worth noting that the schoolchildren in this district still gather acorns. In some years they have a special day's holiday—the Acorn Holiday—to collect them. The acorns are not fed to the pigs as they used to be, but are bought by the Forestry Commission for seed to raise trees. They are paid about threepence halfpenny a pound for them. One of the old people here recalls the old custom of gathering acorns for pig-fodder and comments that payment was not nearly as generous in those days. He got sixpence for a hundredweight-sack full; but he admitted that the farmer was not very particular about their quality.

Although they were not on the whole very good attenders the head teacher rarely missed letting the children have a holiday for their annual 'treat'. This was taken at the beginning of August just before the start of the harvest holidays. The children were taken to Aldeburgh, about six miles away, in big farm wagons. This was a joyful occasion; and to mark it the wagons were decorated with *trimmings* (coloured papers or streamers) and green boughs.

Elizabeth Drewery has given an account of Blaxhall School as it was fifty-six years ago: 'I started at the age of five. My mother insisted I should have my hair cut short like a boy. That was to keep a clean head. I also had to wear thick hobnail boots. They were quite fashionable at that time, and many girls wore them. We were summoned to school by the ringing of the bell. Mr Whitehead was my master, and he was very strict but very thorough in all he taught. When he wanted us to learn something new, he would write it on a large blackboard in chalk; and it was not rubbed off until we all knew it by heart. When we were about eleven years we had to walk, once a week, to the Old School, Snape—the girls for cookery lessons and the boys for woodwork. We children were brought up in the hard way. Each afternoon, after school closed, I had to run home, get a pail and go on a field and pick up so many bushels of stones—three large pails to the bushel. And sometimes my mother would give me a penny for sweets. At school I had many failures, but I worked up to the top standard and left at the age of fourteen. I left on a Friday; and by the next I was on my way in a carrier's cart with my little tin box to seek my own living. I went to a doctor's house at Alderton near Woodbridge, and kept there for three and a half years.'

PART SIX

JOSEPH ROW

21 The Village Inn

The name of Joe Row, one of the oldest men in the parish, was often linked with the Ship Inn, an early eighteenth-century building, the only inn or tavern in the village. Joe Row was a farm-worker or maltster all his working life. His is one of the oldest families in the village, and during the eighteenth century his ancestors were substantial landed people. But the land passed out of their hands at the beginning of the last century and since this time, most of the male members have earned their living as farm-workers. Joe Row had a remarkable memory, a faculty which is often very well developed in people who do not read very much; and he could recall accurately and at will dates and events from the last quarter of the nineteenth century. In his younger days he used to be a frequent singer of the old country songs. He had been singing one traditional song at The Ship for well over fifty years—but only on special occasions: it is the song reserved to welcome the New Year in. It used to be the custom for John Hewitt, the old landlord of The Ship, father of the present one, to enter into the Big Room of the inn just before midnight on New Year's Eve. He carried a log of wood which he threw on the fire, saying at the same time to the accustomed singer: 'Come on, Joe Row; let's have the old *Homestead!*' The Homestead song is not peculiar to this village; neither is it a very old song—it is known elsewhere as *The Miner's Dream*— but it has been appropriated as the ritual song for New Year's

Eve at the Ship Inn; and it is likely that the custom of singing it on this occasion will be kept up now that Joe Row has ceased to attend at this late ceremony.

There are two public rooms in the inn; they are called the Kitchen and the Big Room. Customers used to be referred to either as Kitchen Men or Big Room Men. The Kitchen men favoured the more intimate and smaller room, the others preferred the more formal and usually quieter one. The distinction holds to a certain extent today; but on occasion both groups intermingle, as they recently did when some of the old folksongs were recorded. There has always been a strong tradition of folk-singing here and an interesting local version of the well-known The Barley Mow was one of the most successful recordings. The folk in this village were accustomed to improvise words to the old folk songs, and the chorus of the Barley Mow has a definite local flavour:

> *Good luck, Good luck to the Blaxhall Ship,*
> *And Good luck to the Barley Mow!*

Step-dancing or *steppin'* has also been practised at the Ship Inn. This has usually taken the form of improvised stepping to the tune of an accordion. But recently one of the older women performed a more formal step-dance—the Candlestick Dance—in the *Ship*. This dance appears originally to have involved a series of steps about a lighted candle.

The Big Room was the meeting place of the sheep-clippers; and shepherds from round about came not only to make arrangements with the clippers, but on other occasions just to chat and exchange information. Before the building of the parish hall in the first decade of this century, the Big Room was the only meeting place in the village apart from the school and the church; and it has seen many and varied assemblies since the inn was built. Coroners held their inquests here; in 1841 the Tithe Commissioners made their award here, ending the payment of the tithe in kind, and fixing an agreed money payment for each piece of land. Largesse Spendings, weddings, celebrations and so on were held here; and many clubs, the Rifle Club, the Football Club, the Box Club and the Sickness and Burial Club held meetings regularly in the Big Room. On rare occasions the Parish Council have also met here, the parish clerk turning a blind eye to the regulation that this body should not meet on licensed premises if other accommodation is available.

Not so long ago the inn had as a sign a ship in full sail. But there seems to have been a controversy at one time as to whether *Ship* meant in fact a ship or whether it was the dialect word for sheep. Those who pointed out the names of the nearby Ship Walks and Ship Common as instances of the dialect word appear to have carried the day because now the signboard is a plain one with the bare words SHIP INN upon it.

Many of the old people remember the signboard of the sailing ship very well. It acted as a kind of weather-vane; and although it has long since disappeared it has left a saying which was recalled by Robert Savage: for as it creaked and swung in the breeze coming from the west those who lived near enough to hear it would say: 'There goo the old Ship sign again. It's a-going to rain!'

Although The Ship is called an inn it holds a licence for a tavern or public house; but inns and taverns now perform roughly the same services although at one time their functions were sharply defined. The inn was restricted to putting up travellers by day and night, and its licence would not allow it to provide casual drinks and meals to people: the tavern could only provide casual refreshment and was not licensed to entertain and put up guests. Today, however, you can stop at an inn for a meal or light refreshment; and if the landlord of a public house cares to let someone have a room for the night, he may do so without breaking the law. But an inn-keeper is still compelled to give anyone shelter—provided, of course, that the visitor has the money!— at any time of the day or night.

Underneath the inn is a cellar built for the cool storage of beer and wine; but at one time the cellar stored other commodities as well. Until recent years there were a number of hooks fixed in the beams of the cellar. They were used for hanging up game—partridges and pheasants chiefly. They were kept out of sight in the cellar because they had been poached. This was a very necessary precaution when poaching was punishable by long terms of imprisonment or even by transportation as it was about a hundred years ago. The cellar of an inn overlooking the nearby inlet was also used for the same purpose. In addition the landlord incurred the suspicion of being in league with smugglers. His licence was, therefore, taken away and the inn was closed. The cellar, however, with its wooden trap-door still remains although the house has for many years been a private one.

The fishermen were at one time great poachers in this parish. They worked in the Lowestoft and Aldeburgh fishing smacks for seven or eight months of the year and spent the close season at home. They returned just before Christmas and did not go to sea again until March or April. They relieved the tedium of the winter months by hard drinking bouts and by poaching. They knew the *hards* (fords) down the river and by arranging their poaching expeditions to suit the tide they could avoid the bridge where the police or the keepers would be on the look-out for them. Towards the end of their stay in the village when the money they had earned during the previous season's fishing had long been spent their poaching raids became more frequent and more desperate. The *travellers* (gypsies) were also good poachers. They often stopped on a piece of the common, in a pit called Gipsies' Pit even today. They hobbled their horses on the common and lived as far as they could on the countryside which they raked with their long dogs or greyhounds. The women made pegs from *sallow* wood, little boxes decorated with sea-shells and also lace: these they took round the village with numerous other small articles—packets of pins, collar-studs, hooks-and-eyes—selling them out of their big wicker baskets; but as has already been stated trade was not brisk for them in this area and they tried to make up for it by poaching.

But the fishermen and the travellers were far from being the only poachers. Many a steady workman found it necessary to boost his low wages by selling a surreptitious *bud* or two whenever he could get them. The procedure does not vary greatly from county to county. A moonlit night was chosen and the poacher went with his gun to a remote part of an estate as unobtrusively as he could. From a previous expedition or from a reconnoitre he had a rough idea where the birds roosted; but he approached the trees cautiously, looking round for any man-holes that had been dug underneath the roost to trap night-walkers like himself. When he was right under the tree he fired his gun into the midst of the roosting birds, grabbing as many as he could as they dropped. He then ran from the spot as hard as he could go. A poacher's wife, were she so minded, could tell a story something like this about one of her husband's ex-peditions: 'He used to be out from about midnight until three or four in the morning; and I couldn't rest until he came back. I used to keep a-walking about and worrying, wondering what could have happened to him. And when he came back, like as not he'd be without his cap. It's a rum thing, but he must ha' lost dozens o' caps. He'd shoot into the trees and then he'd run to git away from the keepers—and his head would hit a low branch and off would come his cap! And with his both hands full o' birds and perhaps the keepers not far off he dursn't stop to pick his cap up. So the next morning I had to go into the town special to get him a new one. Sometimes I'd see other women a-buying caps for their husbands and I'd say to myself: "I know, gel, what your ol' man was a-doing on last night." When he brought the pheasants home then there was a job to hide 'em. Sometimes there'd be as many as twenty birds hidden about the house wait-ing to be picked up. I'd dig a hole in the garden and bury some o' them there; or a favourite place was the baby's cot: I'd hang 'em round the sides and cover 'em up with blankets!—We've had many a laugh about it since—Mr X from Y used to call for the birds. He had a game-dealer's licence; and if some one was to see us with the birds I was to swear I was buying the birds off him.

'Mr X used to pay us two shillings or half-a-crown a bird. But the bird had to be whole. I remember my husband once shot the head off a bird, and he didn't want to waste it so he had the idea of sewing it on again. He sat down with needle and thread; and he made a real job of it so that you couldn't tell, unless you looked very close, that the ol' bird's head had been off. He sold it all right; but instead of it going up to London like he thought, it went to Sir Hugh Blank's place who lived over at Whytton—almost next door to us. The bird was all right till the cook came to pluck him. And then . . .! There was a fine row about that. But like everything else it passed over. Then there was another laugh, the time he answered an advertisement in the paper. There was a useful greyhound for sale. It seemed so good that he did a deal and they sent the dog by rail. But the rum thing was that when the dog came he was a white 'un! He went back pretty quick, I can tell you! — All this was a long time ago when the wages were very bad. He don't go out now; he's become what they call respectable.'

Reference should be made to a frolic which was formerly held at Blaxhall Ship. It has been described elsewhere in detail (v. 'The Horse in the Furrow', pp. 220–22). Its full title was *Blaxhall Ship Inn Fair*; and it was held at The Ship every Whitsun Wednesday. It ceased a year or so before the First World War; but there is a tradition at Blaxhall that it had been held on this date for a very long time. The date suggests a *Church Ale*, a mediaeval jollification often held at Whitsuntide, when the churchwardens begged or bought malt and brewed liquor to sell—the money to go towards the upkeep of the church. A seventeenth-century rhyme ('Ex-ale-tation of Ale', 1671) records the practice:

The churches much owe, as we all do knowe;
    For when they be drooping and ready to fail,
By a Whitsun or Church-Ale up again they shall go;
    And owe their repairing to a pot of good ale.

But in spite of the date there is no direct evidence to support the connection between the Blaxhall Fair and the 'Ales' of earlier times.

22 Smuggling

This village is six miles from the coast, but it is nearer than this to a narrow inlet used by small vessels and sea-going barges up to the beginning of the present century. The sea runs through the history of the village like a thread: sea-going apprentices; sailors; barges that used to carry the corn grown in this parish down the estuary and on to London or Newcastle; fishermen; phenomenal tides; and ships' timbers built into many of the cottages. These curved beams are still to be seen, living reminders of the village's close link with the sea.

All these links are lawful ones but as shown in the story of old Liney Richardson there were a number of irregular links as well. In fact, smuggling was practised on this stretch of coast perhaps more than on any other on the eastern seaboard of England. Near the estuary, overlooking the adjacent marshes, is an old inn. During the disastrous floods of February 1953 the rising water in the estuary was closely watched from a window in the roof. For a short time this dormer window became as important as it once used to be; between a hundred and two hundred years ago it was a very important window indeed. From it the signal used to be given to smugglers bringing a cargo up the estuary, telling them that the coast was clear of the 'preventive men'; and that the two red-coats stationed at the inn were safely accounted for. The landlady of the inn, called the *Snape Crown*, would probably be taking care of these two dragoons, suddenly showing a great interest in their welfare, while all the time someone would be upstairs getting ready to give the signal from the window. She would be reminding them that it was very cold out on the marshes. A cold wind was blowing up the estuary and they had better have someting inside to warm them before going out. The result was that while the cargo was being handled the two red-coats would either be fast asleep or too fuddled to stir from their warm corner at the fireside.

Higher up the river in this parish is a long strip of meadow with the unusual name of *The Spong*. It is surrounded by ditches; and not far away, on slightly higher ground there were two wattle and daub cottages, now pulled down. Tom Jay, an old Blaxhall inhabitant, whose family has strong associations with this corner of the parish, remembers that these cottages were once called *Smugglers' Cottages*. At one time it was possible to get cheap spirits there; and on Sunday morning parties of men frequently gathered there to drink. The excise men knew the reputation of the cottages and made a raid. But the smugglers were warned: they hid the barrel of rum they had 'in stock' in one of the full ditches surrounding The Spong: 'The customs men *pritched* for the barrel (poked about with a stick; most probably with an eel-pritch) but they niver did find it.'

Smuggling began very early on the Suffolk coast. It was first practised in the fourteenth century when Edward III put a tax on the sending of wool out of the country. His object was to stop cloth from being made abroad, thus competing with the English cloth-making industry which was so important at the time. But as generally understood smuggling means the bringing in of goods into the country so as to avoid paying the duty imposed on them by the government. It was in the eighteenth century that the Suffolk smugglers were in their hey-day; and the revenue men had a long and hard battle trying to stop them. Their main difficulty was that smuggling was considered almost respectable: nearly everyone was in it—rich and poor—in some way or other. People got tea from the smuggler very much as we now get it from the grocer. And how respectable the *trade* of smuggler was can be judged from this advertisement taken from an eighteenth-century newspaper, *The Ipswich Journal*. It concerns a village three miles away from this one:

'Richard Chaplin, Sudbourn, Suffolk, near Orford, begs leave to acquaint his friends and the public in general, that he has, some time back, declined the branch of Smuggling, and returns thanks for all their past favours. —Also, To be SOLD on Monday, August 8th, 1785, at the dwelling house of Samuel Bathers, Sudbourn, the property of Richard Chaplin aforesaid, A very useful CART, fit for a maltster, ashman, or a smuggler—it will carry 80 half-ankers or tubs; one small ditto that will carry 40 tubs; also two very good wooden Saddles, three Pads, Straps, Bridles, Girth, Horse-cloth, Corn-bin, a very good Vault, and many articles that are very useful to a Smuggler.'

About this time it was said in Parliament that 'all the young, clever fellows in Suffolk are employed by smugglers, and have half-a-crown a day while waiting; and when on horseback, going about the country to dispose of the goods, they have a guinea a day and are well entertained. The gangs are forty to fifty strong and so well horsed that the dragoons could not catch them.' The most famous of these gangs was the Sizewell Gap Gang which operated a little further up the coast from our inlet.

The men who were responsible for catching the smugglers were called preventive men until—in 1856—the Preventive Service was transferred to the Admiralty and the Coastguard established. But whatever name they went under, the Government men had to be very alert and up to all the tricks of the smugglers because they were exceedingly enterprising and always changing their methods. They gave out, for example, that a lonely house on the cliff or the marshes was haunted; they said that a man in a certain cottage was ill with the smallpox, and naturally everyone would avoid it, giving the smugglers plenty of chance to stow their cargo without interruption. On one occasion a vessel anchored off a Suffolk coastal village. Presently the captain came ashore and reported that one of his men had died of the *plague*. He asked permission to bury him. Permission was granted; and the captain suggested that a secret burial at night would be the safest. He knew that few secrets could be kept in a village; and when the *corpse* was brought ashore nearly everyone in the village was there to see it. What they actually saw being buried was a fake coffin weighted with a few stones. While this was going on the real cargo was being landed and taken quite openly through the village street to a pre-arranged place of safety.

It was a dangerous and thankless job watching for the smugglers, and it is not surprising that many of the preventive men found the life too hard and the temptations too great. There are records of many of them being dismissed for 'strong suspicious conduct'—that is, making friends with their enemies the smugglers. One fact gives a vivid picture of one aspect of their lives. When a man was on watch he carried a one-legged seat, something like a modern shooting-stick. It was so designed that if he dozed off in the monotony of staring out onto a dreary stretch of beach he found that the stick supported him no longer and that he had a very fine view of the stars.

It is recorded that one of these *spotsmen* concealed himself on a cliff to watch a suspicious craft. But he himself was spotted by the smugglers. They stole up behind him; seized him and thrust his head into a rabbit burrow, driving a stake between his legs to prevent his getting out. This was a favourite trick of the smugglers; for without injuring a man they effectively stopped him giving the alarm.

But why did so many people turn to smuggling at this time? It is true that the duties on goods were very high, and the difficulties of honest trade during the long Napoleonic Wars were very great; it is also true that there was a good deal of poverty after the Wars. But smuggling was not the work of a number of desperadoes who took to the game when necessity drove them; it was a highly organized business whose roots extended through the whole community. Many people seem to have taken to illicit trade because it gave them a chance of adventure that added spice to their ordinarily dull lives. But the main reason for the wide incidence of this *free trade* was a deeper one: it was to a large extent a protest by the rising middle class—the tradesmen—who resented the continued domination of and the restrictions imposed by the old squirearchy or landed gentry. It is significant, too, that this class formed the spear-head in the fight for legitimate free trade later in the nineteenth century. In our district, for example, some of the most active members of the notorious Sizewell Gap Gang were farmers' sons and small tradesmen. Their chief enemy was according to type: he was Squire Shepherd who owned a very large estate including most of this village (one of his family later built the village school). He was also a magistrate.

Much of this can be gathered from a story discovered in the next village of Tunstall. It was found in an old newspaper cutting of the time. It gives an episode in the history of the Sizewell Gap Gang. The date is 1778, but the account must have been written by a member of the gang a few years later. The story explains itself; but it is worth noting that its opening paragraphs give a perfect glimpse of a man engaged in winter threshing in the type of barn described in a previous chapter. Here, then, is the story told in the smuggler's own words. They are as fresh and as virile as when they were written about 170 years ago, about the time when there were many experiments with the construction of threshing machines mentioned in the text:

THE DOOMED CARGO

'Between Leiston Street and the beach, a distance of about two miles, is a fen or level of marshes called Leiston Common Fen; and it is connected with a Level called Minsmere Level, the upper part of which has been enclosed and is known as Leiston Common Farm. On this farm, held at that time by Mr Doughty as an off-hand farm, was a barn; at one end of the barn a stable; over the stable a loft; in which loft there was a wicket window looking into the upper part of the barn; and another looking out abroad through the loft roof. This homestead, which was surrounded by a haulm wall or fence, is nearly two miles from Sizewell Gap. After I had sold my Geneva, the major part of it belonging to Leiston folk, it was stowed away in what in Suffolk is called the *goaf*—that is the grain in straw packed ready for threshing; which operation generally finds employment (or used to do before the invention of threshing machines) to one labourer—and in this case Crocky Fellows happened to be the man. In fact the gin was deposited under his care, and to be removed when it was wanted, Mr Doughty never troubling himself about the matter as long as he had brandy, raisins and tea without looking for them.

'Now there was a man in the parish called Clumpy, whose name was Bowles, a breeches maker. But the smugglers could never trust him, as he has been found out playing them some slippery trick a year or two before. Bowles had a club-foot; hence his nickname. Crocky was one day looking out at the barn-door and spied Mr Clumpy limping along across the Common with a tub of gin, as he suspected, under his arm; and it at once struck him that he had stolen it. He therefore mounted the goaf and found somebody had been there as the barley was disarranged and a tub had gone. Crocky in an instant decided how to act, for he concluded Bowles would soon be there again; and he was not wrong in his conjecture. Thumping away at his work and keeping his ears open, in about an hour he heard a rustling overhead; dropping his flail, he sprang up the bracket of the cross-beam and on to the goaf in a moment. There was Clumpy crouched in a corner and the stable window wide open. Crocky, approaching him, exclaimed:

' "I'll gin you, you scamp!"

And suiting his action to the word, gave Clumpy what in Suffolk is called a clout of the skull; and catching him by the collar, hurled him clean over the large beam of the barn down to the threshing floor below—enough to break his neck, but for the straw and barley on which Crocky had been at work. The other jumped down and would have commenced pummelling him again, but Bowles swore he would go and lay an information against the goods; and Crocky thought better to desist.

'Bowles left the barn threatening and swearing, and Crocky went up and shut the window; and locking up the barn went into the village to call a council to know what was to be done. The owners (of the hidden cargo) were soon assembled; and some thought Bowles would be afraid to inform; and some thought otherwise. But the conclusion was that the goods should be removed as soon as night came on; when an accidental sight of Bowles by one of the party in close discourse with old Read, the preventive officer, accelerated the moment and all hands set to work.

'At that time there were two horse-soldiers at Leiston *White Horse;* two at East Bridge public house, about two miles off; and no more nearer than *Snape Crown* or Aldbro. The Leiston soldiers were both drunk; and Read—or Old Billy as he was called —was lame; and he told Clumps he must go to East Bridge for the two soldiers there. Off set Bowles limping along as fast as he could; but if any of the smugglers had known his errand, he would never have got to the *Elephant and Castle;* but he did arrive there; and by the greatest chance in the world found the soldiers. The landlady, seeing something was amiss, called the soldiers into the backroom and gave to each two large glasses of Hollands to keep out the cold; for it was a bitter cold day. And this, with the glass they took on their own account before starting, made them about as sober as their comrades at Leiston were.

'By the time old Read had mounted his horse and the soldiers had got ready to go, it was three o'clock in the afternoon; and the smugglers were prepared by the time the Government men arrived. It was dark. Clumps kept out of the way, for he was now frightened at his own folly. Just as the officers and soldiers entered the barn yard, Crocky had put a large padlock on the door.

' "I demand admittance to this barn!" says Mr Read.

' "What for?" says Crocky.

' "To search for smuggled goods," was the reply.

Joseph Row

' "I shall let no man pull my master's property about without his leave," says the other.

' "Then I must order the soldiers to knock the lock off."

' "Knock and be damned," says Fellows, "if you can; but I'll knock down the first man who touches that lock!"

' And one of the soldiers took hold of the lock as if to examine it. Crocky struck him on the breastbone and drove him back. At this instant, Sam Newson of Middleton and a maltster of the name of Wil Thornton, a great cross-made fellow, entered the barn yard; and Thornton, who was called *Quids* from his immoderate use of tobacco, stood behind Crocky. Sam Newson began to wrestle with another soldier; and thus an hour was spent in fighting, laughing, tumbling about and swearing at one another in fun; and pelting each other with barn-door litter. At length a little fellow, a tailor in the village, came and spoke a few words to Crocky, who immediately unlocked the door with the remark that if his master had no objection he had none. The whole party entered and one of the soldiers scrambled up the goaf.

' "Here's the nest," said he; "but, by God, the eggs are all gone!"

' "Why do you say so?" says Old Billy who made an attempt to get up but could not manage it.

'The soldiers were all busy looking about when Sam Newson having been up the stable loft and fastened the wicket on the other side, now came and spoke to Fellows, who slyly slipped out. Shutting the barn door he made the whole of the king's men prisoners. Locking them all in, he and Newson went and themselves made sure the tubs were all gone; and then returned and released the party.

'Read, who saw the trick had been played by removing the goods while his men were engaged in the barn yard, told the soldiers it was plain there was nothing to seize, and they were dismissed. The fact is that the tubs were handed in silence by about twenty smugglers into six two-horse carts and drove clean away to Cold Fair Green, and there deposited in a cart-shed until midnight, when they were carried right back to the barn and placed in a large vault in the barn yard under a dunghill; or, as the Suffolk people call it, a muckheap. About six or eight score of sheep being driven in about the place to obliterate all signs of any other footing than their own. The tubs were piled on each side the vault, and a passage left in the middle at the further end of which was stowed some bales of tobacco and tea; the whole being shut up by a trap door at one end, to get at which a portion of the long horse-muck had to be cut away with a hay knife—this being the mode of concealing goods in the long winter nights against they might be wanted in the summer.

'They were now in a place of safety, and the next thing the smugglers turned their attention to was to prevent any more informing. About a fortnight after the circumstances I have related took place, one night about nine o'clock, a couple of very tall stout men stopped their horses at the door of the cottage where Bowles lived, which was a small house standing in a sand pit close by the Yoxford turnpike, and about a hundred yards from Leiston Street. One of the men alighted, and opened the cottage door: he found all the inmates in a state of terror, as they had heard the horses stop.

' "Is Bowles within?" said the man.

' "No," replied the poor old woman, his landlady.

' "It's a lie!" said the fellow, and he strode across the room and, opening the closet door under the staircase, he forced the screaming, trembling wretch across the room to the door; where the other man sat on horseback. He caught hold of Bowles's arm and jerked him into the pummel of the saddle, his head on one side and his heels on the other. Having got him secure, he struck the spurs into his horse's sides, and the other mounting directly, set off at full gallop through Leiston Street into a lane which leads to Cold Fair Green; and there they dismounted.

'And one man thrust the end of his whip into Bowles's mouth, and the other directly forced the bung of a beer cask in between his teeth, and tied it fast round his head with his neckerchief. They then took his head on one horse and the other took his feet. They then flogged the poor wretch with their heavy whips from Leiston through Friston, Snape, Dunningworth and Blax-hall. Five or six miles at least did they keep on with their bar-barity, till they were tired; and then they threw what they sup-posed to be his dead body over the hedge into a plantation of Squire Shepherd's at Campsey Ash, where he was found by a labourer's dog next morning to all appearance lifeless. But the husbandman, seeing the state he was in, unbound his head; procured assistance; and had him conveyed to Tunstall *Green Man*, where an incident occurred which had the effect of bringing the two ruffians to justice.

'The countryman who found Bowles went on the Sunday morn-ing to see how he was, and was admitted to his bedroom, where he had been attended at Squire Shepherd's expense; and who had ordered everything for him his forlorn state required. For the gentlemen of the neighbourhood took the matter up and were determined to bring the actors to justice if possible. In the course of conversation the man pulled the bung out of his pocket to shew Bowles what it was. The girl of the house, being in the room at the time, took the bung to look at it, and exclaimed:

' " Why, dear me! If that is not the bung Tom Tibbenham asked me to lend him last Monday! I'll swear to it for I cut the notch on it to know which cask it belonged to!"

'The countryman said to the lass:

' "Just stop with this poor man a minute or two."

For he had seen Mr Shepherd ride into the yard, and did not want the girl to see anybody till Mr S had seen her. She did as he requested; and the man asked the Squire into the room, where an examination of Bowles took place; and he declared the men to be Debney and Tibbenham; as he knew them both, having often seen them at Leiston *White Horse*, and in their smuggling vocations.

'The consequence of this information was a warrant issued against each of them; and both were apprehended the same day in the neighbourhood; and were fully committed on the girl's evidence, in conjunction with Bowles's assertion, to Woodbridge Bridewell. It appears they thought very lightly of the matter, as

Cleaver—that is Tibbenham—who was a butcher, admitted the fact in a boasting sort of way; and declared if it had not been for *Nosey* (Debney) he would have served the bloody informer ten times worse.

'After they were put in confinement, it was found necessary to send Bowles right away; and he went to London till the trial, when the poor girl who had got into a sad mess gave her evidence and Bowles gave his. And the two fellows were sentenced to two years' imprisonment in Ipswich gaol. Bowles quitted the country, and I don't think he ever returned to it, as I have never been able to learn anything of him since.

'To return to the goods which were deposited in the vault: they happened to be wanted in a short time after the circumstance occurred. A party of smugglers, among whom was a brother of Debney—I think his name was Sam—and a young fellow of the name of Will Cooper from Tunstall, assembled to *work* the goods as it was termed; and had three or four carts with horses fit to remove them. Crocky Fellows was amongst them and directed whereabouts to cut the muckheap to find the door, which was soon uncovered and opened; and the owners were there of course to deliver them, the same as if it had been a warehouse.

'As soon as the door was opened Crocky said:

' "You had better let the foul air get out!"

'But Cooper, with an oath, replied: "I have enough good stuff in me to repel all the foul air in the world!"

'And he and Debney scrambled down the steps which were nearly perpendicular under the trap door and about sixteen feet deep. The moment they were down all was silent; and Stokes, who was there, called to them but received no answer. A man called Nichols, or Black George, now attempted to go down; but he had just got his head level with the roof of the vault when he held up his arm: Stokes caught it and lugged him out; and he fell down on the ground insensible.

'The whole party now fell to work, and the heap was soon removed, and the roof torn off but it was too late! Cooper was

found lying flat on his face at the farther end of the vault, and
Debney standing leaning on the gin tubs, about halfway along
the passage—both dead and their faces blood-shotten and red as
fire. As soon as they had laid the bodies into one of the carts,
they took the gin, tobacco and tea and conveyed them away, paying but little regard for the concealment, as they were all horror-
struck about the dreadful disaster which had befallen them.

'The bodies were taken to Tunstall, and I never knew whether
a coroner's inquest went over them, or how it was ordered; but
they both lie in one grave; and a large gravestone, nearly in
front of Tunstall Church Park and near the road was erected to
perpetuate their memory, and so far as I know still remains. I
was not at the time in Suffolk, but I had the following particulars
from a friend who was pretty well amongst them all the time.

'And he tells me that it was about twenty of the most desperate of the smugglers swore to punish Bowles; and Debney
and Tibbenham took the job in hand of their own accord; and at
their own opportunity. And the whole seemed to be unfortunate
for the same evening that Cooper and Debney were smothered,
old Ingall, an exciseman living at Saxmundham, having heard
of the death of the two men, concluded that there would be a
removal of the liquor, as it was no secret there was some; and he
thought he could make a seizure.

'The smugglers had for some years paid a man of the name of
Isaac Mayhew, who lived opposite to Ingalls, to watch him of
an evening; and when he saw him go to his stable and take his
pistols from a hole bored in the gable end of the house, saddle
his horse himself, which he could do, Isaac knew that he was
going out after the smugglers. A man was always posted at a
preconcerted spot to whom Isaac repaired with the intelligence;
the man in turn told the smugglers; and Ingall almost always
returned disappointed.

'On the night in question, Isaac could not find the man, and
none came. And the exciseman took the two Saxmundham soldiers with him; and, knowing all the haunts of the smugglers, as
it happened, went right to the spot at Aldringham *Parrot*. In the

yard he made a seizure of six carts, twelve horses, and 300 tubs of gin without the least resistance. The smugglers for the time appearing terror-struck, he got to the excise office at Saxmundham with them; and a short time after, the tubs—as it was the custom at that time—were staved in the yard and the liquor all thrown away.

'And on this occasion which was the last that it was poured down, it ran out of the Custom-house yard; and the people dug a hole outside the gate and carried away the gin in pails—dirt and all. And one man drank so much of the filthy mixture before it had time to settle that he died the same night. Isaac Mayhew lost his berth as watcher, because he was suspected of being paid by both parties and informing when he had an opportunity.

'And I think that I could call this lot of goods by no more appropriate name than *The Doomed Cargo*.'

That is the old smuggler's story, true in nearly every detail as far as can now be checked from records of the time and from local sources. The father of the Debney brothers farmed in Tunstall where the two smugglers lie buried. Cooper's family were millers. The moss and the lichen were recently cleaned away from the tombstone in order to check the inscription. It is still fairly well preserved and reads:

In Memory of
ROBERT DEBNEY and
WILLIAM COOPER who
departed this Life the 22nd of June, 1778
R.D Aged 28 & W.C. 18 years.

All you, dear Friends, that look upon this Stone,
Oh think how quickly both these Lives were gone.
Neither Age nor Sickness brought them to the clay;
Death quickly took their Strength and Sense away.
Both in the Prime of Life they lost their Breath,
And on a Sudden were cast down by Death.

Joseph Row

A cruel Death that could no longer spare
A loving Husband nor a Child most dear.
The loss is great to those they left behind,
But they thro' Christ, 'tis hop'd, true Joys will find.

The inscription gives Debney's age as twenty-eight; but after the parish registers had been examined it was found that he was, in fact, thirty when he died. This, and the fact that Debney's name was Robert and not Sam, appear to be the only inaccuracies in the whole story—small blots, and in no way likely to destroy the picture.

PART SEVEN

VARIOUS OLD PEOPLE

23   Field Names

Most of the information in this section has been gained from various old people of the village—at least in the first place. A certain amount of research in manuscripts, books and old maps afterwards confirmed what had been collected orally; and often this checking amplified the information already received and gave stimulus and pointers to research in other directions. Robert Savage, for instance, when we were discussing the names of the fields in this parish, identified one as *Holly Field*: '*Hulver Field* we used to call it. *Hulver* is the old fashioned word for holly'. Hulver is in fact a dialect word stemming directly from the old Norse word *hulfr*. It was a word once in common use: Thomas Tusser used it in recommending the wood of the holly as being suitable for the making of a flail swingel. But why Hulver Field? This question led to a further search which unearthed an old belief connected with the holly-tree. On one of the farms here there is a field with a holly standing somewhere near its centre. The field would be much easier to farm if the tree were removed; but the farmer will not have it touched as he believes that cutting down a holly tree is always followed by bad luck. Robert Savage also experienced an instance of this veneration of the holly while he was a shepherd at the Grove. Old George Rope would not let any of his workmen cut a branch of the holly: 'The holly-wood made whoolly fine *whip-stalks* (handles for whips). When it was dry it wor as hard as metal; and it would last for a century. You bound the lashes to it with *waxbind* (waxed thread) and it wor better than a bought whip. But ol' George would niver let the men cut branches off the holly-tree. It wor unlucky. You could pull up the young shoots that grew about the trunk of the tree to make your whip-stalks—pull 'em up by the roots; and that we used to do. If you got a young shoot with a piece of root still on it you could use this part of the root for a *crome* (the straight piece or hook at right angles to the handle, often made of bone in a shop-made whip). The groom used to have one and I had one myself: but we dursn't cut the holly-tree to get it.'

This superstition must have been more widespread than it is now; for the field called Hulver is in another part of the parish. No holly grows in this field at present, but the farm still prospers. But what is the explanation of this old belief? Trees were common objects of pagan worship, and it is likely that the superstition is the vestige of an old cult. As Frazer tell us: 'In the religious history of the Aryan race in Europe the worship of trees has played an important part.' Again: 'Sacred groves were common among the ancient Germans, and tree-worship is hardly extinct among their descendants at the present day.' Frazer also tells us that when the tree cult flourished anyone who harmed one of the sacred trees was put to a painful and ignominious death: it is easy to imagine why the superstition—the ghost of the former religion—should survive into the present when the original impulse to believe, or at least to conform, was so overwhelmingly strong. But the holly may have been a guardian tree which Frazer states was to be found in the neighbourhood of every farm in some districts of Sweden: 'No one would pluck a single leaf of the sacred tree, any injury to which was punished by ill-luck or sickness.' Bad luck here is given a specific name; and considering the accessibility of this district of East Anglia to Scandinavian influence in the past, no attempt to track the superstition down could ignore this suggestion of its origin.

Field Names

A good deal has been learned about the past story of this village from a study of the names of the fields. At one time most people in a rural village knew the field names, if not on all the farms, at least on the farm with which they were associated. It was also necessary, forty or fifty years ago for the children to know them accurately as they often had to take their father's *'levenses* or *fourses* out to him when he was working in a particular field. Moreover, they worked on the land themselves at stone-picking and other jobs; and they came to know many of the fields as intimately as their back-gardens. People today do not know the field names as well; and it is therefore important that they be written down wherever possible. In this village two sheets of the Twenty-five Inch Ordnance Survey Map were used to record field names: the Twenty-five Inch was chosen as there is enough space on a map of this scale to write in the alternative names most fields seem to have, as well as to include the short note that many names demand. For instance, the name of a particular field on the Tithe Map of 1837 (or whatever date the award map was made) if it differed from the present-day one could be included; as also could the names taken from any earlier maps that are available. If this is done and the names of a group of fields collected over a period, their progressive corruption can sometimes be traced. In this parish we found that *Park Gate* Walk became *Plackett's*: *Schoolhouse* Walk was changed to *Schol'us*. And in an eighteenth-century map an eight-acre piece of land started off with the name Coney Hill—a good name for it, for up to the myxomatosis plague it was well frequented by rabbits. But the man who made this section of the 1837 Tithe Map could not have been familiar with the dialect for he wrote down *Cunnaugh* Hill as the true name of the field. It is not surprising that today it should be known throughout the village as *Funny Hill*.

Dovehouse Field, a name on a 1796 estate-survey map is worth recording if only as a reminder of the time when the dovecote was an important unit in the manorial economy; when—as Fynes Moryson wrote at the beginning of the seventeenth century—'No kingdom in the world hath so many dove-houses'. *Work'us Common*, adjoining the Old Town House or Poor House—now a farmhouse—is another instance of a piece of history concealed in a name. Another relates to the pre-enclosure period when the Heath or Big Common was much larger in extent than it is now. A group of fields lying in a rough semi-circle to the west of the Heath is called *Walks:* First Ship (sheep) Walk, Mill Walk, West Walk, Scholus Walk, Second Ship Walk, Further Ship Walk, Plackett's Walk and so on. These indicate the former extend of the common grazing or *walking* ground for sheep; and the fact that there are few very old established hedgerow trees within this area seems to confirm that the boundary of the Common once coincided with the outer circumference of these fields now called Walks.

Field names that give a clue to former settlements occur in every parish. *Chapel Field*, in connection with the former church and hamlet of Dunningworth, has already been commented upon. There is also a *Glebe Field* near enough to the site of the old church to postulate a connection with it; while near the supposed site of the 'lost' settlement of Beversham, mentioned in Domesday, there is a field called *First Mill Hill*. An out-of-the-way part of the Heath is called *Landemon's* by the younger generation in the village; and for some time it was thought that this field had some connection with the Devil; for the Old Nick, as he was called, figures in many village legends in Suffolk. But the older people here have corrected this surmise and have called the piece by its original name—*Van Diemen's Land*. It was also pointed out that another remote house, just outside the parish, is called *Botany Cottage* and the copse adjoining it, *Botany Wood*. Van Dieman's Land, as is well known, was the old name for Tasmania; and Botany Bay (Australia) was one of the places where convicts were landed during the first half of last century when the colony was being peopled. Many from this district of East Anglia were sent to the convict settlements for poaching, smuggling and other offences; a few went at the same period as the Tolpuddle Martyrs were transported, and for roughly the same reasons. Margaret Catchpole, a woman from an East Suffolk village, who was transported for stealing a horse to meet her lover, a smuggler, is one of the best-known of the banished people. And she and the people who were sent out with her seem to have made a great impression on their contemporaries in East Anglia, as there are quite a few instances in Cambridgeshire and Suffolk of outlying parts of a parish being referred to, originally no doubt with a kind of ironic humour, as *Botany Bay*.

Old dialect words are often crystallised in field names: one field here is called *The Scuts*. This word is a variant of the word *scoot*, the triangle left within the headlands after a field has been ploughed—a field, that is, of an awkward shape. Robert Savage referred to it as a *box-iron* piece, a piece of land roughly the shape of an old fashioned box-iron used for smoothing linen; and he related that the old ploughmen used to refer to the ploughing of this type of field as *goring work*. A *gore* or *gusset* is, in fact, another name for a scoot.

Another field is called *Houndses* or *Hounces*. This too, is a dialect word, seldom used now: it refers to the yellow and red worsted ornament spread over the collars of horses in a team. It occurs sometimes in old farm catalogues—a fruitful source of old dialect words—notably in one made at Grove Farm during the last century; one item here was listed as *Hounces and Trappers*. The trappers or trappings were the breeching of the cart-harness. There are two *pightles* in this parish, both referring to elongated pieces of land, relics of the time when such shapes were left at the edge of a field after it had been divided up for strip-cultivation. There are also two *Backhouse* fields, both placed where one would expect them—overlooked by the domestic quarters of a farmhouse.

24 *Village Legends, Superstitions and Customs*

Although village legends, old customs and superstitions have none of the status usually accorded to historical fact, they have in many respects a stronger claim to that distinction than many of the transitory incidents often recorded as history. They are important if only for the reason that they put a village and its people of the past few generations into a perspective of human history in a way that no *historical fact* as such could possibly do. It is true that many of these old beliefs are vestigial and that today they have none of the strength they had a few generations ago when they were a real part of the countryside's collective unofficial creed that existed underground to the accepted religion. Yet they still have a surprising power even where there is no longer any reason given for acting upon them other than that to do so brings *luck* and to omit to do so brings its opposite.

For to hold that it is *lucky* to behave in a certain way is often as effective a stimulus to action as a more circumstantial account of the reasons for such an action; and in the same way to label an action *unlucky* may be just as strong a deterrent as a more direct moral prohibition. It is no longer believed, for instance, as it was a few generations ago that a flint with a hole in it has the peculiar quality of warding off evil influences; and no longer do farmers ask their workers to give or sell them such a stone if they discover it while working in the fields; but the holed flint is still considered by the people of this district to be worth acquiring; and it is still hung under eaves or on the stable door; its finder or possessor is still considered to be favoured even although the direction in which his good fortune lies has long since been forgotten.

Village legends, moreover, may also have their direct practical or historical use: they are sometimes real clues to historical fact; and though they often have vague outlines and are covered with many irrelevant accretions they should not be neglected for that reason. One such legend has already been mentioned in discussing the position of the church in this village: another and complementary one concerns the same period—the time of the Great Death of 1348–9. It states that while the village was deserted owing to the ravages of the plague the *Gypsies* moved in and settled here and were never wholly displaced. The legend tells us nothing more about these gypsies—legends are seldom abundant in detail or the accepted kind of logic. But *where there is smoke there is fire:* and the fire in the above legend appears to be this: there are two strains of people in this village; one fair and one very dark with blue-black hair. The legend seems to be a popular or unscientific way of explaining the presence of the dark people.

In this connection the phrase *gypsy blood*, sometimes used by the people here, deserves a note: movement of people in and out of this village has been comparatively rare, at least up to thirty years or so ago; the families have lived here undisturbed for many generations. In most country places a man whose family is well known is judged by his *blood*, in much the same fashion as an animal is judged according to its pedigree. The postmaster here, for instance, after taking a sort of professional interest in Trollope's *Autobiography* made the comment concerning the author's youthful struggles: 'He didn't have much to start with, though look at the tidy sum he earned afterwards. But there, he came of good breed; and that tells!' For according to this realistic country way of looking at the debated question of human behaviour *blood tells* as much in human beings as in animals. But here in this village where most men's forebears are known for generations back, this rough guide has been elevated into a principle and a man's blood—the stock he stems from—is accounted a better indication of his real worth than his overt character which is assumed to be more or less an accidental acquisition, subject to the fluctuations of time and chance circumstance. So to say that a man has gypsy blood in him is to put him down as unreliable, and finally to place him beyond the pale of the true village community—that vague yet organic brotherhood that functions, as it were, underground and keeps its identity through all changes short of the most drastic social reorganization. Even when it suffers this it is doubtful whether it is completely inundated: witness the emergence of small islands of the old culture in an area like the South Wales valleys even after they have been subjected to the dark flood of industrialism for well over a century. A farmer here complained that one of his former workers constantly had to be watched. But he had satisfied himself that the cause of this was beyond his control; and the worker's for that matter. 'Look at his hair,' he said. 'You see how it crinkles. He's got gypsy blood in him, you may depend!' The man had gypsy blood therefore he was a *sport*, someone to whom normal rules do not apply; and for that reason no sleep need be lost over him.

But the accusation of gypsy blood is sometimes more specific, and some of the old people can recall: 'Oh, his grandfather (or great-grandfather) married a travelling woman. The Picketts and the Taylors and the Becketts were the names you used to meet most among the travellers. I believe it was a Pickett he married. They were nice folk but they had a different line o' life entirely to us.' *Pickett*, as Brian Vesey-Fitzgerald has pointed out, is a mis-hearing of the name Beckett, the tribe to which Joe Beckett, the boxer, belonged. The Taylors and the Becketts were, in fact, two of the best-known gypsy tribes in East Anglia.

The old people also remember an old lady called Black Mary who lived here a generation or two ago. Her hair was as black as a raven's right up to her death. But, they say, she knew the gypsy's *hair patent* as she was herself descended from a travelling

208

woman. The lotion was made from the grease of a hedgehog, soot from the chimney, a drop of eau de cologne or lavender water to make it smell sweet and a few drops of olive oil. She used it regularly: 'And even when she was an old woman her hair grew down to her waist and there wasn't a grey strand in it.'

About fifty years ago, as Robert Savage reported, the travellers were turned off their usual pitch on the Common. The reason given for this action was that their horses and donkeys roamed about at night and broke into and spoiled the villagers' common yards. But they also worried the farmers by poaching, and by surreptitiously letting their horses on to the pastures late at night, retrieving them early in the morning before any of the farm people were about. This was a fairly widespread Romany custom, called *pooving* the *grai*.

The Parish Council, on which two or three of the most influential farmers served, was the chief agent in banishing the travellers. Robert Savage was himself a member of the Parish Council for fifty-two years and recalled the occasion: 'All the village didn't want the travellers to be moved off the Common. And I came in for a few shots at the *Ship*, mostly from people who were hinting that I was running in with the farmers in having the travellers turned off. But at the next Council meeting when the chairman asked, "Is there any other business?" I got up and said: "Yes, there's more parish business done at the *Ship* than there's done here!" and I told 'em my mind. Nobody said nawthen to me after that.'

The eviction was accompanied by a kind of ceremony—a ceremony of ejection—that many of the old villagers remember vividly. A body of men, who emphasized that they had nothing against the travellers—'The people wor all right: it wor the horses and the donkeys!'—marched from the *Ship Inn* in a column headed by a trumpet and mouth-organ. This military seeming demonstration, however, met with no resistance; for the travellers had already had word. By the time the column arrived their horses and donkeys were harnessed ready to pull their caravans and carts on to the road. This they did, and the police were waiting on the high road to compel them to move on to another parish. But this purification did not embrace and banish all *gypsy blood* from the village; fortunately some still remains, convenient to wash out the occasional stain that members of this little community sometimes acquire.

Another interesting legend concerns the Blaxhall Stone. This is a huge mass of sandstone weighing about five tons. It lies in the yard of a farm called after it, Stone Farm. As there are no stones in this area larger than flints, this stone has always been something of a landmark and a curiosity. A geologist has identified it as an erratic, a wandering stone, pushed down by the Ice Sheet when it covered the country about 150 thousand years ago. The parent mass of the stone is at Spilsby, Lincolnshire. But the older generation in the village will have none of this: they say that the stone grows. In appearance it is something like a huge flat dish or saucer with its centre part resting on the ground. One old man has said: 'A tidy time ago—I remember it well—a cat could not walk under the lips of that stone. But have a look at it now: a dog could walk under it easily.' Another—a younger man—has said that he can remember the man who found the stone. This man lived at the end of the last century. He was a well-known ploughman, winner of many ploughing matches all over the country. He was also foreman at Stone Farm. It is said that he turned up the stone one day when he was ploughing: seeing that it was different from the flints he usually ploughed up he examined it; put it to one side; and at the end of the day's work carried it and dropped it in the farmyard. It was then no bigger than his two fists. It has lain exactly where he dropped it, growing in the meantime to its present-day size.

What is the use, someone will say, in recording such a fantastic belief as this? How can there be any truth in it? There can be no doubt that the geologist is right: the stone does not grow; on the contrary, it is bound to suffer a certain amount of erosion like all other stones that are exposed to the wind, frost and rain. But the villagers of the past few generations say in support of the legend: 'Flints grow in the ground: why couldn't this stone grow, as well?' and they can point to the belief of some farmers who within living memory used to say that it was no use picking flints off the fields: the land bred them. It is true that flints do absorb the silica that is in the earth around them. The slightly acid rain-water dissolves this element and it collects on the surface of the flint, thereby giving it another *skin*. But a flint can only increase its size by the amount of silica in the soil above or around it—which is not likely to be very much. It is certain that flints do not grow like mushrooms. But the Blaxhall Stone is not even flint: as has already been stated, it is sandstone.

Although the legend, however, tells us nothing factual about the stone it tells us a good deal about the village, if we consider it from the standpoint of the villagers of, for instance, a few centuries ago. Here is a big stone in their midst like an ark that has come from somewhere mysterious. How did it get there? Knowing nothing of pre-history and the Ice Sheet, there was only one explanation short (for them) of the fantastic: the stone grew there. And when it is realized that this is an out-of-the-way village, neglected and to a certain extent despised, with little claim to any distinction at all, it is seen that the inducement to believe in a stone that grows is too strong a temptation to be withstood. The people talked about the legend and were themselves convinced of its truth, because it filled a need—to make the village appear bigger and more important than the rest of the world appeared to think it. And whatever the scientists say, it is still of little use trying to convince the older people here that their version of the history of the stone is not the correct one. The only answer one gets is a definitive and stubborn: 'Ah, but it dew grow!' For them the belief fulfils a need and while the needs lasts they will continue to hold it.

Hag-stones—flints with holes in them—are still to be seen hanging under eaves, or sheds or outhouses; and it is still a common practice to tie a key to one of these small holed flints. As the name suggests, hag-stones were at one time accounted a safeguard against fairies or witches; and they were hung on

211

doors or carried in pockets as witchcraft preventatives. If iron was joined to the stone its potency as a protective charm was increased; and the iron of the key united with the hag-stone to form a powerful safeguard, preventing all evil from entering the house. A hag-stone and key were often hung on a stable door as the old people believed that the Fairies or *Pharisees*, as they called them, rode horses about at night; this explained how a horseman would sometimes find his charges 'all of a sweat' when he went to feed them in the morning. (This strikes one as the sort of belief that the smugglers would be careful to foster, in the same way as it was their custom to people certain houses with conveniently terrifying ghosts.) At one time, too, it was believed that a flint with a hole in it hung above a bedstead was a good preservative against nightmare, also against rheumatism, though by what principle these two complaints were bracketed together it would be hard to discover. Most of the specific beliefs in the efficacy of the holed flint seem, however, to have died out; yet these stones still have fascination for the children of the village. About a year ago a ten-year-old boy discovered a large flint, with an almost circular hole right through it, on a field just after it had been ploughed. In spite of the fact that it weighed nearly a stone he carried it about a mile to school to show his teacher the wonder he had come across.

There is yet another belief in this village connected with stones. The Heath or Big Common is covered with flints; here and on numerous fields in the parish a number of sea-urchin fossils have been discovered. The people of this district call the fossils *Fairy Loaves*. They are, in fact, shaped like daintily marked cottage loaves, the sort of loaf that used to be baked in brick ovens a generation or so ago. People here believed that finding Fairy Loaves was lucky. One old man in this village said as he fingered the Fairy Loaf on his mantelpiece: 'They say that while you have one of these in the house you'll niver want for bread. Neither have I!' Some housewives used to polish these fossils with blacklead and place them on the hob. This action gives a clue to the origin of the belief.

Primitive people still believe that if they themselves imitate the action of Nature they can influence her and help her to bring about the things they want to happen. If they want rain they hold a ritual dance in which the action of rain falling is imitated and forms the central pattern of the dance. After a similar fashion they believe that inanimate things can communicate qualities according to their own intrinsic nature to anyone or anything that comes into contact with them. Frazer has given many examples of how stones have been used in this way; one example, in which the shape of the stone is the quality emphasized, is worth quoting in full: 'In some parts of Melanesia a like belief prevails that certain sacred stones are endowed with miraculous powers which correspond in their nature to the shape of the stone. Thus a piece of water-worn coral on the beach often bears a surprising likeness to bread-fruit. Hence in the Banks Islands a man who finds a coral will lay it at the root of one of his bread-fruit trees in the expectation that it will make the tree bear well.' In the same way the old people in Suffolk placed their Fairy Loaves on the hob in order to induce the dough loaves to rise and imitate the beautiful rounded shapes that were set before them. This is a piece with the old wives' belief that a pregnant woman should look only on beautiful things so that the child in her womb should likewise be born well-favoured. But there is another perfect example of this homeopathic or imitative magic, as Frazer calls it, which still has adherents here: some women believe that cutting their hair at the time of the new moon is a surety that their hair will grow thick—as the moon waxes, so is the belief, in like manner will their hair.

Another belief of the same category was encountered, not in this village, but in the Stratford St Mary district on the southern borders of Suffolk. An enquiry was being made into the old methods of curing hams. In this district they were often malt-cured; that is, they were taken to the local maltings and left for a period on the malting floor covered by the grain. They were then taken out and hung up to dry. While they were drying the hams were to be locked in a room and there was a firm injunc-

tion that 'none of the girls should go near them'. It was believed
—still is, by at least three people who volunteered to give information—that if a menstruating woman touched the hams they
would 'go off' (become bad). Frazer cites many instances of a
similar belief which illustrates just how far removed twentieth-
century Britain is, in many respects, from primitive Uganda or
Costa Rica.

One well-proved pagan custom that survived in this district
into fairly recent times is worth recording. This custom was
bound up with the harvest. The last load of corn from the fields
was decorated with a green bough; and in some villages if a
brave enough—and pretty enough—girl could be found, she
would be hoisted on top of the load. In some districts they
placed the last sheaf of corn gathered in the field on top of the
load after dressing it into a human shape. But whether there was
a girl at the top of the last harvest-load or a puppet made of corn-
straw, the figure represented the same person—Ceres or Perse-
phone, the old pagan Corn Goddess, who was thought to be
responsible for the fertility of the fields and the ripening of the
crops. This old custom, like many another, was honoured long
after the belief it represented had been forgotten. The straw
puppet placed on the last load is sometimes called a Corn Baby
or Corn Dolly. There is one of the old corn-dolly craftsmen still
living in this village. But he and his brother learned the craft
at his home in north Essex. He used to make his dollies out of
the best straw of ripe wheat, taken from the field before it had
become too dry to handle easily. If, however, the corn-straw
tended to split as he worked it he sprinkled the straw with water
and worked with moistened hands. His dollies were not placed
on the last load: they went to church as decorations during the
time of the harvest festival.

Many old customs and traditions have been discovered bound
up with children's games or village pastimes. It is often overlooked that until the beginning of this century, and even later
in some districts, people in villages like this had to make their
own amusements: there were no football matches to watch, no

easy transport to the nearest town, no films to be seen, and there was, of course, no wireless. The games and amusements were the traditional ones handed down from time immemorial, and they are interesting for that reason.

The old people say that marbles was once a great game here —for grown-ups as well as children. Each village seems to have had its own version of the game with its own special terms differing—however slightly—from one village to another. Two forms of the game were played here. The first was the more usual one where the marbles were placed in the centre of a ring drawn roughly on a flat piece of ground that had first been stamped down to make it smooth. Each player then tried to hit the marbles out from the ring by shooting an *alley*—a superior marble—at them. The alley was held between the thumb and the forefinger in the approved way and the knuckles of the hand had to rest on the ground while the player was shooting. The marbles a player hit out of the ring he claimed as his own. This form of the game was called *Round Toy* to distinguish it from *Long Toy*, a much rarer form of the game. In this, single marbles were placed in a long line, as many marbles as there were players, with an equal distance between each marble. The player stood at one end of the line, an agreed distance from the first marble, or *stoney* as it was called. They decided who was to have first turn by rolling their alleys along the line: the one whose alley stopped nearest to a marble was allowed to shoot first. The game was to hit each marble out of the line. If a player shot his alley right up the line of stoneys without hitting one of them this was called a *gull*. Robert Savage recalled: 'Ol' Burch the blacksmith was a rum shot. Nobody would play with him because he'd win 'em all—take all your stoneys. He put some time in at Leiston Works and he knew all the tricks. A *blood alley* was a whoolly fine alley; it was made of hard *stoon* with a pink *strike* through it. It would *half* a glass alley easy—knock chips right off of it. A horse standing on a blood alley couldn't fare to break it. We used to walk to Wickham Market or Woodbridge to get them.'

Various Old People

The marble season began in the spring as soon as the roads were fit after the winter rains. The season went on until Good Friday when there was a definite rule that the game should stop. If a boy saw another playing marbles any time after Good Friday he had full licence to rush up to him, seize the marbles and put them in his pocket, but he must not forget to cry out as he did so: '*Tom Fobble's Day!*' No one here knows how this custom originated and how the day next to Good Friday got this name; nor has research yet discovered a possible explanation. The custom is certainly older than man's memory and it is quite probable that it dates from early times; it might even be a survival from pagan times as it is well known that many pagan customs have found their last refuge in the simple games of children.

The little customs and beliefs commonly cherished among children often give clues to interesting survivals. A boy in this village once told the schoolmistress very proudly that he had been born during the *Chinese Hours*. This statement was taken down for what it was worth, and a certain amount of research was done in an an attempt to discover the boy's meaning. Nothing could be found. Then it was decided to take a leaf from the book of a village lady, the first article in whose creed is: 'If you wait long enough in a village, you'll know everything.' And true enough, the explanation of the boy's boast soon turned up. His mother had meant to tell him that his birth had fallen during the *Chimes Hours:* accordingly he was gifted with second sight, and could discern happenings hidden from the sight of lesser mortals. The belief dates from pre-Reformation days; but the exact times denoted by *The Chimes Hours* appear to be in dispute. Some say that they were the hours of 8 p.m., midnight and 4 a.m., others think differently. Perhaps some light may be thrown on the question by the following quotations: both taken from *The Church Bells of England*, by H. B. Walters: 'The ringing for the canonical hours let the world know the time by day and night; and in those large churches where such a custom was followed, the several bells—as well as the ways in which they were rung for that purpose—told the precise service which was then about to be chanted.' 'At the Reformation ringing at the canonical hours was dropped, except for Mattins and Evensong. We may perhaps, however, discern a trace of it in the custom of playing chimes at the hours of 3, 6, 9, and 12.'

Another belief which probably dates from pre-Reformation times states that it is necessary to give a corpse light. After a coffin had recently been placed in the parish church overnight to await burial next day, there was a certain amount of talk in the village criticising this action. One woman said: 'It's wrong! Him being there all by himself! A corpse should have a bit of company and a light—even if it's only a night light. You should always give a corpse light. I don't know why, but that's what we believe in the country.' Candles, it was hinted, should have been set beside the coffin. These played a big part in the ceremonial of the old religion; and the custom of burning candles is recalled in a saying heard here not long ago: 'You got to hold a candle to the devil now and then': you have to give the devil his due, humour him occasionally and treat him with at least the smallest bit of reverence; a comfortable philosophy and one that has much therapeutic value according to some modern psychologists who rightly point out the dangers of aspiring to excessive goodness.

A much older custom connected with burial is concerned with the placing of a dish of salt either on the corpse or underneath the coffin. 'This,' explained the old lady, who gave the information about it, 'makes sure that you have a good corpse; it makes sure that it doesn't start rising.' The custom has been recorded in other parts of East Anglia, but no explanation of it or link-up with similar customs in other parts of the world is yet forthcoming. Another unusual use of salt has been recorded here. When a child sheds one of his primary teeth salt is immediately sprinkled over the tooth and then it is burned.

Traces of old customs and superstitions may be seen about the village if one knows some of the places in which to look for them. Until about three years ago when the church steeple was repaired and the covering of its flat roof renewed, there were numerous imprints on the lead which had served as a roofing for two or three hundred years. It was the custom for anyone climbing the steeple for the first time to score a mark on the lead by tracing the outline of his foot with a sharp implement like a pocket-knife. After he had done this he traced his initials in the centre of the imprint. The origin of this practice is not known; perhaps it merely grew out of a natural desire of the individual to perpetuate his own memory, a desire which often induces people to carve their names in trees or in the soft stone of some public building. Whatever the explanation the practice had a kind of royal sanction, for it is recorded that when the King of Denmark was a guest of James I of England, he climbed Westminster Abbey and made an imprint of the royal foot.

The custom of covering up mirrors in a thunderstorm still prevails among the older people; and some of the old superstitions about the cure of certain diseases are present in their own peculiar form, as they are in most villages. One belief upholds the qualities of a sliced onion as a kind of disinfectant: 'The onion is cut up and stood in an old tin-plate. Then you place it in the room where the sick child sleeps. The onion draws the complaint into itself, and when the child is better care must be taken to see that the onion is properly burnt.' It would not be difficult to find a parallel in Frazer for a belief such as this whose underlying principle seems to assume that a disease can be charmed into an object that can then be destroyed like an onion or the Gadarene swine.

A cure recommended for whooping-cough seems to be peculiar to this village. It was given to an old lady two generations ago by a travelling woman: 'You place two handfuls of lime on a plate. You next put a flower-pot over the plate and pour a few drops of water through the hole in the flower-pot. The water will slacken the lime. Time it's a-slackin' you put a cloth over the child's head and hold his head over it so that he'll breathe in the fumes. You can hear him a-simmerin' and a-blowin' and a-reekin'. It whoolly drives the phligm up—the phligm that's on the chist. The whoopin' cough will go in May, and it will niver come back. If the child don't get rid of it in May, it will have it all the summer.'

The large spiral irons, shaped something like an elongated S, seen singly or in pairs on the walls of various cottages in Blaxhall, excite little notice as they are commonly supposed to serve the purpose of holding the cottage together; but it appears that their particular shape reveals the fact that they were once considered lightning charms. The double or crossed spiral irons are said to represent the swastika which was known as the Hammer of Thor, the thunder god.

The strength of one practice in this village tempts one to suppose that there are other traces of Norse influence in this area. The Christian ceremony of christening an infant is widespread, and few children are born here without being formally admitted into the Church by this ceremony. There is certainly a greater belief in the efficacy of christening than in any other of the church ceremonies, including that of marriage; and parents who have not themselves attended church for years, who subscribe—as far as is known—to no Christian doctrine and seem to have little intention either of bringing up their children to realize the implication of the ceremony, insist that their children be christened, and make no delay in taking a child to church as soon after its birth as is practicable. Reverence for a Christian ceremony—where reverence is generally lacking—does not seem to be a sufficient explanation for this insistence; and it may well be that here is another of those practices deeply rooted in the old community and drawing its first sustenance from the rich humus of pre-Christian times. For the pagan Norse had a naming ceremony with water, and this was deemed of the highest importance because the right of inheritance hung upon it and the child could not, after this ceremony, be exposed. Again, in the time when witches were feared, and it was believed that evil could be communicated against the will or the knowledge of the victim, christening was held to be a safeguard, preserving the child against all the machinations of the powers of darkness. It is not suggested that any of the above beliefs are consciously present today. It would be absurd to do so. But, as in the case of many already recorded, even where the original impetus for a belief is forgotten, it tends to persist by a kind of inertia: only the shell of the belief remains; but time discovers that the shell is, notwithstanding, as tough and as durable as if it contained the active belief itself.

One more persistent belief here, a belief that can safely be referred to the context of historical time, is that the first vine in England was grown at a local farmhouse—Blaxhall Hall. This statement cannot be true as it stands, for the first people to introduce the vine into Britain are believed to be the Romans; and one writer tells us that vine stems have in fact been found on the site of a Roman villa in Hertfordshire. It is unlikely that the Romans would have first tried out the vine here, in a remote corner of East Anglia: even if they did, it would be just as unlikely that a folk-memory or legend of it would have persisted consciously for over fifteen centuries. But like most of the other legends, this one, too, may have its grain of not-to-be-despised truth: we know that the church in our village both in Saxon and Norman times came under the *soc*—a form of jurisdiction—of the Abbot of Ely who in later times appointed the rectors; and that the Normans knew Ely as *L'isle des Vignes*. Thus the road for the early introduction of the vine, and the creation of the same sort of legend as that surrounding the Blaxhall Stone, was invitingly wide open.

25 Old Words and Old Sayings

There are no more authentic traces of the old village community than the dialect words and sayings still used by the older people, and to a decreasing extent passed on to the next generation. Nothing shows the continuity of the people with their earliest ancestors more than these old words that have come down almost as inevitably as the physical characteristics transmitted by their blood. The world of Chaucer, Spenser, Tusser and Shakespeare is not entirely dead while these old words are used in the identical way they used them: in the writer's own experience Chaucer's world of *The Canterbury Tales* came alive on re-reading the Tales against the background of this small Suffolk community where there are still enough traces of the old way of life to make it a comparatively easy exercise of the imagination to put oneself back into the time the Tales were written. Apart from the actual words that survive from Chaucer's days, the whole atmosphere of village life—difficult to define or give a name—helped to transmute the text and to set up that interplay between fiction and reality, poetry and subjective response, that all great literature deserves, but, in spite of our best endeavours, sometimes fails to get.

Some of the words used by Chaucer and still found in use in slightly modified form are: *yard* (yerd) an allotment or garden; *bent*, a grassy slope in Chaucer, now the coarse grass stalks remaining on a pasture after summer feeding; or as in *bentles* the land where this coarse grass is found. Chaucer's *hoom* (home) is still pronounced exactly as he wrote it; and his *hoolly* is the Suffolk dialect *whoolly* which retains to this day all the colour the old word had nearly six centuries ago. The couplet in *The Canterbury Tales* about those two ancestors of the Suffolk Punch —Brok and Scot—brings up clearly a picture of the Punch's famous *drawing* action which has already been described:

> *This carter thakketh (strokes) his hors upon the croupe*
> *And they bigonne drawen and to-stoupe.*

While a line of two before is the phrase: 'Axe him thyself' which would not sound too archaic even today on the lips of an old Suffolk villager.

Mizzle—a word for a slight, misty drizzle of rain—is at least as old as the writings of Spenser who used it in *The Shepheardes Calender*. *Page* is another word with Spenserian echoes: Robert Savage once talked about the time he was 'page to a shepherd' and brought up instantly the old mediaeval organization of page, squire and knight. *Frorne*, the old past participle of freeze, also found in *The Shepheardes Calender*, was recently used by a ten-year-old boy in this village when he was describing the trees after a hoar-frost.

The Shakespearian words still used are numerous. *Breeches and buskins*, the canvas leggings reaching up to the knees, is a common phrase among farm-workers. *Malkin* or *mawkin*, a slatternly woman or scarecrow, is still frequently heard. To *clapper-claw* someone means to treat him roughly, exactly as it did in Shakespeare's time. *Rend* for tear is common, as in the phrase used by a boy: 'He is rending my *gays*' (coloured prints or pictures). *Abroad* in the old sense is often heard as in the imprecation of an exasperated old woman: 'Throw the mucky ol' cat out abroad, will you?' *Sere whins* is a phrase reminiscent of Macbeth's 'sere and yellow leaf', while the phrase *mewl-hearted* for faint-hearted, is another beautifully descriptive phrase with Shakespearian overtones. *Well-happed* for fortunate

Old Words and Old Sayings

is another. *Tempest*, for a thunderstorm, is a word that can give a pleasurable shock to a newcomer who hears it for the first time in casual everyday conversation. *Stover*, all kinds of clover used as winter cattle-fodder, is a word used by Shakespeare and his near contemporary, Thomas Tusser; and it is still in everyday use here.

A *keeler*, as already described, a large wooden tub used in the making of butter or beer and now demoted to the washing of clothes, or sunk—as in one instance—in a garden to hold flowers is likely to have been the sort of vessel in which 'greasy Joan doth keel the pot'. Some glossaries give '*skims* the pot' as the meaning for keels in this context; but, arguing from the object, also mentioned in Tusser, *washes* seems to be the more likely rendering. In the same manner another obscurity in that identical song from *Love's Labour's Lost* may be cleared up by an appeal to the dialect. In the second verse is the couplet:

> *When roasted crabs hiss in the bowl*
> *Then nightly sings the staring owl*

If we use the modern pronunciation of *bowl* this is the only half-rhyme in the poem; but in this village, as in most of Suffolk, *bowl* is still pronounced so as to make a full rhyme with *owl;* and there seems to be a strong argument for believing that the word was so spoken when the song was first written.

In passing it may be suggested that the Shakespearian student may find it worth his while to get out of his study and occasionally to listen to the dialect in various parts of the country. This is still rich in words that form the groundwork of his researches.

These old words turn up in the most out-of-the-way places: old maps, old people whom no one would, at first acquaintance, associate with any literary heritage worth preserving; old inventories and old farm sale catalogues. There are a number of these in most villages, stored away in drawers and chests, especially in the farmhouses that have been occupied by the same family for generations. In these old catalogues, farm implements

223

and dairy utensils and so on are listed under their old names; and it is possible to learn a great deal from the lists. For instance, an old catalogue of a farm sale which took place here about a hundred and twenty years ago has this item listed under *Stable: Fil-gear*. One of the old people told us that it meant the gear or harness of the *thiller* or *filler*, the horse that was placed between the shafts. He was usually a sedate, quiet old horse, long past his ploughing days. He was the horse that remained in the shafts after the trace-horses had been removed. The thiller or shaft-horse was often called Dobbin in Suffolk. This seems to have been according to a very old tradition because he was so called in Shakespeare's time. In *The Merchant of Venice* Lancelot, the clown, plays a trick on his father Old Gobbo who is blind: it will be recalled that Lancelot approaches with his back towards him and Old Gobbo, trying to identify him by running his hands over his face exclaims:

'Lord worship might he be! what a beard hast thou got! thou hast got more hair on thy chin than Dobbin my fill-horse has on his tail.'

The name Dobbin brings up a picture of a rather shaggy, benevolent old horse who was likely to be a favourite of the family. Perhaps that is the reason the name so frequently occurs in nursery rhymes. At any rate we can see why the boy who wrote in the parish register was so proud at being promised a 'ride on doben tooe'.

The term fil- or fils-gear is often found with a related one, fil- or thill-bells. These are the chain part of the fill-horse's harness, fixed to the wooden seat or forepart of the collar. *Hem-gear* or *hames-gear* was the trace-horse's harness. Another interesting word found in a similar list is *seed-maund*, a basket used for holding the seed when it was sown broadcast: it is sometimes referred to as a seed- or *sid-lip*. The word maund is derived from the O.E. *mand* according to some; one writer, however, connects it with *maundy* money and states that the ceremony gets its name from the baskets in which the royal alms are distributed. The word then is supposed to be corruption of *mandatum*, a

Old Words and Old Sayings

word from the Vulgate used in the context: *Mandatum novum do vobis* (A new *commandment* I give unto you) on the occasion when Christ washed the feet of the disciples.

Old farm catalogues are also worth looking at because they sometimes list the names of the animals to be sold. In an old catalogue of a farm and stock, sold in this village in the year 1812 the following names of horses are included: Dodman, Jolly, Diment (Diamond?) Smiler, Depper and Darby. The cows had names like Gypsy, Violet, Nancy (or Bud); while the more poetic ones were Whiteface, Clowdy and Gardy-good or Gather-good. Some of the village children took the trouble not long ago to collect the present-day names of the animals on the farms. They compared them with the names on the above catalogue and with those on two other farm catalogues, one dated 1873, the other 1919. The first of these had the following names for horses: Boxer, Matchet, Dapper, Scot (a name with a lineage at least as old as Chaucer) Diamond, Darby, Sharper, Captain, Proctor, Briton, Smiler, Dragon, Doughty, Gyp, Moggy. The cows were Cherry, Brindy and Cowslip. There were only cows' names in the 1919 catalogue. They were Snape, Violet, Comly, Cherry and Strawberry. The children found that many of the old names had been kept but naturally a number of new ones, such as Frisky, Fay, Titania and Babs, had crept in. The newest of all was a cow's name—Mercedes.

It has been said that nothing in England seems to have withstood the changes of time so effectively as the names for everyday things about the farm. Experience here bears this out: many of the words used by Thomas Tusser are still alive in this village; and an intelligent Suffolk farmer of the old school could read most of Tusser, and understand him, without the use of a glossary. *Mother*, Tusser's word for a young girl, is still known in Suffolk, slightly altered to *mawther*; tumbril, or *tumbrell*, is still common while *fyeing out* or *bottomfyeing* is used regularly by the hedgers and ditchers. Robert Savage regularly referred to animals as *things*, exactly as did the Elizabethans; and a *didall*, a triangular shaped ditching tool described by Tusser, turned up

not long ago in an exhibition of old farm tools organized for a
County Show.

Many of these old words, which would be regarded as too
poetical or literary for everyday use, are spoken naturally in the
dialect; and apart from the scholarly interest they arouse these
words are good in themselves, rhythmical, evoking clear cut
images, and shaped to the tongue as smoothly as the old implements have been worn to the hand. The countryman, contrary to
accepted belief, has a feeling for words, and in the dialect he
gives his love of repetition and alliteration a loose rein, often
with better effect than in the consciously literary use of the language. He will say *sad and sorrowful, fled and flown, coach and
cossett* because he likes the sound of the words; and even in the
nicknames he bestows he tries to strike a balance between the
apt and the euphonious: for instance, Croppy Ling, Tabbler
Cable, Handky Smith and Darcher Poacher.

The mention of this character leads to a story which illustrates what has been said about continuity with the past in a
village. An old pit, part of a playing-field scheme here, was
recently converted into an open-air theatre for which it is naturally suited. The pit had once been a marl-pit but in more recent
times gravel had been taken from it, notably by an old man,
called Darcher Poacher, and his cart and donkey, or *dicky* as a
donkey is known in the dialect. The first play chosen for produc-
tion in this experimental theatre was *A Midsummer Night's
Dream*. Many of the people were seeing a full length play for the
first time, and judging from the way they reacted they greatly
liked what they saw. The 'rude mechanicals' had a heartening
reception, and when the translated Bottom first showed his head
one of the older people at the back said in a loud and delighted
whisper: "Ere comes Darcher's Dicky!'—the sort of comment
that might have been made by one of the Elizabethan ground-
lings.

Many of the words undoubtedly used by them are still in currency here: *enow* for enough, *sculp* for to scoop out—'The old
crones couldn't sculp the roots out as they got no teeth, so we

had to cut them up fust with a beet-chopper'; *mavis*, the beautiful word for the thrush; *discern* meaning to see—I discarned him a-coming across the field; to *homage* in the sense of to greet or acknowledge as when a short-sighted lady once said to her friend: 'If I don't homage you when I'm out a-walking, dew yew homage me.'; *chance times* meaning occasionally: 'Chance times I used to meet him a-coming home, and I'd jes' give him the *sele o' the day*,' *Sele*, Old English *sael* meaning time or season, as in *haysel*, the time of the hay harvest, which is still the usual word in Suffolk.

A number of these words also give clues to old customs and practices: a *traveller*, the euphemism for a gypsy or tramp, may possibly have originated in Shakespeare's *'vagrom men'*—the people displaced by the sixteenth-century suppression of the monasteries and the changeover from arable to sheep farming; the word would certainly be tinged with a little of the meaning attached to paupers shuttle-cocked from parish to parish as a result of seventeenth-century poor-law legislation. *Groops* (Old Norse *Grop*) are the little runnels cut in land to take off surface water. In old records the word is sometimes written as *gripe;* and *griping* or *re-grooping* his strip of land was at one time obligatory for each holder of land in the common field. *Mere* is an interesting word that has the meaning of boundary in addition to its usual meaning of lake or pond. One writer quotes 'the evidence of *meres* which are mentioned as Old English boundmarks and are still also to be seen, such as Rushmoor Pond on the bounds of Bradley (Hants) and Rockmoor Pond where Hants, Berks and Wilts now meet'. There are a number of places in England called *Mere* because they are situated near a boundary; and perhaps the best-known of these boundary towns is Mere on the Wilts-Somerset-Dorset border. Whatever the connection between the two meanings of the word *mere* Robert Savage recently used it to indicate the division between the *yards* on the Common. 'They called them *meres:* they were usually made wide enough so that each man could have a load o' muck taken to his yard. When they built the cottage—as they did on many of the yards—the meres became *drifts.*' The drifts are the lanes which now exist between the scattered cottages originally built by the squatters on the Common. *Flags* for turf (already mentioned) is associated with eighteenth-century poor-law practices and also with the old farming.

Old forms and usages of interest to the philologist are still frequently heard: examples are *dove* for dived—sometimes also *deeved*; *hew* for hoed and *gon* for given. *Innocent* is sometimes used in its old, pejorative sense of absurd or 'a bit lacking', as in the phrase, *the innocent mawther* (the stupid girl!). *Vexed* in the sense of grieved or sorry (I was vexed when I saw how ill he was looking) is another archaic usage.

Another feature of the dialect is the expressive vigour of many of the words and phrases: to *putter*, to nag or talk querulously; *squat* (pronounced with a very broad *a*) hidden or quiet: 'He knows all about it, but he's the one to keep it squat'. 'A *shanny* young thing' is the description of a high-spirited, rather flighty girl. *Dizzy* (O.E. *dysig*: M.E. *dysy*) meaning stupid, foolish, even half-witted is often heard in the form *duzzy*, as in a Suffolk Methodist's judgment on members of the Established Church: 'The pore duzzy creeturs!' The word *maggot* is used figuratively: 'He said he would buy me a hat and I told him we'd wait until they got the new 'uns in; but when we come to it a week or two later he wouldn't spend his money. It was my fault! I should hev let him while he had the *maggot* in him'.

The phrase *a sloe-wind*, meaning a cold wind, gives the clue to an old belief which is mentioned every year in this village. The belief is enshrined in the proverb: '*Sloe-hatching* time is the coldest time in the year'. This is the time when the blackthorn breaks in its spectacular blossom; and, strangely enough, within the writer's experience, this period often coincides with a cold spell distinguished by east or north-east winds. It is likely, however, that the coming together of the cold and the blackthorn blossom is one of accident; and it is probable that the belief is another vestige of the primitive form of reasoning displayed in the examples already given of homeopathic or imitative magic. Like produces like: the blackthorn in spring simulates the depths of winter—A blackthorn hedge in full bloom does, in fact, look as if it is covered with snow or a thick hoar-frost—therefore according to the old principle cold weather is an inevitable and logical consequence.

The countryman takes a great interest in the weather: he has to because his living is bound up with it; and he observes it as closely as a scientist watching a long and intricate experiment. The hypotheses, formed after his observations, are many; but most of them are related to the empirical findings of a long tradition and the world is spared a too individualistic interpretation of some of Nature's more self-willed manifestations. During the disastrous, wet and cold summer of 1954, an old villager here stated with an air of one who could produce an explanation for most of the weather's eccentricities: 'We read that thou shalt not tell summer from winter except by the leaves on the trees. Look!' he said, as he pointed to the foliage swept by a cold and persistent north-easter. 'It's true, isn't it?' Another man said: 'It amuses me to write down things about the weather. On the 17th November I was up at Friston, and I saw Joe Knights, him who carts logs and that, riding up the road in his shirt sleeves. I said to my boy: "I'll write that down when I get home," and I did.'

There are a few weather rhymes used in the village. Nearly all concern the moon:

> *On Saturday new*
> *On Sunday full*
> *Has never brought good*
> *Nor never 'ull (will).*

Another is:

> *Near burr, far rain;*
> *Far burr, near rain.*

The *burr* is the ring round the moon. Another belief is: if, after an indifferent new moon the third day is fine, the weather will change for the better in the moon's *second* quarter. One belief, still widely held, concerns the sun: If the wind is in a certain quarter when the sun crosses the line (March 21st, the vernal equinox) it will not veer far from that quarter until June 21st (the summer solstice). If it does, it will soon come back to it. A *roger* or *Roger's blast*, the small whirlwind sometimes seen disturbing the dust on the road or the corn in a field when no other wind is about, is thought by some to be a sign of approaching rain; but the writer has also heard it quoted as a portent—correct, too, on this occasion—of fine weather.

The sayings of country people, sometimes tinged with poetry, always rich in concrete images and braced with the vigour and rhythm that gives them long life, are worth recording. The ones quoted below can be imagined against the background of the village which has already been described:

Soap is the only good thing in the world you should shut your eyes to.

Pride must abide. Said by a mother to her daughter as she vigorously combed her hair, her meaning being: If you want to be proud and look beautiful you must abide a little discomfort.

The quaking spoke is the last to go.

If poverty gets into the stable it will soon be all over the house. One of the sayings of John Goddard, the old farmer who worked horses until well after the coming of the tractor.

You are no white hen's chick: you were born under a black crow. Used by a mother gently to scold her son.

I saw a cloud coming up no bigger'n a load of hay.

Picking the words out of his mouth. 'The lil' ol' boy sat on his father's knee while he wor a-telling him a story. And he kept lookin' at him as though he wor a-pickin' the words out of his mouth.' 'We made up a new road and *then came the floods along.*' The poetic inversion in this phrase sounded perfectly natural in the speech of one of the men who had helped to make the road.

You'll niver make a woman in the world unless you say good morning to folk. An old lady reproving a child who had omitted to return her greeting.

Old Words and Old Sayings

They say, Let the morrer look after itself; but I'm a-going to help it a bit and make sure.

Said by an old man preparing for the next day's work by carefully packing his dinner.

And the following have been picked out of the turmoil of village disputation:

I was just going to tell her what I thought of her, but God governed my tongue.

It was bound to come out: I had to say it; it lay kind o' uppermost in my mind.

When I shet Mrs Smith's door and gate, I shet in har business.

Spoken by a woman defending herself from the charge of gossip.

I said nothing, though I could ha' done: I wasn't going to empty my hid to fill hers!

There he was a-sitting there like a scaly old bull.

After he married thet woman he fare cussed his way through life.

The lil' ol' boy turned up a bit quick: he come jus' in time to hev a slice of his mother's wedding cake.

He wor as lousy as a cuckoo: no disrespect to him now that he's gone, but he had so many fleas they wouldn't let him inside the pub. He had to hev his beer a-sitting outside on the bench.

I'm a straight man up and down. A farm worker's view of himself. The farmer's point of view was rather different: 'Venables. Venables! Don't talk about him: he's the slyest man in the parish.'

The following story is told not so much to emphasize the ordinary villager's feeling for words as to underline his cunning under a cover of artless seeming simplicity. A dealer in agricultural machinery took a beet-cutter to demonstrate to a farmer. The farmer called one of his men and said: 'Here, George, you have a go at it. Tell me what you think on it.' An old worker, after giving the machine a jaundiced look, turned the handle and tried it with a few roots. Asked what he thought of it he said with conviction: 'It's some stiff, maaster. It whoolly sticks when you turn thet wheel: I fare to think it wants greasin'.' 'Send for Copping (the dealer); he's just across the field a-looking at that

231

harrow,' said the farmer. The verdict *It wants greasin'* was repeated to the dealer; but as he was a Suffolk man himself he summed up the situation in a moment. So as soon as the farmer's back was turned he slipped a shilling into the old boy's palm— 'Six pints o' beer at that time o' day'—and said to him: 'Just yew have a go at it now, bo'.' On being asked the second time by the farmer how the machine worked, the old worker said: 'It be wholly fine now, maaster. It dew go like a rick on fire.'

Which perhaps helps to disprove the prejudiced ethnography of a *furrina* to Suffolk: 'The Angles, you understand, all settled in this part of England; but after a time all the acute Angles moved away to the north and the west. The obtuse Angles just stayed where they were in Suffolk.'

An interesting sidelight on the enquiry into old word-survivals here is the frequency of American sounding words used in the dialect. Coming from old Suffolk natives these words sound strange to someone whose first knowledge of spoken American English was gained from the early talking pictures. The peculiarly adverbial use of the word *some*, often heard in Suffolk, is an example: The well is some deep. That's some rum (very queer). A similar usage is found in many parts of the United States. The same applies to the word *bor* or *bo'*: this word, once common in the tough American 'Westerns', sounds—and is—pure Suffolk. Forms of words that are obsolete here, except in the dialect, still persist in the U.S.A. Such a word is *roiled* (to be angry or irritated), commonly used in Suffolk and in parts of America in preference to the more usual form *riled*. It is probable that like many other obsolete words still in use in America it was taken there by the early settlers from Eastern England, and that those words have remained alive in pockets of that country in a way analogous to the old English folk songs discovered by Cecil Sharp in the Alleghany Mountains. The 'Deep South' may well be another of those areas in America, judging from some of the words used by the novelists of that region. *Skillet*, for instance, a word that occurs in one of William Faulkner's books for a cooking utensil, is not used here now; but one frequently comes across it in eighteenth-century lists of domestic equipment.

Ezra Pound, the American poet and critic, has long ago recognized this correspondence. He writes: 'The American New England dialect, and many other forms of the so-called American accent, are accents of different English Counties and districts.' This, too, has been noticed by some American servicemen, especially those stationed in Eastern England; and the story is told of how an American airman, travelling in Lincolnshire, jumped up suddenly when the train stopped at a station because he thought he had heard someone speaking American. But the only man on the platform was the porter who was announcing branch stations along the local line.

But this correspondence between the East Anglian dialect and American common speech has been noticed long ago by a number of people. John Bright, speaking on the Slavery and Secession question at Rochdale in 1863, told the story of the East Anglian who visited the United States: when he stepped from the steamer onto the quay at New York. he found that 'everybody spoke Suffolk'. ('Speeches on Questions of Public Policy', 1869.)

An Essex clergyman, Edward Gepp, made a close study of the similarity, and came to the conclusion that 'the common tongue of Georgia and Virginia represents English Speech at the end of the sixteenth century—the best period; the other northern settlements represent the speech of East Anglia in the various periods of the seventeenth'. It was Gepp's theory that the negroes of the Southern States maintained, even to this century, words and expressions handed down from the early English settlers. To prove the frequency of Essex words in the speech of the negro of the Southern States, Gepp took ('A Contribution to an Essex Dialect Dictionary', 1922) that accurate record of negro speech, Joe Chandler Harris's *Uncle Remus*, and went through it, picking out the words still used in the Essex dialect. It is possible, using the same book, to point to words still heard in the Norfolk and Suffolk as well as the Essex dialect: 'ast' for asked, also 'ax'; 'bait', a dish of food; 'cotch' for catch; 'crep' or 'crope' as the past tense of creep; 'cowcumber' for cucumber; 'feared' for afraid; 'forrerd' for forward; 'fudder' for further; 'helve' for handle; 'het' for heated (cf. the American phrase, 'all het up'); 'hull' for husk; 'skeer' for scare; 'mess' a meal of food; 'sparrer-grass' for asparagus; 'ellum' for elm; 'bor' or 'bo'' for friend, or mate (O.E. *(ge)bur*: husbandman; gossip. Neighbour: a friend who lives nigh).

An American service-man, stationed in one of the East Anglian bases, recently told the writer that when he first came to East Anglia he noticed the simularity between his own and the local speech. At first he used to look at a person sitting opposite him in a bus or train and speculate, after hearing him speak, whether he was a fellow-countryman. An airman's wife whose home is in Texas, mentioned that they called the place where they cured bacon 'the Smoky House'—the usual Suffolk term, as already stated, for the little outhouse known to be used for this purpose as early as the sixteenth century.

Undoubtedly, the East Anglian dialects and American common speech are rich in expressions used by all classes in this country three and four hundred years ago. And although there is a dash of wry rhetoric in the claim of the American poet, James Russell Lowell, 'Our ancestors unhappily could bring over no English better than Shakespeare's', it has, nevertheless, enough truth in it to deserve a serious reading. Alistair Cooke made the same point later: 'When you hear an expression that seems a little odd to you, don't assume it was invented by a music-hall comedian trying to be smart. It was probably spoken by Lincoln or Paul Jones. And when you hear a strange pronunciation, remember you are not hearing a chaotic speech that anyone has deliberately changed . . . It is the cultivated speech of a New England gentleman of 1934, and it happens in essentials also to be the cultivated speech you would hear in London over 200 years ago.' At the time Alistair Cooke was writing, the talking-pictures had only just made American speech part of our common experience; and the tone of his remarks reflects the impact it made when it was first heard in this country to any extent.

But we still tend to condemn many unusual words and new sounding expressions as ugly American neologisms, when in fact they are often old words and phrases that have been preserved in American common speech for centuries and often have their counterparts in the English regional dialects. To give some examples: the phrase 'I've no edge for it' (I'm not keen: I've no zest) sounds a typically modern American expression. But it was in use in England during the seventeenth century ('The King—James 1st—had no edge for the play, and retired early to bed'). Similarly, the American 'yeah' is often condemned as an ugly debasing of the word 'yes'. It may sound ugly, but it is salutary to note that 'yeah' is probably the way 'yea' was pronounced in England three or four hundred years ago. The affirmative in the East Anglian dialect is 'yeh', which is undoubtedly not a corruption of yes, but a true survival of the early 'ye' ('Let youre ye be ye, and youre naye naye' of Tindal's Bible). 'Oh, he's a real *heel*,' is an expression that is instantly recognized as American; but a *heeler* in the Suffolk dialect is also a worthless fellow—a word that was in use in England during the seventeenth century. On the other hand, 'putting on his parts'—making a show or an exhibition of himself, as in the comment: 'G., of course must go and put on his parts and spoil the whole evening!'—may also sound American, but it is a good old Blaxhall expression, heard by the writer nowhere outside this village.

It is likely, however, that a fair case could be made out for the similarity of more than one of the English regional dialects with American common speech. But the statement that the speech of the early East Anglian emigrants had a special influence—both in accent and vocabulary—upon the formation of the American tongue has very strong support.

Conclusion

Six years after this book was first written I ask myself again: what was the purpose or the use of writing it? Has it made a contribution to the village that Blaxhall, for instance, will become? I am bound to answer: very little. But a recent visit to a group of Young Farmers has given me a kind of retrospective justification. While talking to them about the way of life that has so recently been displaced—chiefly the farming followed by their grandfathers—I was struck by their almost complete unawareness of the temper and framework of rural life at the beginning of the century. The leader of the group, a farmer of middle years, also found their unawareness very revealing; and later he volunteered the probable reason for it: 'When I was these lads' age I often used to go into the stable on wet days, or for half an hour at the end of the afternoon, and listen to the old horsemen or stockmen talking. They'd pick on some incident that had perhaps happened during the day, and around it they'd built up a picture of one side of farming or of the life they led in their early days. But today there are few men on the farm to tell these youngsters how they used to go on in the past; and there's little opportunity to do so. And with the machine and television competing for their time and interest the young ones haven't much ear for the past either. There's been a more or less complete break; and it wasn't until I saw how little these lads knew about the old way of farming that I realized how nearly complete the break has been.'

The break, as the farmer suggested, has chiefly been in the oral tradition: a farm-worker of the old school, a horseman for instance, had latterly no apprentice to take up his lore; and the young—the true bearers of the tradition—have in this respect been receiving a speedily diminishing heritage. It is not so much that they are not interested in the pre-machine farming: they have now so few points of reference against which to measure it that they find the old economy almost incomprehensible. That a little of the tradition has been written down in the present book is perhaps a piece of salvage work that will not be without its uses.

Yet, although the book may have little direct relevance to the village of the future—the village that is becoming—it has, I think, certain implications that should be looked at closely to see if we can infer what direction this development will take.

The old pre-machine village community in Blaxhall was a tightly knit group, integrated for the carrying out of a particular work—the farming of the land and the many subsidiary trades and crafts directly connected with that farming. Mutual dependence, close ties among neighbours, was not merely a virtue: it was a necessity. Owing to the nature of the old hand-tool economy, farming could not be carried on except by the aid of a large group of people. At harvest-time, for example, there were crowds of reapers in the field, crowds also of women and children tying up the sheafs of corn and doing other light but necessary jobs. The whole village concentrated its efforts to see that the harvest went smoothly. Everybody was involved; and if something went wrong—a broken trace, a cracked felloe on a wagon-wheel or a horse dropping a shoe—someone in the village was ready to put it right; and the ritual of the harvest made it a truly communal occasion. Today, the harvest in the most highly mechanized districts is merely the chief incident in the rural year. Where twenty men formerly spent three weeks with scythes or binders harvesting the corn, today a couple of

237

men with a combine-harvester will do the same work in a few afternoons; and if something goes wrong while they are at their task, the farmer will probably have to send to the nearest town, perhaps even further, to get the spare parts for his combine. Full mechanization, that is, has had two main effects: it has gradually made most of the labour and many of the old village trades redundant; but—just as important—it has thrown back the virtual boundaries of the village so that it would be very difficult to say where exactly those boundaries lie today.

We can, moreover, be fairly sure that the pressure of the machine on the old village groupings will increase greatly in the future. The efficiency of the machine is likely to improve, and the character of the farming which uses the machine will itself be changed by it. It seems almost inevitable that arable farming in the future will take on the nature of a purely business economy; and this process is certain to quicken if Britain enters the wider European grouping. Farming will pay less and less regard to the old traditional unit of the parish; and will be rationalized to conform to the new dictates of a changed market. In most Suffolk villages, even at this stage, the percentage of residents who are engaged in farming, or in occupations directly connected with it, is very small: it is likely to become very much smaller as time goes on.

The 'becoming' village, therefore, cannot look to the traditional work of farming to solve the problem of its re-integration. A new type of village is already growing; and farming is having a decreasing influence on its development. It follows that any attempt to 'fix' a village in the past, to preserve the old ways and customs artificially, is misguided romanticism, wrong in its conception and impossible of application. It cannot be stated too emphatically that there is nothing to be gained by bemoaning the passing of the old community. The village has never stood still; its form has never been constant; and although the speed of recent change is making village life today both uncomfortable and disturbing, it does offer in addition an interesting challenge to those who are convinced that the small rural village has a future and who are actively concerned with helping it to evolve a new form.

But we can point to two great advantages which the machine has already brought to the countryside. It has largely taken the back-breaking and debasing toil out of farming—a tremendous gain in itself; and it has given to the farm-worker the conditions for better living. Again, as already stated, the machine has shattered the boundaries of the old village and admitted it to a larger environment. How great a gain this is can be shown by two examples of the negative side of the closeness of the old village community. It was self-sufficient, a compact rural unit; but it was also parochial in the worst sense of the word. The people who lived in the next parish were strangers, even 'foreigners'; and were treated as such in all dealings with them. Ordinary commerce was sometimes inevitable, but any intimacy was frowned upon: to be married to one of them was almost a crime. An old lady in the parish of Needham Market recalled her young days when she was rash enough to walk out with a man from the next parish. Her father's command, although ultimately ineffective, was direct enough: 'You must not do it! I can't have a daughter o' mine a-courting one o' those owd Creeting *jackdaws*.' Creeting is a village less than half a mile away, at the other side of the river.

A Benhall man in his sixties not long ago also recalled a story to illustrate this intense parochialism: 'My grandfather, John Edmunds, only once went out of this parish—and I dare say there were many more like him. The occasion was when he took a load of corn with a tumbril and two horses to the mill at Wickham Market—five or six miles away. He didn't like what he saw; and as soon as he got back on this side of Farnham Bridge he lit up his pipe and said: "Thank God I'm back in good owd England!" *Owd England* he was called for the rest of his life; and he did not again go out of the parish.'

Most parishes have now grown out of this stage of inbred isolationism; and today when there is talk of an European comity, and even of a world community, to have evolved to the point where three or four parishes can lie together as bedfellows without kicking one another is at least a little way forward towards it.

The village, having first lost its self-sufficiency, has necessarily also lost a great deal of its independence; and in the future it is likely that groupings of small villages nucleated in a larger one will become the viable units in the countryside. This development has already taken place in education largely owing to the foresight of Henry Morris who saw the process emerging and began to administer for it in the Cambridgeshire village colleges over thirty years ago.

Another example of the village's loss of self-sufficiency is the village hall. However well designed and up-to-date the hall in a small village is today, it cannot hope to hold the young against the pull of the amusements of the town. But a large community centre equipped (ideally) with cinema, dance-hall, library, gymnasium, playing-field and swimming-bath—built for the use of a *convillation* or group of villages—could well compete with most of the town's allurements. But this is not to say that the old village hall has out-lived its usefulness: it will still be needed for a dozen village functions such as wedding-receptions, Women's Institute meetings, parties and clubs. But one cannot expect a building, which in its scale and essence was one of the products of the pre-machine age of farming, to be able fully to serve the needs of modern country youth. This changed status of the village hall is probably typical of the new village: many of its old institutions will be displaced but they will not be altogether superseded. Pluralism, for instance, has returned; but this does not mean the elimination of either the church or the parson from any particular village.

Yet there is one institution to which the changing village will give a great new opportunity. This, aptly enough, is one of the village institutions with a very long history—the parish council. And the fact that parish administration is comparatively primitive could at this stage be as much of an asset as a liability; for the parish council could be adapted, both through its statutory powers and its customary functions, to the needs of the rapidly evolving new community. But before discussing the part the parish council could play in the changing village it would be as well to state again as clearly as possible the difficulty the new village is having to face, even if this means courting the dangers of over-simplification.

A community is not formed by a number of people living together in chance association. The old village was integrated, in spite of the inescapable tensions due to class divisions and a prolonged farming depression, because its inhabitants had to work together within the framework laid down by the necessities of the time. A more or less common work bound the people together; and out of this work grew the organism which was the old community. But what common work can a village embrace under modern conditions? Blaxhall is a village that well illustrates the problem raised. Not long ago it was almost entirely agricultural with the greatest percentage of its workers directly engaged on the land or at the nearby maltings in the next village of Snape. Today, a number of people from Blaxhall work on the American-occupied aerodrome a few miles away: many more work in nearby towns, and travel to work daily. The people who are still working on the land are in a very small minority. What then can bind together the different kinds of people in a modern village—the workers on the spot, the commuters, the retired people—and give them some sense of purpose, conscious or implicit?

As there is no common work, it is clear that the task of integrating the new village will fall on some body or institution which will go out consciously to do so. It seems to me that the parish council is the only body able adequately to fill this role. But a parish council, it will be objected, is the smallest and weakest unit of local government in England. How can a body like this hope to carry out such a difficult task of helping to create a new community? This may seem to be the ultimate objection. But it must be remembered that since the parish councils have learned the powers given to them by voluntary combination (The National Association of Parish Councils was formed in 1947) it would be more accurate to talk of strength in this connection rather than weakness. Again, the parish council though small is potentially the healthiest member in the trinity of local government because it is most representative and in the closest touch with the people it speaks for. It meets in the evening, and no one is debarred from serving owing to difficulties of transport or the demands of daily work—disabilities which have determined that the members of the two other bodies in local government should largely be drawn from a comparatively small section of the rural population.

It has often been stated that one of the reasons for the decay of the village community is that its natural leaders have deserted it—through no fault of their own, it must be added. The squire ceased to reside in the parish because he could no longer live off the rent; the parson has now become responsible for three or four parishes and has less and less time to devote to the secular affairs even of one of them; the village school-master has become one of the rare rural birds, and one of uncertain passage, ready and straining his wings to take off almost as soon as he settles. These, it is said, have left a vacuum which has never adequately been filled.

But it is within the power of the parish council to supply leadership to a village, a true leadership of ability and interest and not one solely of status or of wealth. After working for a number of years in rural parish councils I am convinced that there is plenty of latent ability in the small rural village if only a proper climate is induced for its exercise. A good parish council can create this climate, and at the same time root out the mentality of the Big Name, the dead hand of the old dispensation which is still heavy in many rural villages, and is expressed in the attitude: 'Nothing is done in this village. It's dead because there are no big names.'

But few parish councils, with only their present statutory powers, can hope to revivify the village and absorb the new elements. These powers, again, are more appropriate to the old

Conclusion

hand-tool stage of rural economy than to the day of the combine-harvester and the multi-purpose tractor. Yet apart from this desired increase in status, a parish council would need to concern itself not only with its statutory powers and permissive duties, but with anything and everything that is likely to promote the welfare of the village it represents. In this way it will gain the confidence of the new residents, whatever their job or status, and will live down the period when election was by show of hands, and the parish council sat constantly under the minatory eye of rural privilege—to the country at large an object of derision, to the cynical one of the most curious and transparent pieces in the rococo facade of British democracy.

Yet even with its present status a parish council is as good—and to a certain degree—as powerful as its members care to make it. For in addition to its statutory powers it has great powers of complaint; and if the council has a parish solidly behind it, it can go a long way towards making the village a desirable and socially healthy place to live in. In so doing it will transform itself and weld the village into something like a true community, with the full consciousness of a closely shared achievement.

Appendix

The parish of Blaxhall is just over 2,000 acres in extent and is mainly arable land, the only extensive pastures being on the low-lying ground, or marshes, bordering the River Alde which forms for the most part its north-eastern boundary. The village's name has been variously put down in its long, though sparsely recorded, history; and it is likely that the present-day spelling is the most inaccurate of all. For the *h* is never sounded by the natives of the village; and *Blaxhall* appears to be an arbitrary attempt to give it a name that would make it sound more solid and respectable than it really was; and that would give, at the same time, some sort of support to an unlucky attempt at a derivation.

It is an isolated village well off one of the main routes that run roughly north and south through the county. It lies in the middle of the old Sandlands, the coastal strip of light, sandy soil that has been cultivated since earliest times but much of which remained heathland until the enclosures of the eighteenth and nineteenth centuries. As far as is known, the earliest settlement in this village was just off the flood plain of the river and near its lowest fordable point, just below the highest reach of the tide that comes up the estuary. Here Roman coins and pottery have been discovered in a field adjoining a farm; and the next field to this is still known as Kiln or Kiln Hill field. But the present village is extremely scattered with no apparent reason for its shape. The church is about a quarter of a mile from the nearest focal point in the village, and about a mile from the inn and the school which form another focus. There is a legend relating to this remote position of the church. It says that at one time the village was situated near the church, but that a great plague came and most of the people died: the rest left the village. When they came back a year or so later, they burned down the old cottages to 'kill the plague' and built new ones well away from the old site.

But there are many nearby villages similarly shaped, and one historian goes so far as to say that the isolated church, 'with farms scattered or gathered at a Green' some distance away from the church itself is the normal feature in East Suffolk.

Yet there is some evidence to show that at one time there was, in fact, a settlement near the church in this village. An old estate map, dated 1796, gives the name of the field adjoining the church as the *Ham*. This word is the Old English *hamm*, a pasture or meadow enclosed with a ditch. Under the old open-field system of farming the ham was the stinted pasture, the field where the villagers who had land in the open-field grazed their cattle—a fixed number of cattle in proportion to the size and number of their strips of arable land. In mediaeval times the ham was invariably the nearest field to the settlement, probably because in this position the cattle were easy of access, would be less likely to be attacked by wolves and other wild beasts and could more readily be watched by the herdsman or hayward. But there is a tradition, too, that the old settlement was situated on this same field called *The Ham*. If this was the actual site, *ham* could then be interpreted in its more usual sense of a village or a township. There are also two isolated cottages near the church, with a triangular piece of rough green just opposite them. The old people know this green as *The Knoll*, quite a common name in Suffolk for such a piece of land. But the usual place for a knoll is somewhere near the centre of the village, so that it forms a natural platform for many of the village activities.

Appendix

Old documents, however, will probably give the true reason for the scattered nature of the village: this is bound up with the kind of tenure and the method of farming the land. We know that there was no manor in this village in Saxon times: instead there were a number of little holdings. The character of these holdings is brought out in the 1086 (Domesday) Survey about which the old Anglo-Saxon chronicler wrote wistfully: 'So very narrowly did he (the Norman, King William) cause it to be traced out, that there was not one single hide, nor one yard of land, nor even—it is shame to tell, though it seemed to him no shame to do—an ox, nor a cow, nor a swine was left that was not set down in his writ. And the writings were brought to him afterwards.' From the Domesday Survey we know that instead of a number of serfs owing service to a lord, and therefore grouped closely round his manor, there were numerous small freemen holding parcels of land in their own right. Here are a few of a number of similar entries taken out of the 1086 Survey: 'In Blachessala Ulricus, a free man, holds four acres. In the same (village) Edricus Grim, a free man, holds twenty acres. In Blachessala Brotho, a free man, holds twelve acres: in the same (village) two free men hold eight acres'.

As has already been stated, there are a number of these scattered villages in East Suffolk, especially on the seaboard; and the manorial system of the Saxons and the Normans does not appear to have been as well established in this part of the country as it was further west. The probable reason is that at the time of the Norman conquest this coastal area was more Norse or Danish than Saxon; and these comparatively newly settled sea-men, adventurers by nature, had not yet been absorbed into the community method of farming which had been practised by the Saxons and which remained the basis of the Norman system. Although there was bound to be, owing to the nature of farming in those times, a great degree of co-operation among these freeholders of land, and though their methods of cultivation must have been similar to those practised in the Saxon manor, they naturally preferred wherever possible to hold the land without

the encumbrances of forced service. They could protect themselves, and, as adventurers, would care to be bound as little as
possible by ties to any community. Some historians believe that
each of these pieces of land—called a *manslot*—was allotted to a
soldier when raiding turned into settlement. Therefore there
would be more freedom in this area, the old *Danelaw*, than there
would be, for instance, in the Midlands where the manorial
system was more rigidly established. A manor was, in fact, set
up in Blaxhall during the time of Edward I; but this was carved
out of the various small holdings listed in the 1086 Survey. And
it came, it appears, too late to give the village that physical
character usually associated with the manor—the more or less
compact grouping of homesteads around or near the manor-
farm, with the church somewhere near the centre.

Yet in spite of the apparent independent nature of these
coastal settlers a great deal of their work had to be done in common. For a village is fundamentally a community organized for
work; and however far it diverges from this purpose in its later
history it was certainly such a community in its origin. The
Domesday Survey gives us an idea of the kind of organization
necessary in this village. One entry says: 'Six free men hold sixty
acres' and this is followed by the phrase *'semper 2 carucae'*—
always two plough-teams; another says: 'two free men hold
fourteen acres' and there is the accompanying phrase, *'semper
dimidia caruca'* always half a plough-team.

The general belief is that the mediaeval plough-team consisted of eight oxen. The *caruca* or plough was a huge, cumber-
some implement that had to be dragged through the soil; and
the power required to use it effectively must have been considerable. It was impossible for a small freeman to own the
requisite number of oxen, and therefore co-operation with his
fellows was a necessity and not a choice. Some writers maintain
that the plough-teams ranged from one yoke to six (twelve
oxen) which were necessary for the heavy or difficult land; two
yoke being the usual number. It is likely that four oxen would
have been sufficient for a plough-team on the fairly flat, light

land of this village; but even four draught beasts would have beyond the means of a small cultivator, apart from the question of the ownership of the plough, therefore he would be forced to combine with his neighbours.

But their co-operation would not have ended here. They ploughed their land in common according to the three field or open-field system. Each man's share of the arable land was in long ploughed strips, placed at different parts of the field so that the good and bad land would then be equally divided. At least this was, up to a short time ago, the most popular reason given for the scattering of a man's strips over different parts of the field. But present-day mediaeval scholarship is in such a flux that it would be a bold man who would bring forward any long-standing and widely accepted belief as his strongest support for his views on manorial farming. A theory that the strips were placed according to the organization of the plough-team may soon be as popular as the one just stated. This later theory claims that the man who owned the plough would take the first acre of the field, the owner of the first two oxen the second acre, and so on until every man who shared the team had a strip. This process would then be repeated until the land was completely divided up. It is worth noting that the strip was commonly a furlong in length and a chain in width, its area becoming the English acre of 4,840 sq. yards (220 x 22); and it has been suggested that a *furlong*—or furrow-long—was the distance a team of oxen could comfortably plough without taking a break.

Yet undoubtedly the long nature of the strips in the open-field was conditioned by the shape and manner of working of the *caruca*, the heavy type of plough used in the Middle Ages. It was not different in fundamentals from the modern general purpose plough, usually drawn by a tractor. A vertical cut is first made in the soil by the *coulter* or knife; the *share* makes the horizontal slice that determines the width of the furrow; and the *mouldboard* guides the slice over to the right hand side of the plough. It would not be possible with this type of machine simply to plough up and down the field: if this were done the slice turned over by the mouldboard would continually be placed on unploughed land; and at the end of the work only half the soil of a field would thus be turned over. The mediaeval ploughman, therefore, was forced, like a man ploughing with a tractor today, to divide his field first of all into *lands* or *stetches*—as they all called in Suffolk —of about twenty-two yards wide. (At the present day this width is conditioned by the draining capabilities of the soil.) Then he began in the middle of his stetch and threw up a ridge by laying two furrow slices together; then by ploughing round and round this centre ridge the whole stetch was completed and all the topsoil neatly turned over. In this type of ploughing the fewer turns the plough made at the end of the stetches the more time was saved and the easier it was for the ploughman and his team, especially when the team might be five or six yoke of oxen: the way to ensure fewer turns in a given area of land, open and quite hedgeless, was simply to lengthen the strips to the longest practicable distance.

In the mediaeval open-field the strips were divided from one another by turf balks. All the land of a community was most commonly divided into three fields: wheat or rye would be sown in the autumn on one field; on the second would be spring-sown crops of barley, oats, beans or peas. The third field would lie fallow, being grazed by cattle which would crop some of the weeds. But there were also three ploughings of the fallow to keep down the weeds: the first in the autumn when the stubble would be turned in; the second or *twy-fallow* was done in the spring; the *thry-fallow* or third ploughing was done in the following summer.

The eighteenth and early nineteenth centuries saw the final break-up of the three-field system. The discoveries and practices of such men as Sir Richard Weston, Lord (Turnip) Townshend and Tull made it possible to rotate the crops: to allow arable land to recover without leaving it unused for a whole year. It became more profitable for each man to farm his own separate holding, fenced in and planned and worked without the direct help of his neighbour. By the beginning of the last century most land had been enclosed. But even today traces of the old three-field system can still be seen. There is, of course, the classic example of Laxton in Nottinghamshire where three-field farming, along with many of the mediaeval usages, is still practised. But in innumerable parishes up and down the country it is still possible to trace the old ridge and furrow of the open-field. These strips can best be seen in land that has long been laid down to grass. But often they can be picked out underlying the modern field pattern, as in parts of Leicestershire. Air-photographs often reveal them, as sometimes does a light fall of snow, or the slanting rays of a late sun. The typical shape of the furrows is a curve like an elongated S—a shape that was again conditioned by the plough and the unwieldy teams of oxen. Vertical air-photographs of our parish show no trace of the old ridge and furrow; but that is not to say that there is none there. It is quite possible that low-level oblique air-photography, if taken at a favourable time of the year when crop marks might be visible, would reveal patterns of the mediaeval farming.

It is interesting to note that until recent years and the coming of the motor-tractor, farms in our village were still known by the number of plough-teams they could muster, in a way analogous to the listing in Norman times. Lime Tree, a 500-acre farm, was known as an eighteen-horse farm; that meant it carried six or seven ploughs, requiring fourteen horses, the rest being used for *jobbing*-carting, or doing odd jobs about the farm. The Grove, a 200-acre farm, was known as a six-horse farm: it had three plough-teams with two or three extra horses for jobbing.

There is another survival from open-field times in a village near our own. Here the marshes along the river are *stinted* in very much the same way as was the mediaeval pasture or *ham*. Farmers from the village graze their cattle on the marshes which are used as a common; but each farmer is entitled to graze only a fixed number. This right, in which the number of cattle is definitely stated, goes with each farm: it is called *goings*. A farmer who is allowed to graze ten head of cattle on the marshes is said to have ten *goings*. This custom is probably so termed so as to form a rough opposite to *outgoings* which is a definite charge on a farm. For instance, Red House Farm in our parish has outgoings of £57 10s per annum. This is the Sir Michael Stanhope Charity, a seventeenth century charity paid to the people of the nearby village of Orford.

This part of Suffolk does not appear to have been very much affected by the big enclosure movement of the eighteenth and nineteenth centuries; and the present-day shape of the Blaxhall fields and the main lines of the landscape were probably established well before this. For this was an important sheep-rearing district in mediaeval times. and the open-field system had been abandoned and most of the common fields enclosed to make sheep-walks by the end of the sixteenth century. But there *were* enclosures in the early nineteenth century, chiefly of common pastures and heathlands still left uncultivated and used—as we saw in the chapter on *Field Names*—as common sheep-walks, where fuel (whins, broom and heather) could also be collected. These late enclosures may not have affected the general pattern of the landscape as much here as elsewhere, but they certainly helped to shape this village. For it was then that most of the squatters' cottages—of which there are many in Blaxhall—first began to be erected.

These were put up according to the ancient custom whereby a man could set up a home on waste land or common provided that he did it quickly. He believed that if he lit a fire on the hearth and sent smoke up the chimney of a cottage he had constructed—all between sunset and sunrise—no authority could dispossess him. After the first dramatic building he could improve on his dwelling at leisure. The existing squatters' cottages in Blaxhall were made in a less spectacular but just as effective a way. A man built a rough pigsty or chicken-house on the waste ground not far from where he was living—probably in a tied cottage—and at first the structure was only a temporary shack used to house animals only at certain times of the year. But gradually as its existence was connived at by the neighbours it took on a more permanent form. Then a chicken run was perhaps constructed near it; at first a few pieces of board or wire between or around a clump of gorse bushes. Next a hedge was planted—hawthorn perhaps—or as in one or two cases a screen of unassuming lilac. Then a few tentative gooseberry bushes began to sprout outside the hedge; and after a year or two it might be moved forward again. By degrees a piece of common land was fenced off, becoming a common *yard* or allotment which was eventually put on a kind of official status by the payment of a nominal quit-rent of sixpence a year to the lord of the manor. Very soon after this a new dwelling place would begin to appear.

There is at least one cottage here that was, within living memory, a pigsty. It now has two storeys and is a small but comfortable-looking two-roomed cottage. But it could not have been very comfortable for its early occupants who at the end of the last century brought up a family of seventeen children in it. It is true that the couple bought an old shepherd's hut and erected it nearby to relieve some of the pressure as the children grew up; but even with this, and the children's sleeping across the bed instead of along its length, space must have been almost a non-existent dimension. Yet overcrowding in those days appears to have been usual here; and where the norm is not unequivocally stated the *usual* tends to take its place and is sometimes even elevated into a principle. 'For what'—it was asked at the time—'could families do with bigger cottages? They can hardly pay the rent on the ones they live in now!' And a state of things in which the animals were more comfortable in their stables than the average family in its cottage was accepted as being one of the less illuminated ways of Providence.

The conditions of these shacks and cottages in the early stages of their development may be inferred from what one of their occupants is reported to have said about his own cottage: 'You can shut the door and the windows close enough, but you won't keep the cat out.' And some of the tied cottages, it appears, were at that time not very much better. The land on which these squatter's dwellings were built is sometimes called *Poor'us* (Poorhouse) *Land* here; and the squatters, dispossessed of their own small holding or common grazing land, would seize a few rods of it to grow their bit of produce: it is also known as *'Croached Land* from the way it was encroached or won from the common.

The enclosing of the common pastures was perhaps a necessary step in the development of agriculture here as elsewhere, but it was carried through in most areas and in most periods with little regard for the people displaced by the new farming. Distress, of which the hardships and discomforts of the original squatters is a small measure, invariably went with the enclosures; and it is not surprising that they have left a legacy of bitterness that still exists in the villages. The following rhyme is not infrequently quoted in this district:

> *They hang the man and flog the woman*
> *Who steals the goose from off the Common;*
> *But let the greater criminal loose*
> *Who steals the Common from the goose.*

The enclosure movement gained great impetus from about 1760 onwards; and there is evidence from the adjoining village of Snape that enclosure of the commons was a question much fought over here. Part of the story is told by a monument in Snape churchyard. It is the tomb of Jonathan Woolnough, the village carpenter, who lived at Snape from 1732 to 1817. The inscription on the monument reads:

IN THE YEAR 1776 THE DECEASED

JONATHAN WOOLNOUGH

SUPPORTED THREE LAW SUITS &

SECURED TO THIS PARISH THE

RIGHT OF COMMONAGE EXCLUDING

THE TENANTS OF

LORD STRAFFARD

A search has failed to reveal any legal records of this dispute;

but it can be reconstructed in part from the Manor of Snape Court Books (1738–1779). These are the records of the manorial Courts Baron. The Lord of the Manor was Lord Strafford whose family name was Wentworth; but the stone-mason in cutting the lettering on the monument put it down as *Straffard*—probably a true rendering of the dialect version of the name. Woolnough, and another Snape man, John Wynter, were the *homage*, or jury, at the manorial court during the year of the dispute. But there is no direct mention of the controversy here or in any other entry in the book. In the following year, however, there are two entries indicating the dispute's successful outcome—successful, at least from the standpoint of the homage and the other users of the common.

The first entry is referred to in the Index to the 1738–1779 parchment volume of the Court records as 'A presentment for committing waste':

'AT THIS COURT it is presented by the homage that John Birkingdale, an Inhabitant of Snape, has made an Incroachment upon the Common of Snape lying within this Manor by Inclosing a part thereof.'

The second entry shows how the enclosures were probably halted:

'Thomas Barmby is granted a parcel of waste land lying in Snape upon which a cottage has lately been built . . . to have and to hold the premises aforesaid . . . according to the Custom of this Manor by yearly Rent of Sixpence, payable at the usual time to the Lord of the Manor for the time being, for ever and ever, and the Sum of Five Shillings to be paid as and for a fine on the admission of every Tenant after a Death or an Alienation when the same shall from time to time happen, and by such fealty and Suit of Court as are due from and accustomed to be done by copyhold tenants of this Manor *but without right of commonage*; and he pays to the Lord the Sum of Five Shillings as and for a fine on this his Grant and he is admitted Tenant accordingly.'

It is clear that by debarring the tenants of the Lord from

exercising common rights the main threat to the commons was stopped. For few tenants wanted simply a cottage, even if it had a piece of garden attached to it. Somewhere to graze their small stock—a cow, pigs, a donkey, and perhaps a few geese—was just as essential as a roof over their heads; and without grazing rights a cottager was at the greatest possible disadvantage. For at this period, and for many years to come, it was only by keeping stock of his own to supplement his day-wages that the ordinary villager was able to live and to bring up his family.

Jonathan Woolnough was evidently the leader and most active of the villagers who stood out against the filching of the common with the connivance, or perhaps at the instigation, of the Lord of the Manor. He had been churchwarden for a number of years prior to the dispute; but in 1778, two years after his skirmishes with the Lord, he expanded and was Warden, Village Constable, and Surveyor of the Highways all at the same time.

The yearly rent of sixpence paid to the Lord of the Manor by any tenant who received a grant of common land seems to have been the usual amount in this area. In Blaxhall the present name, common yards, is a pointer to the origin of these pieces. As far as is known they were taken out of the common land and granted to villagers under the Allotments Act of 1832 (they all appear in the Tithe Award Map of a few years later). Moreover, the rent at Blaxhall even to this day is sixpence for an allotment of about a quarter of an acre; and it is still payable to the Lord of the Manor.

Written Sources

PART ONE

Shepherds of Britain. Adelaide Gosset. (*Constable*)
Thomas Tusser. Ed. Dorothy Hartley. (*Country Life*)
History of the Homeland. Hy. Hamilton. (*Allen & Unwin*)
The English Countryman: A Study of the English Tradition. H. J.
   Massingham. (*Batsford*)
Farmer's Tour Through the East of England. (*Arthur Young*)
The Shepherd of Banbury's Rules. (*Country Life*)

PART TWO

English Country Crafts. Norman Wymer. (*Batsford*)
Country Relics. H. J. Massingham. (*Cambridge Univ. Press*)
Crafts of the Countryside. E. J. Stowe. (*Longmans*)
Rural Crafts of England. K. S. Woods. (*Harrap*)
North East Suffolk. Allan Jobson. (*Coldharbour Press*)
Household Crafts. Allan Jobson. (*Elek*)
The English Countrywoman. G. E. & F. R. Fussell. (*Melrose*)

PART THREE

English Farming Past and Present. Lord Ernle. (*Longmans*)
English Husbandry. R. Trow-Smith. (*Faber*)
The Evolution of the English Farm. M. E. Seebohm
The English Countryman. G. E. & F. R. Fussell. (*Melrose*)
The Farmer's Tools. G. E. Fussell. (*Melrose*)
The Story of Farm Tools: Beecham & Higgs. (*Evans Bros.*)
The Story of Farm Buildings. N. Harvey. (*Evans Bros.*)
Change on the Farm. Thomas Hennell. (*Cambridge Univ. Press*)
The Village Labourer. J. L. & Barbara Hammond. (*Longmans*)
The History of the English Agricultural Labourer. F. E. Green
The History of the Agricultural Labourer. W. Hasbach
General View of the Agriculture of Suffolk. Arthur Young
The History of Hawstead (Suffolk). Sir John Cullum
Suffolk in the XIX Century. John Glyde
A New Suffolk Garland. John Glyde (Junior)

Written Sources

The Agriculture of Suffolk. William & Hugh Raynbird
Notes on Aldeburgh. N. F. Hele (1870)
This Suffolk. Allan Jobson. Heath Cranton
The Mingay-Rope Papers. East Suffolk County Archives
The English Village. V. Bonham-Carter. (*Penguin Books*)
The Agricultural History Review. Vol. 1. 1953: Vol. III, 1955

PART FOUR

Suffolk Churches. H. M. Cautley. (*Batsford*)
The Parish Church. P. Thornhill. (*Methuen*)
The Parish Chest. W. E. Tate. (*Cambridge Univ. Press*)
The History of the Art of Change Ringing. E. Morris. (*Chapman &
Hall*)
Church Bells of England. H. B. Walters. (*Oxford Univ. Press*)
The Alde Estuary. W. G. Arnott. (*Adlard, Ipswich*)
Blaxhall Parish Chest
The Fitch MSS. Ipswich Borough Archives

PART FIVE

English Letters of the XIX Century. James Aitken. (*Penguin Books*)
English Social History. G. M. Trevelyan. (*Longmans*)
Blaxhall School XIX Century Log Book

PART SIX

English Inns. Thomas Burke. (*Collins*)
Storm Warriors of the Suffolk Coast. E. Cooper. (*Heath Cranton*)
This Suffolk. Allan Jobson. (*Heath Cranton*)
Tunstall Parish Registers

PART SEVEN

Tithe Map for the Parish of Blaxhall (1837)
Plan of Ash Park Estate of John Revett. Surveyed by Isaac Johnson,
1796
Suffolk Folk Lore. P. Gurdon
A New Suffolk Garland. John Glyde (Junior)
The Golden Bough. Sir James Frazer (*Macmillan*)
The English Festivals. Laurence Whistler. (*Heinemann*)
English Folk Lore. Christina Hole
Suffolk Words. Edward Moor (1823)
Vocabulary of East Anglia. Rev. R. Forby (1830)
Chapters on the East Anglian Coast. J. G. Nall
The English Dialect Dictionary. Joseph Wright
Thomas Tusser. Ed. by Dorothy Hartley. (*Country Life*)
Rustic Speech and Folk Lore. E. M. Wright

Written Sources

The Agricultural History Review. Vol. III. 1955

The Suffolk Dialect of the Twentieth Century. A. O. D. Claxton. (*Adlard, Ipswich*)

Antiquity. Vol. XXV. 1951

A B C of Reading. Ezra Pound. (*Faber*)

Gypsies of Britain. Brian Vesey-Fitzgerald. (*Chapman & Hall*)

APPENDIX

Local History Series. Standing Conference for Local History. National Council of Social Service

The Lost Villages of England. Maurice Beresford. (*Lutterworth Press*)

Manors of Suffolk. Copinger

Suffolk. Lilian J. Redstone

The Anatomy of the Village. Thomas Sharp. (*Penguin Books*)

Antiquity. Vol. XXVII. 1953

English Society in the Early Middle Ages. D. M. Stenton. (*Penguin Books*)

How to Write a Parish History. R. B. Pugh. (*Allen & Unwin*)

Index

Index

Index

Index